Road Tripped

**A comical misadventure
with a dash of larceny
and a twist of romance**

Ron Fugere

Dear shipmates,

I hope you enjoy this story of misadventure!

Your Skipper,

Road Tripped

Aaron and Jake are lifelong friends, quite content to live the simple life of a couple of country hicks in rural Washington State where they were born and raised. They are also top executives a hugely successful video game company. On the eve of the initial public offering of stock, which would make them instant millionaires, they suddenly find everything they had or ever dreamed of snatched from their grasp by an unscrupulous business tycoon.

What to do when your world falls apart? Road trip! Leaving navigation to chance, circumstance, and whims, they embark on a journey which eventually finds them stranded in southern Mexico, where fate reunites them with old flames, and long smoldering fires are soon rekindled.

They stumble on a plot involving none other than their old nemesis. Soon they hatch a plan to foil the plot, recover their lost fortunes, and take their revenge.

It all comes together in an action packed climax in which they will either find triumph, love, and fortune or failure, heartbreak, and an untimely demise.

Boring legalese

This is a work of fiction. Names, characters, businesses, places, events, locales, and incidents are either the products of the author's imagination or used in a fictitious manner. Any resemblance to actual persons, living or dead (or nearly dead) or actual events is purely coincidental.

Furthermore, the author accepts no responsibility should excessive laughter cause heart palpitations. Readers with heart conditions should seek the advice of their doctor. Reader discretion is advised.

Blah, blah, blah.

Chapter One

Aaron ran out and jumped behind the wheel of *Ingrid,* his ancient Volvo station wagon. He retrieved the key from its clever place of concealment over the sun visor, inserted it in the ignition, and gave it a turn, only to be rewarded with a whirring noise as the starter motor spun but did not engage. Nonplused, he stepped on the clutch pedal, put the shift lever into second gear, and released the brake. *Ingrid* gathered momentum as she rattled down the twin ruts and potholes that passed for a driveway. When she'd gained enough speed, he popped the clutch and the engine roared to life. Well, maybe roared is too powerful a word, really it was more of an asthmatic wheeze. He continued through a meadow of tall yellowed grass and weeds that once might have been considered a lawn and skidded to a stop at the end of the driveway to check for traffic, allowing the billowing cloud of blue exhaust smoke to catch up, engulfing the car. Turning left, he drove down Olalla Valley Road. The weak morning light held no clue as to what the weather would be, but then what would one expect? After all, the valley lay in the Pacific Northwest, where wearing sunglasses with a raincoat is not considered odd in the least.

Groves of alder trees flanked the road on either side. The trees leaned far out over the road forming a tunnel as their branches jostled for position to steal what meager sunlight they could. The silver bark of their slender trunks stood in stark contrast to the gloom of the tunnel where the pavement would remain damp with the morning dew long into the day. Here and there, clusters of bigleaf maple trees released their helicopter seeds that fluttered to the ground like swarms of insects. Although the leaves had not yet begun to turn, they had lost their bright green sheen and just looked dirty and old.

Reaching into the back seat, Aaron retrieved a mildew scented towel with which he wiped the growing fog of condensation from the inside of the windshield. He banged on the dashboard with his fist until the defroster fan began to turn with a pathetic squeal.

He continued past scattered farms sprinkled with neglected tractors and abandoned cars. One could gauge how long a vehicle had sat idle by the extent to which the encroaching blackberry brambles had engulfed it. In the untended orchards, the fruit trees had grown tall, leaving what meager fruit they still produced well out of reach. The top-heavy trees leaned at crazy angles as they gradually surrendered to the inexorable pull of gravity. Soon the remaining apples and pears would be rotting on the ground together with un-raked leaves.

On higher ground were stands of majestic Douglas fir trees that had already been old and proud when the farms were young and thriving. In the bottom land down by the creek were cedar and cottonwood trees draped with moss, and a thick undergrowth of ferns, huckleberry, and salal. The brush had once served to conceal Aaron's dad's illicit fishing expeditions on which he used the tried and true pitchfork method of luring the spawning salmon onto the bank and the dinner table. Although it was illegal, he figured that the fish were so plentiful that a few would never be missed. These days, only a few lonely fish found their way up the creek.

Interspersed among the farms, a few gleaming new homes with their ubiquitous 3-car garages had begun to appear as the modern world tried to gain a foothold. Each had its own perfectly manicured patch of lawn. In search of the perfect shade of emerald green, the newcomers installed in-ground automatic irrigation systems which would generously water the lawns, rain or shine. They liberally applied fertilizer, creating the perfect environment for dandelions and other weeds to flourish, to which they responded by deploying an arsenal of chemical herbicides to combat the blight. Meanwhile, they fought an ongoing battle with armies of moles whose mounds were a pox on their oases of perfection. The skirmish lines waxed and waned day by day, but neither traps nor poison would long fend off the relentless onslaught of the burrowing rodents.

Aaron, on the other hand, like many local yokels had long known the futility of trying to ward off the moles. The whirling blades of his riding mower were beaten dull by their repeated encounters with the dirt and stones of the molehills. Once a year, he and the neighbors would trudge around their property pulling or spaying Tanzy Ragwort after they received their reminder from the county to kill this noxious weed that is poisonous to non-existent livestock. The rest of his weeding he did with a chainsaw. In only about ten years, the blink of an eye in Olalla time, the alder "weeds" could reach forty feet or more in height. Fortunately, alder makes good firewood, and today the air was scented with smoke rising lazily from a few chimneys.

For the newcomers, it was de rigueur to have an F350 Super-Ultra-Mega-Duty 4X4 dually Phase II double-mega-turbo Powerstroke diesel pick-em-up truck parked in the driveway as befitted the desired image of country gentlemen these urban refugees sought to achieve. Inserted in the receiver hitches would be a cluster of trailer balls intended to tow the boats, travel trailers, and other toys they had no time to use. Instead, they served to leave distinctive marks on other cars they encountered in the parking lots of grocery stores and scars on the shins of those who walked too close. Of course the heaviest load these behemoths were ever likely to carry was a bag of groceries, lest they soil the pristine bed of the truck. When school let out, the line of vehicles waiting to retrieve their spawn looked like a powderpuff monster truck rally.

Continuing along the valley, Aaron passed the little league field, where the reader board still touted the annual Olalla bluegrass festival which had taken place there months ago. He had once tried out for the local team, but was soon banished the bench in favor of the coach's son, who was of course the star pitcher. Aaron's baseball career lasted all of three weekends.

He arrived at Jake's place, which had not quite acquired the patina of the surrounding farms, although it had been some time since it had seen the business end of a paint brush. As he pulled into the driveway bleating the horn, Jake emerged from the front door and dashed down the rickety steps while the door slammed shut behind him. Clenched in his teeth was a half-eaten piece of toast. He pulled on one arm of his jacket while juggling his travel mug and his genuine artificial imitation faux leather brief case, which was a relic from the thrift store bargain bin. He rushed out to the car and Aaron reached across to open the door as he approached. Jake tossed his case into the back and hopped onto the cracked vinyl passenger seat. As they lurched into motion, the door slammed shut behind him. They slewed around spraying gravel and headed for Southworth, a few miles away. Jake clutched his mug between his legs while he finished pulling on his jacket. Through the toast still clamped in his teeth, he said, "Ya better gas it or we're gonna miss the ferry again!" He opened the door and slammed it again to get it to latch, then tried to persuade the seat belt to reach across his chest. After a bit of fiddling, he was belted in and his hand was finally free to pull the toast from his mouth. He took another bite and with a full mouth said, "When ya gonna get a new car, anyway?"

"What for?" Aaron glanced at the odometer. "*Ingrid's* only got 468,000 miles on her; she should be good for at least double that!" He lovingly patted the dashboard. "Be nice when you talk about my sweetheart; ya might heart her feelings."

"Ya ever wanna get laid? Yer never gonna get any in this old heap! And them ewes're gettin' tired o' puttin' out!" Jake said while poking his thumb at the flock of sheep as they sped past the Alber's farm in Frog Holler.

Well at least I ain't chasin' the ram around the pasture tryin' t' git me sum!' Aaron retorted, punching Jake on the shoulder.

***

This lively banter had been going on for as long as either could remember. They had met on the first day of kindergarten and had been best friends ever since. In fact each considered the other to be better than a brother. Before they had even abandoned their training wheels, their bicycle tires had worn grooves in the shoulder of the road as they made their way back and forth between their houses.

Soon after they outgrew the training wheels, they had set up a motocross course where they would pedal around furiously while mimicking the sounds of racing engines. Their moms kept a ready supply of band-aids for the inevitable spills. Later still they got real motorcycles, and the band-aids became bigger. Jake was always a Honda man, if for no other reason than he liked their red racing colors. Aaron preferred Suzuki yellow. Jake seemed to have a knack for tuning his bikes for more speed, but Aaron usually got the best of him by methodically analyzing the moisture content of the soil and its effect on traction, the atmospheric pressure and its effect on the fuel-air mixture, and the performance parameters of his adversary's mount relative to his own. Or he would just ride crazier. Both of their parents regularly got calls from the neighbors complaining about the noise and dust.

Then one day, they were tearing down the road with Deputy Martin in hot pursuit in his squad car. He was gaining fast, when they peeled off into the woods and Martin screeched to a stop unable to follow. The two hooligans then took one of their familiar trails home and hid their mounts behind the barn at Aaron's house. They walked around the side of the barn laughing about their escapade, when they bumped right into the deputy who stood with his arms crossed and his feet planted. He did not look happy.

With their motorcycles locked up for the summer as punishment, the boys turned to other means of entertainment. Rummaging around in the barn, Aaron and Jake had discovered a treasure trove of old tube type radios. In no time at all, they had succeeded in making one work. Soon they had one capable of

Road Tripped

picking up the police channels and then Air Traffic Control at Seatac airport. They then started monitoring the military channels. They succeeded in rigging one as a transmitter, and managed to raise McChord Air Force Base, who did not find their crank calls humorous in the least. When the military police showed up for a chat with Aaron's dad, they left with the radios in hand. To this day, Aaron's dad's eyes will twinkle whenever he retells the story.

By this time, the boys had reached that age when their raging hormones took over control of their minds. Their thoughts turned to girls, for Aaron, one girl in particular. Renée, a girl who lived down the road a piece had been a classmate for several years. When they were little, he used to take delight in teasing her. She would act offended, but in reality, she liked the attention. She would overtly flirt to which he would respond by pointedly acting disinterested. Then over the previous summer, she had miraculously sprouted breasts and hips and things changed. In fact he and Jake had been showing off for Renée on their motorcycles when someone had called the cops again, leading to the loss of their motorcycle privileges.

Renée had a shock of wavy blonde hair that cascaded to the middle of her back. Long eyelashes highlighted her deep blue almond shaped eyes. When she smiled, her white teeth shone like the moon on a cold, clear night.

Over the course of the summer, they regularly found excuses to go to Al's Market for their moms, but really it was just an excuse to go by Renée's house. Renée's friend Allison would often be hanging out there. She had a mop of curly red hair and a sprinkle of freckles across her nose. She was cute as a button, but she just couldn't hold a candle to Renée's assets. She

7

had not yet blossomed as Renée had and remained skinny and flat chested.

Aaron liked Renée but was reluctant to admit that he "liked" liked her, and was completely unaware that she felt the same for him. Both were unwilling to say what they felt for fear of rejection at best or being ridiculed at worst. Allison would fawn all over Jake, who was completely oblivious of her attentions, despite her none too subtle flirtations. To Jake, Allison was no more than his best friend's girlfriend's best friend. She may as well have been invisible. At best, he found her only mildly annoying. In this love quadrangle, all were completely clueless and would not have recognized the signs had they been written in plain English.

Then one fateful day on one of their "shopping excursions" to Al's, a new contraption had replaced the antiquated pin-ball machine that had resided in the back of the store for as long as the guys could remember. Soon the Pac Man machine was consuming all of their meager allowances. They had discovered video games.

***

Aaron looked at his watch and stepped harder on the throttle. They were just rounding the last bend before the ferry landing when he heard the siren. He looked in the rear-view mirror to see it filled with flashing blue lights.

"Shit!" Aaron groaned as he pulled to the shoulder and stopped. He rolled down the window as the officer approached.

"Will you please shut off your engine sir?" Deputy Michael Martin Jr. asked.

Aaron turned the key, and *Ingrid's* engine sputtered to a stop.

"License and registration please."

Road Tripped

"Aw come on Mikey; can't ya see we're trying to catch the ferry?" Aaron groused while rifling through the glove box for the registration. He pulled his license from his wallet and handed it together with the registration to the deputy.

"Do you have any idea how fast you were going sir?"

"Not fast enough, I guess!" Aaron grumbled as he watched the ferry approach the dock.

"You were doing nearly forty and this is a thirty-five mile an hour zone. Please wait here while I run your plates."

"Run the plates? Are ya kiddin' Mikey? You rode in this car with me and my folks when you were still fillin' yer diapers!"

Deputy Martin strode slowly back to his squad car, but rather than reaching for the radio, he took off his mirrored Ray-ban aviator sunglasses, pulled a handkerchief from his pocket, and commenced to slowly and methodically polish them to a high luster while leaning casually on his squad car. He glanced at his watch and waited for a moment. The ferry blasted its whistle and began to leave the dock. Martin then strode back up and handed the license and registration back to Aaron.

"I'm going to let you off with a warning this time, Mr. Skandish. Try to be a bit more careful in the future."

"Thanks a lot. Mikey; now we missed the ferry!"

"You're welcome Mr. Skandish. One more thing?"

"What now?"

"It's *Deputy* Michael Martin." He said as he turned on his heel and headed for his car.

"He's as bad as his ol' man was!" Jake said.

"What an asshole!" Aaron agreed, his blood at a low simmer. He turned the key and the solenoid clicked, but the starter refused to turn. "Shit! Ya wanna give me a push?"

"Damn it!" Jake grumbled as he got out and went to the back of *Ingrid*. "Ya ready?"

"Yep."

Jake leaned into it and *Ingrid* began to gain speed. Aaron popped the clutch, and the motor chugged a few times, before backfiring and belching a huge plume of black smoke that engulfed poor Jake. The echo from the backfire came back from Blake Island as Aaron said, "Oops; I had her in reverse. Try it again."

"Damn it Aaron!" Jake said as he gave another shove. This time when Aaron popped the clutch the engine caught, but the backfire had split the muffler wide open, and *Ingrid's* exhaust note was now deafening. Jake ran to catch up and hopped in while the car was still moving.

They made their way down to the Southworth ferry toll booth dragging the remains of the muffler and tailpipe behind. They paid their fare to the toll taker who was of the school of thought that a if a little make-up was a good thing, a lot was way better. Thick clumps of mascara clung to her lashes, her eyebrows looked like they were drawn with a magic marker, and her eye shadow was a shade of blue not found in nature. The overall effect while striking, did little to hide her canyon size wrinkles.

They proceeded down lane four to wait for the next ferry. Aaron pulled to a stop right next to a sign that read: "Idling pollutes. Please stop your engine." He ignored the sign because he had no confidence that the engine would restart. So for close to an hour, the guys endured the glare of the surrounding commuters annoyed by their throbbing exhaust. Aaron watched the temperature gauge climb higher and higher until steam started escaping from under the hood.

Road Tripped

At last the ferry arrived and they drove aboard the Washington State ferry *Klahowya*. A crew member directed Aaron to a spot in the very front of the ferry, beyond where the upper deck and passenger lounge covered the car deck. Aaron turned off the key and *Ingrid's* overheated engine coughed and sputtered to a stop.

Klahowya got under way with her hull shuddering to the throb of her huge diesel engines. A blast of her whistle startled a Great Blue Herron from its perch atop a nearby piling. It squawked raucously as it took flight, beating its huge wings vigorously. As it flew over the open bow, it unleashed a stream of poop that spattered across *Ingrid*'s windshield. Now if you've ever seen a heron do its business, you know that they can produce a considerable volume of….. "Shit!" Aaron exclaimed while turning on the windshield washer. A meager dribble of water did not quite reach the windshield, and the wiper just smeared the mess around, completely obscuring the view.

The ferry headed across Colvos Passage toward Vashon Island, a couple of miles away. Some commuters climbed the stairs to the passenger cabin on the upper deck while others remained in their cars reading or napping. Recorded messages about security and emergency procedures played over the loudspeakers and were generally ignored by everyone.

"I'll be right back," Aaron said. He went up to the passenger lounge where some of the commuters were stretched out sleeping on the vinyl upholstered benches while others perused the newspapers. A jigsaw puzzle was partially assembled on a table for any and all to try to find a the right piece. A group of shipyard workers sat together in a booth telling dirty jokes and leering at the sweet young thing who was walking laps around the passenger cabin listening to her ipod

11

through her ear buds. Aaron found a garbage can and rummaged through it looking for something to hold water. A mother shooed her children away saying, "Don't stare kids, some of us are less fortunate than others." He found a discarded Big-gulp cup which he filled in the restroom.

Returning to *Ingrid*, He stood by the front fender and told Jake to turn on the windshield wipers, then began to pour the water on the windshield. The first sweep of the blades flung water mixed with the heron poop all over the front of his pants, giving him the appearance of someone with a bladder control problem. "Aw gawd damn it!" He said as he looked in dismay at his jeans. Climbing back into the driver's seat muttering obscenities under his breath, he used his defroster towel to dry himself off a bit while Jake laughed at his dilemma.

A voice over the PA system announced their arrival at Vashon Island, where a few cars and passengers disembarked and others got on. Soon they were under way again, ignoring the same recording as they headed for Fauntleroy, West Seattle.

The morning overcast had begun to lift and from their vantage point, they could see Mount Rainier in all its splendor off to the south, its permanent snowcap glistening with the first dusting of new snow. Whitecaps sprinkled the surface of the water of Puget Sound. Seagulls soared alongside the ferry, snatching kernels of popcorn out of the air that were tossed by kids from the upper deck. A heavily laden container ship lumbered by heading south for Tacoma to disgorge her cargo of cheap products imported from China, while a tugboat headed north pulling a gravel barge.

As the ferry neared its destination, the guys were startled by the ringing of the claxon bells followed by several blasts of the ship's whistle. The captain came over the PA system announcing an emergency drill and asking all passengers to proceed to their muster stations and to follow all instructions given by the crew.

"Damn it! Are we ever gonna get there?" Aaron fumed.

"We're gonna catch so much shit." Jake muttered as they joined the other passengers at their muster station, where a bored crew member instructed the gathered passengers how to don their life jackets. The ferry shuddered as the captain reversed propulsion to bring the ship to a stop. A couple of crew members clambered into a rescue boat while others began lowering it from the davits. It circled the ferry a couple of times before coming back alongside so the crew could hoist it back up on deck. The captain came back on the PA to announce the conclusion of the drill and thanked everyone for their cooperation. After missing the ferry, Aaron's blood had been at a low simmer. With the added delay it had reached a boil when at long last they arrived at their destination, Fauntleroy.

After the foot passengers disembarked, a crew member signaled for Aaron to proceed. As one might have guessed, *Ingrid* refused to start, and the drivers behind honked their horns, impatient to be on their way. Together with the crew, Jake helped push *Ingrid* aside so the other cars could get off. As they streamed past, the displeasure of the other drivers was plain to see in their expressions. While a deckhand cleaned up the oil and coolant *Ingrid* had leaked on the deck, Aaron opened the hood and another crew member brought a jumper box. He hooked up the cables and said, "OK, Give it a try." *Ingrid* belched a cloud of smoke that was carried away on the salty breeze while the sound of her un-muffled exhaust reverberated through the steel enshrouded car deck. As *Ingrid* started up the ramp, she deposited the remains of her battered muffler on the deck. A deckhand shook his head as he dragged it up the ramp to the dumpster.

They proceeded up the dock to Fauntleroy Way, where a Washington State Patrol Cadet signaled for them to stop. With a couple tweets of his whistle, he then waved for the backed up traffic to proceed in both directions. It seemed to take an eternity for the long streams of cars to pass. Bringing up the rear was a northbound Seattle Metro bus and one last car, a white Toyota Camry. The lady driver was so short that she peered through the steering wheel rather than over it, and she held the wheel in a death grip at the ten and two o'clock positions.

The cadet at last signaled for Aaron to proceed and he turned left and fell in behind the Toyota. From behind, the driver's blue curly perm was not even visible over the headrest, giving the impression that the car had no driver. The license plate frame on the Toyota proudly proclaimed: "I (heart symbol) my poodle." The Toyota gradually accelerated up to the breakneck speed of about sixteen miles an hour while weaving from lane edge to lane edge. Her left turn signal was on and was likely to remain so permanently.

On their left, they passed by Lincoln Park where cars waiting to board the westbound ferry lined the curb, slowly creeping ahead. To their right were neat, tidy brick homes sprinkled with the occasional rambler.

Aaron looked for the first opportunity to pass the Toyota, but the solid double stripes on the road indicated that it was a no passing zone. After having had one run-in with the law already, he was not about to push his luck. The bus had moved ahead, but when it came to the first stop, the lady stopped too, even though she could have easily gone around. Of course she stopped straddling the center line, leaving no room for Aaron to pass.

Road Tripped

After a clearly inebriated passenger slowly ambled onto the bus lugging bags of belongings, it accelerated away, leaving the Toyota behind as it's driver ever so slowly gathered speed.

At last the dashed stripe indicated that it was OK to pass. Aaron floored *Ingrid* and had nearly gotten alongside when the lady swerved abruptly left as if to avoid an imaginary obstacle, nearly colliding with *Ingrid* and forcing Aaron to stab the brakes and fall in behind once more. They caught up to the bus at its next stop. It proceeded to stop at every... single... stop... along... the... way.

They had to stop again at the crosswalk in front of a retirement center while a young lady in staff uniform helped an elderly man wearing a blue flannel bath robe and bedroom slippers cross with his walker, which was equipped with the obligatory tennis balls on the legs. He stopped mid-way across to honk a clown horn attached to the handlebar of his walker and wink and smile at the lady in the Toyota

Then they came to the school zone, where the lady would have had to accelerate to reach the 20 MPH speed limit. Instead, she slowed further still. By now, Aaron's blood was at a full rolling boil.

Eventually, they made it to the traffic light at the junction of California Avenue and Fauntleroy Way. The light was green, but as the Toyota approached it, she slowed. The light turned yellow as she got closer, and she applied her brakes. Then, just as the light turned red, she gunned it into oncoming traffic. A car skidded and swerved, narrowly avoiding T-boning her but was unable to avoid a light pole. It hit with a resounding crash and the light pole toppled over as if in slow motion to block the road. That was the last straw. Aaron's blood exploded in a volcanic eruption of a magnitude that put Mount St. Helens to shame. He unleashed a torrent of profanity that would cause the saltiest sailor to blush, at a volume that could be heard from the mid Pacific. In a submarine.

After Aaron got his blood pressure in check, he gave his information to the driver of the wrecked car in case he was needed as a witness. Meanwhile, Jake walked over to the Thriftway store and returned with doughnuts. When they were again on their way, Jake said, "Ya know, I've heard all those words before but I never heard 'em put together quite so eloquently. You should write a book!" Aaron's look made it clear that it probably wasn't the best time for humor. They rode on in silence, munching doughnuts.

As they crossed the Duwamish River and Harbor Island on the hi-rise West Seattle Bridge, huge cranes resembling transformer dinosaurs could be seen looming over the bustling Port of Seattle, as they disgorged the contents of the many ships in the harbor and transferred it to numerous trains and trucks lining the pier.

They swung onto northbound highway 99, passing the twin stadiums, Safeco Field, where the Seattle Mariners play, and the Seattle Seahawks stadium, Century Link Field, formerly Quest Field, soon to be known as Who-Knows-What Field. Yes friends, now you too, for the low, low price of only (enter price) can have a sports stadium named in your honor! But wait, there's more! Order now and receive a free "Twelfth Man" t-shirt!

Skirting downtown Seattle on the aging, soon to be demolished Alaskan Way Viaduct, tall skyscrapers loomed to their right and the waters of Elliot Bay stretched off to their left. The jagged Olympic Mountains defined the horizon to the west.

Ingrid's exhaust echoed as she wove through the Battery Street Tunnel. As they continued across the Aurora Bridge, to their left lay Salmon Bay where the fishing fleet lay idle following the season in Alaska. Sparks from a cutting torch sprayed from a ship in the dry-dock at Foss Shipyard, while others were wrapped in plastic like huge Christmas presents as shipyard workers applied new paint. To their right lay Lake Union and the rusting hulk of the historic coal gas plant at Gasworks Park. A week or so ago, the city had applied a new coat of rust colored paint, but the graffiti "artists" only saw this as a blank canvas and had already defaced it before the new paint was even dry. Immediately after the bridge, they turned east and made their way along potholed Northlake Way past derelict motor homes and vans in which vagrants lived like modern day gypsies. They approached a gleaming modern building which stood in stark contrast to its surroundings.

They turned into the parking lot of *Live It, Unlimited.* Passing by the assorted Mercedes, Porches, and BMWs, *Ingrid* made her way to the head of the parking lot and rattled to a stop in the spot reserved for Aaron Skandish, Senior Vice President. To the right was an empty spot reserved for Jacob Overbee, Vice President, and to the left, closest to the grand main entrance was the spot reserved for V. I. Petrovinski, President and CEO, but neither his Lamborghini nor his Maserati was anywhere to be seen. Maybe Vlad was running late too, they hoped. They hastily grabbed their brief cases from the back seat and dashed into the building past the reception desk where Monique was fastidiously filing her nails.

They hurried through the elegantly appointed foyer with its soaring sunlit atrium. The gigantic chandelier suspended high overhead had been crafted just down the street by none other than world renowned glass artist, Dale Chihuly. When the irascible Chihuly, sporting his eye patch and unkempt mop of curly hair had toured the building during construction, he had shown no interest whatsoever in doing the chandelier. But V. I. Petrovinski could be very persuasive, and indeed all of the wall sconces and overhead lights throughout the building were Chihuly's.

The cost of the building permits alone would have bankrupt many large companies. The rooftop even boasted a helicopter landing pad, much to the chagrin of the neighbors. Their objections had gone unheeded by public officials; money talks.

Aaron and Jake rushed into the gleaming stainless steel and rosewood elevator, where Jake impatiently jabbed the button for the fourth and top floor.

The elevator opened onto the executive floor. To the left was Vlad's secretary's desk in front of the closed door of his palatial office. To the right were Aaron's and Jake's. In the middle, the double doors of the conference room were standing wide open.

Through the huge picture window at the end of the conference room, they could see Vlad's gleaming yacht, the *Illusion,* which dwarfed the Boeing Company's corporate yacht *Daedalus*, which was moored across the lake. The company's dock, constructed to accommodate *Illusion* was built over the objections of the EPA and the Army Corp of Engineers who seemed to consider each piling to be a dagger driven strait into the heart of Mother Earth herself. Who knows what kind of behind closed door shenanigans had finally convinced them to approve the project.

Right down the center of the gleaming rosewood conference table was the reflected image of the Space Needle, surrounded by the skyline of Seattle. When the Space Needle was built for the sixty-two world's fair, it had been a vision of what the world would be like in the twenty-first century. When the corporate headquarters of *Live It, Unlimited* had been built, it was strategically oriented to focus on the Space Needle and its promise of the future.

In contrast to this opulence, beyond the dock, a fleet of humble sailboats was taking advantage of the late morning breeze on Lake Union.

Aaron hurried over to his secretary's desk and said, "G'mornin' Mary; ya got my briefs?"

Mary replied, "Good morning Aaron. Didn't you get my email?"

"I guess not."

"What about the voice mails I left you?"

Aaron fumbled through his pockets looking for his cell phone. It was nowhere to be found.

"Argh! I left my cell phone on the charger! What's happening?"

"Mr. Petrovinski is unable to make it, so the meeting will need to be rescheduled."

Jake's secretary's deck was empty. Mary said, "I'm sorry Mr. Overbee, but Jane called in sick today. Didn't Monique contact you?"

"Nope; she must've been too busy," he said, with a note of sarcasm.

The guys strode into the conference room where the brain trust of the company were gathered drinking their Starbucks grande cappuccinos with extra shots of shade grown espresso and steamed milk from free-range cows and organic fair trade cane sugar hand harvested by monks. The various executives and managers with their perfectly groomed hair, beautifully tailored Armani suits, and polished Italian shoes took in the incongruous scene of Aaron and Jake entering with their unkempt hair, faded jeans, plaid flannel shirts, and, cheap sneakers. Aaron, a bit shy of six feet tall and well proportioned had dark brown hair and even darker brown eyes and sported a couple days growth of beard. Jake, a couple of inches taller, had sandy brown hair, hazel eyes, and was rail thin.

"Dudes' didn't you guys get the memo? Grunge died in the 90s!" Alexander Michaels, Managing Director of Something or Other said.

"Nice tie, Al," Jake said while straitening and tightening Alex's maroon Prada silk tie. Alexander loosened it again so he could breathe and slinked away to the other side of the conference room.

Although it was only eleven, Mitchell Adams, Executive Director of Nothing Important, said sarcastically, "Good afternoon gentlemen. Glad you could join us," while glancing at his gold Rolex.

Aaron smiled, showing his deep dimples and replied, "Mornin' Mitch. How's progress on your contribution to the Thunderclap project?"

Adams stammered, "Uh, we're right on target; we've got a real winner here!" He replied as he edged toward the door. The rest of the group suddenly remembered that they had other places to be. Soon the two old friends had the conference room to themselves.

"We've got a winner, Eh?!" Aaron quipped. "Let's see; what has ol' Mitch contributed so far?"

"Near as I can tell, a whole lotta too much o' nuthin'," said Jake.

Road Tripped

Chapter Two

When Aaron and Jake had first laid their hands on the controls of the Pac Man machine, they were immediately hooked. After cutting their teeth on Pac Man, they went on to master Donkey Kong, Super Mario Brothers, and all the other arcade games that were to follow.

They saved their allowances together with birthday and Christmas money, which they pooled to buy an obsolete version of a Nintendo game from a classmate. They bartered and traded games for the machine with friends. The most sophisticated games of the time presented no challenge to the pair, and they began to look for ways to improve the experience.

Aaron and Jake visualized the effect that they desired. Aaron managed to break the codes of the games and reprogram them to add levels the original game developers had never imagined possible. He had an innate programming ability that bordered on genius. It was as if he thought in binary code.

Jake on the other hand, possessed entirely different abilities. He could troubleshoot mechanical or electrical problems intuitively. His mom had bought a new car, and she had been having problems with it stalling. It was an intermittent problem that had the factory trained technicians baffled. Without even popping the hood, he had suggested that they check an electronic emissions related gizmo. The technician decided to humor the precocious kid and tried what he suggested. Viola! The problem was fixed.

Jake could fabricate just about anything that he or Aaron could conceive. Aaron imagined a new style of controller and mentioned it to Jake. In no time, he had built a working prototype that worked perfectly, but was so crude in appearance that it would not have looked out of place at a steampunk convention. Together, they refined the unit's aesthetics and ergonomics as well as the wireless interface with the game consoles. When it was perfected, they began producing replicas to be sold to friends together with Aaron's reprogrammed games.

With the proceeds of the sale of their products, they would buy the latest in a succession of ever more sophisticated game machines. The introduction of each new generation of Nintendo, PlayStation, Sega, and X-Box was eagerly anticipated by the pair, and they were always the first in line at the stores when the new units were released. Usually they had mastered the new games before most consumers had even opened the box. As they continued to hone their development skills, they improved these as well.

Whereas their class mates were interested mostly in girls and cars, the guys took only a passing interest in such things and remained focused on their games. This continued through graduation.

Eventually, their interest, no obsession with video games put them in contact with many like-minded people. With the advent of personal computers and the internet, the game industry exploded. The dot-com bust left a great number of computer techs unemployed in and around Seattle with little to do but play video games. A small group of these gamers had gradually formed. Over beers at Seattle dive bars they lamented the fact that none of the current games available were challenging enough for them. Aaron became the de facto leader of the group, who looked at him as their guru and Jake his acolyte. Their yin and yang approach made them a formidable team. The ragtag group discussed how things would be different if they ran Nintendo. The time was ripe for a new contender in the game industry and they knew it. All that was missing was one small ingredient: Money.

During one of their beer fueled bar-room discussions, they met a Russian immigrant with an obscure past. Vladimir Igor Petrovinski had recently come to America to expand his fortune. He had become obscenely wealthy on the black market by selling surplus military arms which seemed to have been misplaced after the collapse of the Soviet Union. Although he had little need for more money, what he did need was a way to launder the money he had so he could enjoy his fortune in a place where everything a person could ever dream of was available in huge quantities. He'd happened into the bar after wrapping up some more or less legitimate business dealings at the port.

Sitting at the bar, he had overheard some of the things being discussed by the group of young men at the adjacent table. Vladimir approached the table and asked to join them with the offer of another round. The guys shrugged and scooted over to make room for the stranger. They were in the right place at the right time.

Over that first round of beers and the many that followed, the nucleus of a new contender for domination of the video game world was conceived. Conceived is an appropriate choice of words, since as you will find, it involves someone getting screwed.

Within just a few years of that chance meeting, *Live It, Unlimited* had indeed erupted on the scene to challenge the established giants in the video game industry. The name of the company reflected the vision of its founders that video games should be so realistic as to put the player into the game, as if they were experiencing it in real life, as if they were living it. The suffix, Unlimited was chosen because the video world was a world without limits and "Inc." or "LLC" just sounded too, well, corporate for lack of a better word.

The products that *Live It* sold were little more than bits of information on the web, and youth of the day no longer had to wait in line to buy the hardware to play the games. A fantasy world of games was available with a few simple keystrokes and clicks of the mouse to anyone with a computer, internet access, and a credit card. Download the programs and you were playing in minutes.

Aaron and Jake applied their talent and enthusiasm for video games to develop the type of games that appealed to the masses as well as game connoisseurs. They collaborated to design and develop more sophisticated versions of the simple controllers they'd built in their youth. They were not vital; the games could be played with a mouse, but they served to enhance the experience and add value. "Order now and receive a controller valued at $349.99 for only $ 34.99!" one could almost hear Billy Mays shouting over the airwaves. "But wait, there's more! Order in the next 30 minutes and your order will be delivered to your doorstep tomorrow! That's right, next day shipping for absolutely free!!!" With the financial clout afforded by their huge sales volume, they were able to secure manufacturing agreements in China, where the controllers could be produced for only a couple of dollars per unit. The shipping costs, paid by the company, actually far exceeded the manufacturing cost of the controllers themselves.

Together, Aaron and Jake developed a marketing strategy with allowed customers to sample the games for free on a seven day trial basis before committing to the purchase. They reasoned that seven days was just enough time to sink the hook, but not enough for potential buyers to master the games, in much the same way that drug dealers give away drugs for free to get the junkies hooked and thereby increase their customer base. The marketing plan was hugely successful and soon the money was pouring in faster than the numbers could scroll on a computer screen.

The core group from that first meeting was soon pulling down the kind of income they could never have imagined in their wildest dreams. Most of them indulged in all that their newfound prosperity promised; the luxury cars that filled the parking lot stood witness to that. Sharing the dock with *Illusion* were the thousand horsepower replicas of offshore racing boats owned by junior executives. The lumpy idle of their huge engines could be heard all across Lake Union as they maintained the seven knot speed limit out to Webster Point where they could unleash the snarling beasts. Their booming exhaust could be heard for miles over the water of Lake Washington as they flew up and down the lake at over a hundred miles an hour. Also at the dock were the ski boats of middle managers, some of whom commuted to the office in their boats from their luxurious waterfront homes on Lake Washington. The boats bristled with toy racks filled with skis, wakeboards, and stereo speakers which served to attract a succession of bikini clad bimbos eager to succumb to the charms of the nouveau riche. Nestled up close to shore at the head of the dock was a solitary classic wooden rowboat with her fine shear and wineglass transom which belonged to Zak, an intern from the University of Washington, who considered rowing to be a Zen thing. When Mitch would encounter Zak on the dock, he would taunt him, "Duuude, how's your Karma maaan?" The caterers who brought in the gourmet lunches for the board meetings would also have to bring fruit and vegetable smoothies for the intern. "Glop," the arrogant junior executives called his diet. They scoffed at the modern day hippie's inclusion in the board meetings at Aaron and Jake's insistence, who felt a certain bohemian kinship with him.

For an undisclosed amount reputed to be tens of millions of dollars, Vlad acquired a beautiful Tudor mansion in Medina, on the eastern shore of Lake Washington. He had the lovely old home demolished to make way for a home that better suited his east European taste. An article in the Seattle Times home and garden issue described his new home as "a monstrosity with all of the charm of a dentist office." Among his neighbors were several Microsoft billionaires, including none other than Bill Gates himself.

The talk around the office, the buzz on Wall Street, and throughout the entire game industry was that the company would soon go public. It was never a question of *if* they would go public, but *when*.

When it had all begun, all of the principals and staff were offered the opportunity to take stock options in lieu of salary, a concept pioneered by Microsoft that had resulted in many low-level executives becoming instant billionaires when the company had been floated on the stock market. Most of the execs at *Live It* had chosen to take the money sooner rather than later. A bird in the hand is worth two in the bush, they reasoned. Unlike the rest, Aaron and Jake had absolutely no doubt about the future of *Live It*, and had chosen to take the stock options and a modest salary. Most of what they did earn in salary was put back into voluntary 401K contributions or into exercising their stock options. While several of their compatriots drove cars that cost more than many houses, Aaron had dilapidated old *Ingrid* while Jake's car sat on blocks in the driveway of his house. Whereas many of their fellow executives lived in McMansions, Aaron's sole concession to luxury was the purchase of a brand new mobile home which had been delivered only weeks ago to the property where he had grown up. The old family home, humble at best, had finally succumbed to the ravages of time. The mobile home would suffice until sometime in the future when he would build a modern replica of the old house. Jake still lived in the home he had inherited from his parents. When the company did go public, the friends would instantly become multi-millionaires, but until then, they were quite content to live the simple life of a couple of country bumkins.

Chapter Three

Aaron and Jake spent the next few weeks working from home. As executives in the company, it was vital for them to keep their fingers on the pulse of their target audience in order to anticipate future trends and open potential new markets. They took an active role in beta testing their new products before they went live. They needed to analyze the performance of their competitor's products relative to their own in order to develop their marketing strategy. So their "work" consisted of playing video games.

They immersed themselves in *Thunderclap*, the game that would render all that came before obsolete. They had conceived a game in which players would have their own unique video persona. When purchasing the game, buyers would be asked to upload digital photos of themselves and answer a few questions about age, weight, and sex, which Live It's computers would use to create their avatar. They could take a Rorschach ink blot test and answer a few more questions to help the computer tailor their character to their personality. If buyers preferred, they could manually input their data, should they wish to add an inch here or lose a pound there. The characters would be unique for each individual player, so when a new player joined a network, he and his character would both be strangers to others in the network. The characters would learn together with the players to evolve and grow over time. In most video games, there are levels that must be mastered before the player can proceed onto the next. Once mastered, there is little reason to go back. In Thunderclap, there would be no levels. Each game session would be unique, just as every day is a bit different. With advancements in video technology, 3D would give players an experience of near virtual reality. Its introduction would likely correspond with the imminent announcement of the company going public; that is if Mitch could expend as much effort on his job as he did at chiding poor Zak.

Autumn in western Washington could be a bit wet and it rained for several days straight while the leaves in the orchard turned golden and those of the maple trees exuberant shades of red, orange, and yellow.

Sometimes even the most avid video gamer wants a bit of fresh air, so the guys resurrected their old motorcycles and braved the elements. They proceeded to taint the fresh fall air with unburned hydrocarbons as they tore around Jake's pasture, churning it to mud. Jake had nearly gotten the better of Aaron when his over stressed engine abruptly locked up with Aaron hot on his tail. Aaron took evasive action, narrowly avoiding colliding with Jake, instead plowing headlong into the brambles that encroached on the edge of the pasture. He eventually extracted himself with a stream of curses while Jake laughed.

They abandoned their mounts where they lay for the blackberry vines soon to claim.

Without their motorcycles to distract them, the guys cabin fever returned, and they were actually relieved when at last their secretaries contacted them to announce that the postponed meeting had been rescheduled for Wednesday at ten am, two days hence. All of the key executives were required to attend, but none of the middle management was invited. Could this be the meeting in which the Initial Public Offering would be announced?

Aaron took *Ingrid* down to Kitsap Muffler and Brakes to have the exhaust replaced and while they were at it, they replaced the battery and alternator.

Wednesday morning, Aaron picked Jake up at 7:30. In the early light of day, the clouds hung low in the sky and the air was crisp. They had decided to take the land route rather than risking a repeat of the ferry delays of their last trip. So instead of heading north for the ferry dock, they headed south toward the Tacoma Narrows on highway 16. As they proceeded south, the sky grew brighter and as they passed Purdy, there were a few patches of blue peeking sheepishly through the clouds. They passed Gig Harbor, which had been a quiet fishing village when they were kids but was now a tourist destination and bedroom community for the wealthy. Most of the fishing fleet had been replaced by sleek white yachts. The remnants of the fishing fleet had become little more than photo props for the tourists.

They stopped at the booth to pay their toll before proceeding on to the new "second" Narrows Bridge that had been built alongside the old bridge. In reality, it was the third bridge. The original "Galloping Gertie" had blown down in a storm just months after its completion in 1940. The new and improved replacement bridge was completed in 1950 and the second (third) bridge on which they drove opened for traffic in 2007.

To the north, the low gray overcast had been replaced by billowing white clouds. Over the bridge deck of the first bridge near Point Defiance, the Salmon Beach community was visible, crowded against the base of a tall cliff by the swift flowing current of the narrows. When Salmon Beach had first been settled back in the forties, it had been a small cluster of ramshackle squatters shacks perched on the beach or pilings, inhabited by the outcasts of society. In the sixties and seventies, it had become a hippie haven. Aaron and Jake probably would have fit right in back in the day.

To the south, one could see a cluster of islands extending to the Nisqually delta in the far reaches of the Puget Sound. In the east, the clouds had parted and "the mountain was out," which is a local colloquialism meaning that Mount Rainier was visible. More snow had accumulated on its flanks and now sprinkled the foothills at its base. The view from the bridge was breathtaking by any standard. The support towers over which the suspension cables were draped soared hundreds of feet over their heads. Together with the sweeping arch of the cables, it created a dramatic scene. Nearly 200 feet below, a solitary sailboat's white sails stood in sharp contrast against the deep blue of the water.

They wove through the S-turns of the Nalley Valley Viaduct and merged onto northbound Interstate 5 where they encountered the usual slow traffic as they neared the Tacoma Dome. Traffic began to flow again as they crossed the Puyallup River. They continued past Fife, which had once been a farming community but now auto dealerships flanked the freeway on either side and huge warehouses choked the once fertile land.

Ron Fugere

One last farm had held out as long as possible, but when the bulldozers arrived mere days before the last harvest, there was to be no stay of execution, and the crops were crushed beneath their clanking tracks.

In their parent's lifetimes, the inexorable march of progress had consumed the last open spaces between the various town and cities along the I-5 corridor. The expanding communities growth was constrained on the west by the Puget Sound and to the east by the Cascade Mountains. Today the boundary between the towns was blurred, defined only by signs. The Puget Sound metropolitan area had come to be known collectively as the "Pugetroplis." Perhaps in Aaron's and Jake's lifetimes, even their sanctuary in Olalla would be overrun by development. Progress marches on.

Eventually Seattle came into view and again traffic slowed to a crawl. Nonetheless, they were still on schedule. They passed Boeing Field where several historic aircraft at the Museum of Flight were visible from the freeway. The display included a Concorde supersonic airliner, mere yards from where Boeing had once boldly painted the life-size image of their proposed supersonic transport (SST) across the front of a huge hanger. The Boeing SST project never got off the ground (pardon the pun). Not even a single prototype was completed and the image was eventually painted over. The very first 747 was also on display, an aircraft that enjoyed much greater success. As they continued along the length of the field, a brand new 737, still wearing its green primer touched down on its way to the facility where paint would be applied and final assembly completed.

Boeing had long been the driving force behind the economy of the entire Puget Sound region. In addition to the tens of thousands of people directly employed by the company as

32

managers, engineers, and production workers, many more jobs depended on the dollars that the company brought into the area. Aaron's dad, Marvin, was still a Boeing engineer who wore the obligatory white button down shirt to which he clipped his photo identity badge. In his shirt pocket, he carried a plastic pocket protector filled with pens and pencils. His desk was one of hundreds in a warren of identical cubicles washed in the harsh glare of the overhead florescent lights. On his desk along with his stained coffee cup he had a Dilbert desk calendar. His day always started with a cup of stale coffee from the pot near the time clock and a chuckle as he tore off the previous day's page from his calendar and shared the new day's installment with the other minions in the surrounding cubicles. The Dilbert character could have been modeled on Marvin himself. With no more than a glance at the institutional clock on the wall, he could tell you at any time how many days, hours, and minutes remained before he could retire from the company and move to Florida. That is if he didn't follow the example of many of his co-workers who exited the company feet first on a gurney. Shortly after Aaron graduated from high school, his dad had grown tired of the long commute and had moved closer to his office. He and Aaron's mom, Cecilia now lived in a stereotypical 70's vintage split entry 3-bedroom house in a subdivision in Kent where Cecilia busied herself doing volunteer work.

The traffic went from a crawl to stop and go, which was just part of everyday life for Seattle commuters. They passed by a cluster of skyscrapers before passing under the Washington State Convention Center where a stand of trees grew atop a platform above the freeway itself and from which vines hung down to brush the taller trucks as they passed.

Emerging from beneath the Convention Center, they crossed the soaring Ship Canal Bridge. To the right they could see Portage Bay and the University of Washington campus, including Husky Stadium. To the left over Lake Union, they could see the KOMO 4, KING 5, and KIRO 7 news helicopters jockeying for position over the north end of the lake near *Live It's* headquarters. Could the news of a local company going public be that big a story? Their anticipation grew as they neared the office. They talked animatedly about how they would spend their millions.

Exiting the freeway at north 45th, they went through the Wallingford district before making their way down toward Northlake. Ahead on Northlake, they could see blue lights flashing. At Gasworks Park the road was closed, so they parked in the lot at the park and walked the last couple of blocks. They strode into the parking lot of *Live It, Unlimited* to see a number of black SUVs and vans with magnetic blue lights flashing on their roofs. They watched as a crew of workers dressed in dark blue coveralls rolled file cabinets and computer hardware on hand-trucks out the door and down a ramp to the waiting vans. Emblazoned across their back in bold white were the letters FBI.

They approached the yellow police line tape and found their way blocked by a burly plainclothes officer.

"What's going on?" Aaron asked the officer.

"Nothing to see here, move along," he replied curtly.

"We're Vice Presidents of this company; I think we have a right to know what's happening here," Aaron replied.

The officer took in the appearance of the two men. They looked more like some of the homeless people who had scattered like hens from a fox when the police had arrived at the scene than the executives they claimed to be. "Can I see your IDs please?"

Aaron and Jake pulled out their licenses and handed them to the officer, who turned his back and held his hand up to his ear as he spoke into a wire at his cheek. He then turned back to the guys and said, "Will you please come with me?" Holding up the police tape, he waved them through. They strode through the foyer past Monique's reception desk where as usual, she sat filing her nails as the unanswered phone buzzed incessantly. A police woman stood stone faced by her side.

They took the elevator to the fourth floor, all the while exchanging nervous glances. The elevator doors opened upon a scene of pandemonium. There were a large number of plainclothes and uniformed officers, and people dressed in coveralls. All of the desks had been moved from their customary spots and their drawers removed. Officers wearing rubber gloves were examining the contents of the drawers meticulously. One officer closely examined an un-opened tampon he found in a secretary's desk drawer and deposited it a zip-lock evidence bag while another carefully disassembled each individual pen as if they might contain an illicit substance. Through the windows on the closed doors of the conference room, they could see the rest of the corporate officers gathered. All looked nervous, but none were speaking. Perhaps the police officer standing at parade rest watching them was discouraging any conversation.

The officer escorting them turned Jake and his ID over to another officer, then taking Aaron by the elbow let him into his own office. All of the contents of the room were gone except the frame of his desk and a couple of chairs from the lobby. The officer handed Aaron's license to a man seated at what remained of his deck. He examined it, then stood and said, "Mr. Skandish, will you please have a seat?"

Aaron sat on the wrong side of his desk, and the officer sat down in Aaron's chair. He said, "I am Special Agent, Mathew Cromwell of the FBI," while showing him his badge.

"Can you please tell me what the hell is going on?" Aaron asked.

"I'll ask the questions here. You would do well to cooperate."

"Am I being charged with anything?"

"No no Mr. Skandish. But we would very much appreciate your help. Do you know this man or his whereabouts?" He slid an eight by ten photo of Vlad across the desk.

Aaron looked at the picture and said, "That is Vladimir Petrovinski, the president of our company." He then glanced at his watch and said, "He should be here any minute; we have a meeting scheduled for today."

"When did you last see him?"

"I don't rightly recall, maybe a month or two ago."

"Then you don't see him on a regular basis?"

"No; we usually work from home. With the internet we can work anywhere."

"I see. And what do you know of the extra pennies?"

"Huh?"

"The extra pennies. When you sell your product, the price is say 39.98, but when a customer's credit card is charged, he is billed 39.99. Have you ever seen the film Office Space?"

"Of course; by the way, where's my red stapler?" Aaron said somewhat sarcastically. He tried in vain to calculate the number of dollars that it could add up to. At the rate the products were selling, it could be thousands of dollars a minute.

Road Tripped

Agent Cromwell went on, "It seems that Mr. Petrovinski has fled the country with a sizable fortune. Do you have any idea where he may have gone?"

"He's originally from Russia; could he have gone back there?"

"We don't think so. To say that he does not have a lot of friends there would be a gross understatement. By the way Mr. Skandish, we have found records of stock options that you have exercised and a 401K account into which you have contributed a considerable sum."

"Yeah, I just got my statements the other day. I have a couple million dollars in my various accounts with the company."

Agent Cromwell glanced at a piece of paper and said, "2,768,452 dollars More or less."

"And?"

"I'm sorry to tell you that the statements you have been receiving are a sham. No such accounts exist. You have nothing."

Aaron felt his mouth go dry and the room began to spin.

The agent looked at him and said, "Are you alright Mr. Skandish?" He signaled the other agent to bring Aaron a glass of water. He accepted the water but his hand was shaking so bad that he spilled it all over himself.

Aaron asked, "What of the others?"

"Well it would appear that you and Mr. Overbee were the biggest victims. Most of the rest have of course lost their jobs, but they had not invested as you did. They'll be alright."

"Wait a minute! Just because the president of the company ripped me and Jake off doesn't mean that the company can't stay afloat. We can still sell our product."

Ron Fugere

"I'm afraid it is not that simple Mr. Skandish. Mr. Petrovinski had recently received an offer from a competitor of yours. They had forwarded a sizeable deposit as a sign of good faith while they exercised due diligence. It was for much less than the net worth of the company but nonetheless a considerable sum. The funds have disappeared with Mr. Petrovinski. Your company no longer exists."

Aaron's mouth hung open, but it was a few moments before he could speak. At last he said, "But how? He couldn't sell the company without the approval of the board. Jake and I *are* the board!"

"We're still trying to figure it out ourselves. He is obviously quite devious and cunning."

Agent Cromwell stood and said, "That will be all for now; you can go. Thank you, Mr. Skandish. If you have any contact with Mr. Petrovinski or have any ideas where he may be, please contact me." He handed Aaron his card.

Outside the office, Jake was leaning on a chair, obviously in a state of shock. They took the elevator down to the lobby and shuffled past Monique's desk where she was meticulously painting her nails. As they walked out the exit, they passed by a reporter, camera man, and sound technician who were interviewing the executives of the company with Mitch grabbing the spotlight as the news helicopters hovered overhead. The news team hustled Aaron and Jake out of the way, assuming them to be vagrants who had stumbled into the camera shot.

Aaron and Jake walked in silence back to Gasworks Park. They approached the spot where they had left *Ingrid* but all that remained was a puddle of oil and anti-freeze. They stood dumbfounded staring at the spot. Nearby a park maintenance worker was blowing leaves with a loud backpack blower. He shut it off and ambled over. "Lookin' for yer Volvo guys?" He asked. They just continued to stare at the puddle. The worker pointed at the handicapped parking only sign and said, "Can't ya read? Yer car got impounded."

At last they were able to speak. "I guess we're gonna have to call a cab." Jake said while reaching for his cell phone. It was a company provided phone, as was Aaron's. Their phone service had been cut off.

They walked a mile or so over to Fremont where they stood at the bus stop with commuters, students, vagrants, and drunks. They managed to scrape together enough cash for the fare and caught a bus that was heading south, but they had no idea how to get from Fremont to Fauntleroy. A regular bus commuter could see that they were perplexed, and explained where they should get off and which bus to catch next. She told them not to lose their transfer tickets or they would have to pay again to get on the next bus. They made their transfer, sitting next to a bum who smelled of stale urine, alcohol, tobacco, and vomit. They got off the bus at the Fauntleroy ferry terminal and approached the window of the toll booth. The bored ticket taker asked, "Where ya headin'?"

"Southworth," Aaron replied.

"That'll be fourteen dollars."

Aaron handed his company credit card through the window. The man swiped the card. "I'm sorry, but your card has been declined."

"Can you try it again? The man complied and got the same results.

"Here, try mine," Jake offered. His too was declined.

Ron Fugere

Aaron remembered that he had his vehicle commuter pass in his wallet which still had a several uses left. "Can we use my vehicle pass?"

"Where's yer car?"

"It got towed."

"Then you'll have to buy tickets."

"But we don't have the cash."

"Bummer! Ya wanna move aside? It's rush hour."

"But I'm offering you thirty dollars worth of passes for fourteen dollars worth of tickets."

"I'm gonna have to ask you to move aside," He said again while with his eyes he sought out the police officer directing traffic whom he could summon if these two bums caused any trouble.

The first car in line honked his horn and glared at the guys as if they were the scum of the earth.

They walked back along the line discussing what to do. They approached a car a few back and tapped on the window. The driver ignored them, pointedly avoiding looking their way. The driver of the next car acted like they were invisible too. When they approached another car, the lady at the wheel lowered the window an inch or so and dropped a couple dollar bills to the pavement. Aaron picked them up and slipped them back through the crack.

"We're not beggars, ma'am; we're just trying to get home!"

The lady looked at them in surprise, taking in their pathetic appearance.

"Please ma'am; we've had a pretty bad day," he said. At least she had acknowledged their existence. "I have a vehicle commuter pass with probably ten or fifteen uses left on it. I'll give it to you if you'll just give us a ride home."

Road Tripped

"Where d'ya live?" She asked.

"Olalla Valley road."

She read the look on their faces a moment before taking pity and saying, "Get in."

They hopped in, thanking her profusely.

"Not so fast. I have to be sure that this pass is valid."

Their turn came at the toll booth. The same bored ticket taker scanned the pass which still had thirteen uses left, a value of 195.00. She paid the fourteen dollar fare for her passengers in cash and slipped the commuter pass into her purse. It looked like they were going to make it home after all. The bus fare had been $2.50 each, making the cost of their trip home a nice round $200.00. And they weren't home yet!

Chapter Four

The gray sky gradually darkened, threatening rain. In the dying light, the tall evergreen trees loomed like grim sentinels of despair over the stark bare branches of the deciduous trees. Just a few short days ago, they'd seemed so vibrant and beautiful, resplendent in their fall colors. The few withered remnants that clung to the branches did little to lift the pall of gloom that had descended over Aaron and Jake like a cold wet blanket.

Mildred, the kind lady who had come to their rescue, drove down Olalla Valley road. As they neared home, their spirits lifted a bit. When the rest of the world seemed so desolate, they could always count on the comfort and sanctuary of their homes. But as they approached Aaron's driveway, a truck was pulling out with Aaron's brand new trailer in tow! Aaron shouted, "Mildred Stop! She brought her car to a stop and Aaron leaped out yelling to the driver of the truck, "Hey! Where ya goin' with my house?!"

As he engaged second gear, the driver yelled back, "Yer check bounced asshole!" Aaron ran after the truck as it continued on its way dragging pipes and wires behind. Finally he stopped as the tail lights disappeared from sight.

He walked dejectedly over to where all of his worldly possessions had been unceremoniously deposited among the leaf litter on the ground under the maple tree. He stood in the detritus; shoulders hunched and head down as he dejectedly surveyed the pile of what remained of his world. The last solitary leaf that clung to the maple tree surrendered its grip to join the others decaying on the ground at Aaron's feet, just as the sky opened up and rain began to fall in torrents.

Jake walked up behind him and putting his hand on his shoulder, said, "C'mon dude you can crash on my couch."

From her car, Mildred said, "C'mon you guys; get in before ya catch yer death!" They walked dejectedly over and got in. "You boys hungry?"

Neither Aaron nor Jake had even thought about food since their world had been turned upside down. But then they realized that they hadn't eaten since breakfast and their stomachs growled. She said, "I'll fix us some dinner."

They made a quick stop at Al's market, and Mildred came out with a bag of groceries. She put it in the trunk and they headed for her house a couple of miles away.

It was dark by the time they pulled into the driveway of her humble Craftsman style home. The warm glow of a light illuminated the covered porch in a scene reminiscent of a Thomas Kinkade painting. A Basset Hound bayed his greeting while the guys helped carry the groceries into the house. "C'mon Abner," Mildred called and her dog ambled in.

"Just put the stuff on the counter and take a load off," Mildred said, waving her hand toward the breakfast nook in the bay window. She turned on an old 19" TV on the end of the faux marble formica countertop of the white painted cabinets and switched to KIRO 7 eyewitness news. She slipped a floral apron over her head and tied it behind her back. Her gray hair was cropped short and done up in a curly perm. She stood all of five feet nuthin' tall and was a bit stout of build. She wore a homemade cotton dress and practical shoes. Her wire rim glasses had thick lenses but could not hide the ever present twinkle in her eyes. She looked like anybody's grandma would in a Norman Rockwell painting. "How's spaghetti sound boys?" She asked.

"Sounds great," they said together.

She put away some of the things she had bought at Al's and hummed a tune while she browned some sausage in a cast iron skillet. Next she chopped garlic, onions, mushrooms, and bell peppers.

"So tell me what was so bad about your day. You guys were already in a funk even before you found out that your house was repossessed," she inquired.

Before either could reply, her attention was drawn to the TV by news anchor Steve Raible saying, "And now for an update on today's top story. The whereabouts of this man, (a photo was shown on the screen) Vladimir Petrovinski, a Russian immigrant and Seattle business mogul remains a mystery. Petrovinski is wanted for questioning in the disappearance of millions of dollars of funds belonging to *Live It, Unlimited*, the hugely successful Seattle based video game company. He is believed to have fled the country. Let's join reporter Jeff Dubois on the scene earlier today."

Mildred added the vegetables, herbs, tomato sauce, and paste to the meat and turned it down to simmer.

Road Tripped

On the TV, the scene cut to a reporter wearing a yellow and black Helly Hansen parka and holding a microphone with the KIRO 7 logo prominently displayed on it. He was interviewing an executive in a neat three piece suit in front of a sign bearing the *Live It* corporate logo.

As she put on water to boil, Mildred glanced again at the screen and said, "Tsk, tsk; why can't people just make an honest living?" Suddenly her attention was riveted to the screen as she saw her two houseguests shuffle past the camera like a couple of zombies. She looked back and forth between the guys and the TV to be sure. "Oh my!" she said.

She set the table and served the guys a delicious meal, although in their present state, they really had little appreciation for the wonderful flavor and aroma of the meal.

Over dinner, the guys told Mildred of the events of the day. She listened attentively to their tale of woe. When they'd finished, she slid a step stool over to reach the cupboard above the refrigerator, from which she extracted a bottle of brandy. She blew off a layer of dust and said, "My Henry always said a shot of brandy was good for the nerves. I never much cared for it, but maybe it'll help you feel better." She poured a dram in a couple of snifters and set them in front of her guests. "Warm the glasses in your hands and breathe the fumes before you drink," she instructed.

Mildred climbed back on the step stool again and rummaged around in the far reaches of the cupboard. She extracted an old shoe box. She brought it to the table and brushed the dust from the top before wiping her hands on her apron. Written on the top in a neat hand with a fountain pen was a short phrase. She turned it toward her guests. Aaron it aloud: "Pieces of string too short to save." Mildred lifted the lid, revealing a wad of multi-colored string, yarn and twine. She pulled a small batch from the wad and teased out a few strands, the longest of which was no more than six or seven inches in length.

The guys looked at each other with a puzzled expression. "If they're too short to save, why save them?" Jake asked.

"When I was a little girl, we had a farm in Arkansas. We weren't what you'd call well off, but we got by. That is until the drought came. We lost our crops one year and then the next. The next year, when we were done plowing, the wind came and carried all the soil away."

"The dust bowl," Aaron said.

"Yes," She said. "We finally had to give up and leave. There wasn't enough soil left to grow a weed. Our farm had blown away on the wind. We went to California where Pa looked for work, but with the depression on, jobs were few and far between. He left Ma and us kids with my aunt while he joined the CCC. They sent him to Washington State."

"The CCC? What's that?" Jake asked.

"The Civilian Conservation Corp," She answered. "It was a government program to give men jobs when there weren't any. Ma took in cleaning and sewing to help out. No one could afford new clothes so they mended what they had. When they were too far gone, she saved the rags, buttons, or even scraps of thread... these threads."

"I think I understand now," Jake said. "When you got nuthin', even a piece of string can give you hope."

"Just remember boys, you had nothing when you started, so what have you really lost?" She pulled a single strand from the wad, and took Jake's hand in hers. She put the string in his palm, curled his fingers around it, and patted it gently, smiling wistfully.

"May I?" Aaron asked while pulling another strand from the box. The guys put them in their wallets.

"Kinda puts things in perspective, don't it Aaron," Jake said.

"Here's to you, Mildred; for coming to our rescue today and reminding us that things aren't so bad after all," Aaron said while he and Jake held their glasses up to her. They downed them in a gulp.

"So what're ya gonna do now? She asked while pouring another round.

"We'll come up with somethin'," Jake said.

"Hmm," Mildred said thoughtfully. "Are you guys any good with tools?"

"I can twist a wrench," Jake said.

"I don't mean that kind of tool; I mean like woodworking tools and paint brushes and such. My house could use a little fixin' up."

"Is this like the CCC?" Aaron asked suspiciously.

"No," she said. "With Henry gone, I could use the help. Try as we might, we never had any kids, so I can't call on them."

"You don't have any other family?" Aaron asked.

"Just my sister. Her husband died too. Her daughter is divorced and lives back east somewhere. And her daughter, my grand niece, is grown and off living her life somewhere. Besides, I wouldn't want to be a bother."

"But we don't want to take advantage of you," Aaron said.

"Nonsense. It sounds like you guys could use a bit of money, and believe me, I'll get my money's worth," she said confidently.

Aaron and Jake shrugged and said, "Sure; why not?"

"It's settled then. I'll pay you each ten bucks an hour, cash under the table. You can start tomorrow. I'll pick you up at eight. Now let's get you guys home so you can get some rest."

A few minutes later, she dropped them off at Jake's house. He fumbled with his keys in the dark and finally managed to unlock the door. He reached in and flipped the light switch, only to discover that the power had been turned off. He felt around, searching in vain for a candle or some other means of illumination. In the dark, he couldn't find any dry kindling to light a fire either. He gave up and felt his way through the refrigerator for the beers he knew were there. They sat in the dark shivering as they polished off the better part of a case of beer.

Mildred pulled into the driveway at 8: 00 sharp and honked her horn. The guys stumbled out bleary eyed. It had been a cold night and neither of them had gotten much sleep. To make matters worse, with the power out, they didn't even have a way to make coffee. They felt every bit as pathetic as they looked. When they got to Mildred's house, they discussed what was to be done over a welcome pot of coffee and a hearty breakfast.

"OK guys, its 9: 00. You're on the clock; now let's get to it! You can start by raking leaves."

Raking leaves proved to be therapeutic for the guys. The sound of the metal rake tines on the ground and the smell of the damp leaves brought back memories of simpler times. The air was a bit chilly, but soon the physical exertion had them shedding their jackets. While they raked, Abner ambled around sniffing at the pile. Jake tossed a stick and said, "Fetch Abner; fetch." Abner wandered over to the stick, sniffed it, and gave

Jake a look as if asking, "What do you expect me to do with this?"

Over the next few weeks, the routine was very much the same. Mildred seemed to enjoy having the guys around and she was glad to have so many little projects taken care of. The guys felt good about helping her out and were it not for their financial dilemma they probably would have refused payment. As it was, they managed to earn enough money for Jake to get his power turned back on and buy a few groceries.

As the last item was crossed off of the list they had written, Mildred announced that that was all she could afford to have done for now. The guys could see that there was much left to do and offered to continue to work for free, but she said, "Nonsense! You boys work hard and you deserve to get paid. I'll have ya come back when I've had a chance to refill my piggybank."

When she dropped them off for the last time, she gave them a fresh baked apple pie and made them promise to come by for coffee on a regular basis. They both gave her a hug and assured her they would. Mildred was a dear old soul who helped to renew Aaron and Jake's faith in humanity. In a way she had become a bit of a surrogate grandmother to them.

Chapter Five

Aaron strode up the hill toward the old barn with Jake in tow. The cedar board and batten siding was silvered from exposure to the elements, but here and there, traces of the red iron oxide paint could still be found clinging in the crevasses. Its gambrel roof was covered with corrugated metal, from which most of the galvanizing had long ago succumbed to the ravages of time, leaving the bare steel to rust. Here and there, entire roof panels were missing, exposing the rafters and skip sheeting, which gave the barn the appearance of a rotting carcass whose skeleton had been picked over by scavengers. The cupola clung precariously to the peak of the roof which sagged in the middle like a sway backed old nag. Atop the cupola, the old wind vane stood askew and pointed perpetually to the southwest.

They approached the barn doors upon which the X-braces had been attached with square nails, dating the building in the nineteenth century. Aaron pulled the crooked old bolt that took the place of a padlock in the hasp and tossed it aside. With Jake's help, he swung the creaking doors open. The upper hinge on one of the doors broke off and they had to support the weight of the door as it reluctantly opened. Disturbed by their noisy entry, a barn owl took wing with a cry and swooped low over their heads on silent wing as it glided past.

They stepped in and allowed their eyes to adjust to the gloom. Beams of weak sunlight streamed in through cracked and missing boards. Scattered on the earthen floor were long forgotten farm implements, discarded household furnishings, broken appliances, and piles of old crates. The smell of dust mingled with that of musty gunnysacks, mildewed hay, and the old grease on the implements.

"What are we lookin' for in here?" Jake asked.

"You'll see." He led Jake to the back and began clearing away some of the rubbish to reveal something enshrouded in a rotted old canvas tarpaulin. "Remember when we used to go camping with my folks?"

"Yeah."

"Ta da!" He exclaimed as he yanked the tarp free and was showered with mouse droppings and the guano of countless pigeons. He coughed and said, "Behold *Gertrude*!"

Through the dust, the beams of sunlight illuminated a treasure from the past. The first thing Jake could make out was a tarnished VW emblem. Soon he could make out the sweeping arch where the contrasting shades of faded green paint came together. *Gertrude*.

Gertrude was a vintage Volkswagen micro bus. When they were kids, Aaron's parents used to take them camping from time to time. As they drove to their destination, the boys would look up through the open roof at the clouds as they passed, or out the row of small windows along the sides of the roof. The total number of individual glass panes was twenty-one; they had counted them all. The boys would sleep in a pup tent nearby while the adults slept on the back seat that folded out into a bed. Aaron's mom had sewn paisley curtains for the windows and they had used kerosene lanterns for light. Their meals were prepared either over an open fire or on a Coleman white gas stove. Seeing the old bus brought back many happy memories. Aaron's mom had liked to call them four peas in a pod on their camping trips.

"Damn!" Jake exclaimed. "I didn't know ya still had her. When was the last time she ran?"

"I dunno; it's been a long time."

The left front tire was flat and the rest of the tires were cracked with age. Aaron grabbed a bicycle tire pump from where it had always hung above the cluttered workbench and commenced to try to get some air into the tire. The old fashioned pump had a leather piston which had dried and shrunk to the point where it would barely pump, but eventually he was able to get just enough air into the tire for it to roll.

They cleared away more of the stuff so they could get to the driver's side door. The door opened with a groan and it was immediately apparent that squirrels had made their home inside. Aaron brushed away the debris from the cracked vinyl seat with his hand. He reached over and put the shifter into neutral, then checked to be sure the parking brake was off. Clearing away more stuff, they tried to make their way to the back so they could push, but unfortunately, she had been parked right back against the wall. Instead, Aaron found a piece of hemp rope which he tied to the front bumper. "C'mon, pull!" He said. They leaned into it and *Gertrude* had just begun to move when the rotted old rope parted and they fell flat on their butts in a cloud of dust. At least they had moved her far enough that they could get behind her and push. Aaron opened the door and hopped into the driver's seat. As usual, Jake had to push. With her nearly flat tires, it wasn't easy, but eventually, she rolled out into the weak autumn sunshine.

Outside the barn there was a bit of a slope and *Gertrude* began to move on her own. Aaron stepped on the brake, but the pedal went right to the floor. He pumped the pedal furiously but to no avail and she began to gain speed. Giving up, he steered her toward the shallow gully that ran across the property. She had enough momentum that she rolled up the other side, slowed, and started to roll backward. She again gained speed and rolled back up the grade, slowed to a stop once more, and then rolled ahead to a stop in the bottom of the gully.

The guys stood back to survey her condition. The retractable canvas roof was rotted, but at least there was enough of it left to serve as a pattern for a new one. She would clearly need all new or at least newer tires. Obviously the brakes would need attention, but all in all, she looked pretty good. They opened the hatch on the rear to reveal her air-cooled boxer engine. The squirrels had been at work there too. Aside from a cracked generator belt and ignition wires that the squirrels had munched on, it looked pretty good. Even the oil on the dipstick looked clean. Jake twisted off the gas cap and took a sniff, expecting to smell gas turned to varnish. Instead he smelled only stale air. He slid under her to look at the fuel tank and could see the stains where the fuel had leaked out through pinholes where rust had eaten through. The good news was that that would mean the carburetor would not be all gummed up.

"So what ya gonna do with her?" Jake asked.

"Ya mean what're we gonna do with her!

"OK, what're we gonna do with her?"

"ROAD TRIP!"

Their attention was drawn back to the barn by a creaking sound. As they watched, the barn began to lean to one side. Some boards popped off and clattered to the ground. And then, with a sustained rending groan accompanied by the screaming protest of nails pulling free, the barn that had stood for well over a hundred years crashed to the ground. The billowing cloud of dust from its collapse began to settle, revealing the cupola still standing erect, although now at ground level. The only remaining sound was the squeaking of the wind vane, which was turning for the first time in many, many years, as it spun forlornly over the rubble. Soon it too was silent. The guys stood in shock surveying the ruins.

With *Ingrid* missing in action, Jake had finally found it necessary invest in tires and get his car down off the blocks. The next morning, he arrived in his car and parked near *Gertrude*. He opened the trunk and began to unload the blocks. Soon *Gertrude* was up on the blocks without her wheels. They piled the wheels in the trunk of Jake's car as best they could and secured the lid with a length of baling wire.

Together they made a list of the things they would need to get *Gertrude* running. They covered *Gertrude*'s roof with a blue poly tarp that usually covered Aaron's riding mower and weighted it down with plastic milk jugs filled with water tied to the corners. They tossed a five gallon gas can in the back seat of Jake's car and set out for "Po Dunk" (Port Orchard) to get parts and supplies.

At the wrecking yard, they found four reasonably good tires, three of which actually matched. A half rack of Coors was enough to get them mounted and balanced. Back at Aaron's place, they replaced the belt, installed new points, plugs, condenser, rotor, cap, and wires. They replaced the air filter and installed an in-line fuel filter. The pinholes in the bottom of the tank were sealed with epoxy. They changed the brake fluid and while the wheels were off, inspected and adjusted the brakes. When they had bled the air from the system, it was time to put the wheels back on. They installed a new battery and poured fuel in the tank. With that, Aaron hopped behind the wheel and Jake went back to watch for any problems in the engine compartment. Aaron reached up and retrieved the key from where it had been on top of the sun visor for many years. Inserting the key in the ignition, he said, "Here goes nothin'!" He pulled the choke, pumped the accelerator a few times and turned the key. The starter motor turned her over smoothly, but the engine did not start. From the rear, Jake called, "Try her again; the fuel filter is still filling up. After a few more turns, the engine coughed a bit. Aaron pumped the accelerator again and turned the key. The engine caught and he eased the choke in part way, keeping the engine revved up a bit. After a few minutes, he was able to open the choke fully and let the engine idle down. She purred like a kitten.

Aaron got out and he and Jake walked around and looked her over. Everything looked in good working order. With a whoop, they gave each other a high five and hopped in. They drove down to Jake's house, along the way checking the brakes. There they washed off years worth of grime, vacuumed out the interior thoroughly and surveyed their work. *Gertrude* looked good. Damn good.

Their first excursion took them only as far as Mildred's place. When they pulled into her driveway, Abner bayed at the sight of an unfamiliar car, but as soon as he recognized the guys, he wagged his tail in greeting. Mildred stepped out onto the porch, wiping her hands on her apron. She hugged the guys and walked around inspecting the van.

"Mildred, meet *Gertrude!*" Aaron said.

"So this is what you boys have been up to!"

"Do you think you could do us a favor? We need new canvas for the sun roof."

Mildred looked it over and said, "I've got just the thing."

They took off the rotted old top and left it for her to use as a pattern.

"Say guys, while you're here, could you take a look at the kitchen sink drain?" While they were inside, she took measurements of the seats. When they came back out, she said, "OK guys, I should have your top made in a couple of days. Now you skedaddle so I can get to work on it."

They gave her hugs and kisses on her cheeks and were on their way.

Aaron and Jake were outside raking up the last of the fall leaves when Mildred's car pulled in. She got out and opened the trunk from which she extracted a pile of green and yellow floral pattern fabric. She unfolded the largest piece to reveal the new top for *Gertrude*. The guys grinned at the flamboyant pattern, but it seemed only fitting to have a top like this on a genuine authentic early American hippie van. While the guys fitted the new top, Mildred fitted the seat covers she had made as a surprise. Mildred was a bit sentimental about the Sunbrella fabric she had used. She had bought it years ago to upholster a porch swing her and Henry had planned to build together. But the cancer took him before it was done, so the fabric had been waiting for the right time to come out. As soon as she saw *Gertrude*, she knew why she'd kept it.

Road Tripped

"She really looks great Mildred!" Aaron exclaimed. "What do we owe you?"

"There ain't nothin' I need. How about a hug for an ol' lady?"

"Shoot Mildred, you get those for free."

Although they couldn't persuade Mildred to take anything for her work, the guys knew that she would need some more firewood for the winter, so they borrowed a friend's pick-up and cut, split and stacked a couple of chords of dry maple for her. They went by the old abandoned shake mill down Frageria road where they found piles of rejected cedar shakes which they split into kindling and put in paper sacks in the basement. She was most grateful and it felt good knowing she would stay warm over the winter.

To prepare for their impending departure, Aaron and Jake resurrected the old Coleman white gas stove from the wreckage of the barn. They would use it to prepare their meals and more importantly, coffee, without which they were unlikely to survive a day. Mildred found an old fashioned aluminum coffee percolator and showed them how to use it. They found an old kerosene lantern in the attic of Jake's house in case they needed light, but for the most part, they figured that daylight would serve most of their needs. They planned to bathe in lakes, rivers, and streams whenever possible, but in the event that none were to be found, they would use the galvanized steel watering can that Jake's mom had used to water her flowers as a shower. Perishable provisions, and more importantly beer, would be stored in a classic metal cooler and non-perishables would be stowed in a Rubbermaid tub. Without a particular destination or route in mind, they had to pack clothes for any occasion, so both packed jeans, tee shirts, and flannel shirts.

"Heads we go north, tails we go south." Aaron said as he tossed the coin. He caught it in his right hand and slapped it onto the back of his left. They looked at it together. It had come up heads.

"Winter's just around the corner; ain't a good time to be goin' north. Toss it again," Jake said.

The next toss came up tails.

Road Tripped

Chapter Six

In the weeks since leaving Olalla, the guys travelled through all of the western states. Along the way they adapted to life on the road.

Gertrude proved to be a willing accomplice, taking it all in stride. For the most part, all they had to do was refuel her, add oil from time to time, air up the tires, and wash the windshield. On flat ground, she could only muster about fifty miles an hour, and on hills, she was only good for about thirty-five, even less in the high passes. Her underwhelming performance didn't bother the guys; they were in no hurry, and traveling at a slower pace allowed more time to enjoy the scenery. Her leisurely pace did tend to incite rage in drivers forced to follow until they could find a way past. Often they would wave as they went by, but only with one finger.

The first leg of their journey carried them east through the gorge separating Washington and Oregon, where the Columbia River cuts through the Cascade Mountains. Towering hexagonal basalt columns soared to hundreds or even thousands of feet in height and thin threads of water fell from the vertical cliffs. The ever present west wind at their tail gave them a nice boost, and at least once, Aaron saw the speedometer needle swing over to near sixty. As soon as they cleared the gorge, they took the first opportunity to break away from the main highway to meander the back roads more suited to their agenda and *Gertrude*'s pace.

East of the mountains, the topography changed. The evergreen forests of western Washington gave way to rolling hills and wheat fields that stretched to the horizon of eastern Oregon. The wheat had already been harvested, leaving fields of stubble. Scattered about the huge fields were farmhouses clustered with barns, silos, and equipment sheds that were protected by rows of poplar trees permanently deformed by the wind. The hustle and bustle of large cities was replaced by sleepy little towns. The signs welcoming them to town often proudly displayed populations in the dozens or hundreds rather than thousands. Tree shaded streets were lined with neat whitewashed Craftsman homes. The main street (often the only street) usually had a number of small businesses owned and operated by descendents of the founding family for which the town was named. The fruit doesn't fall far from the tree.

In Bakerville, they stopped for a burger at Ma Baker's Cafe. They sat on round topped stools at the lunch counter elbow to elbow with local farm hands. Ma herself took their orders and placed their ticket on a spinner in the window of the kitchen. Through the window, they could see the cook who bore a strong resemblance to Ma working the griddle like a maestro tickling the ivory keys of his grand piano. Ma prepared their milkshakes and served them in the frosty stainless steel cups in which they were made along with an equally frosty glass cups and long spoons. The smells of the food being served had the effect of sharpening the guys' appetites. Every time the cook rang the bell that another order was ready, they salivated like Pavlov's dogs. When their orders arrived, the buns, unadorned with sesame seeds glistened with a sheen of grease spattered from the grille. A steaming mountain of French fries was garnished with a sprig of fresh parsley. They attacked their meals with the gusto of a pack of ravenous dogs. The food tasted as good as it smelled. With a twinkle in her eyes, Ma said, "If ya eat those plates, it'll cost you extra!" They could not resist Ma's offer of huge slices of fresh, homemade pie to complete their meals.

Next, they stopped for fuel at Baker and Son's Service Station. The appearance of the building had them wondering if they'd been transported back in time to the '50s, a time before service stations had become only gas stations. As they pulled up to the pump, a young man who bore a resemblance to Ma from the cafe stepped out from under the car on the rack, wiping his hands on a rag from the back pocket of his greasy coveralls with the name *Hank* embroidered above the breast pocket. Hank greeted them and asked, "What'll it be?" They still could not get used to being met at the pump. In Washington State, the profession of gas station attendant had long since gone the way of the dinosaurs, but in Oregon they discovered it was illegal to pump your own gas.

"Fill 'er up with regular, please," Aaron answered.

"Will do." While the tank was filling, Hank went to the front of *Gertrude* and asked Aaron to pop the hood. He was surprised to learn that the engine was in the back. "Well I'll be darn. I ain't never heard o' such a thing!" he exclaimed. He accepted their cash and went back to work in the garage.

With their bellies and the tank full, they continued on their way. Sometime later, Aaron felt *Gertrude* begin to wallow around and handle oddly. There was no shoulder, but he found a wide spot in the road and pulled over. He and Jake got out to see what was amiss. Much to their dismay, they found that the left front tire was deflating. Upon closer inspection, Jake found a nail protruding from the tread. He grabbed it and wiggled it out. "Here's the culprit," he exclaimed, holding it up triumphantly. They became aware of the hiss of escaping air, and the tire began to deflate much more rapidly. "Oops, maybe I should've left it there. In just a few moments, *Gertrude* was resting on her rim.

"Well, I best get the jack," Aaron said and began rummaging around trying to find where it was stowed. At home, they'd used a floor jack they found in the wreckage of the barn, so they had no idea where the jack was or even if there was one. Try as he might, none could be found. "Shit, no jack. Now what're we gonna do?"

Jake scanned the surrounding area and spotted a stack of wooden fence posts nearby. "Come'ere and gimme a hand," he beckoned Aaron over to the pile. They began sorting through the pile, and Jake selected the longest and sturdiest posts. After a couple of trips, they had a stack of posts near *Gertrude*.

"What're ya gonna do now, build us a cabin?" Aaron asked.

"Shut up and let's put the ol' two man stare on it," their code for thinking something out together.

After a bit of head scratching, Jake laid a short, thick post alongside *Gertrude* and wedged the longest pole over it and under *Gertrude*'s frame. "Now all ya gotta do is lever her off the ground while I block her up."

Aaron looked skeptical. "Why do I have to do it?" he asked.

"You're more capable."

"How so?"

"You weigh more."

"Oh." He sat on the end of the post, and sure enough, the wheel lifted off the ground while Jake positioned blocks under the frame.

"I'll be damned, it worked," Aaron said.

"Well, ya know what they say…"

"If it's stupid and it works, it ain't stupid!" they said in unison, reciting one of their familiar truisms.

"Gimme the lug wrench," Jake said.

Aaron went back to rummaging. He could be heard muttering to himself. "Ah ha!" he exclaimed and handed Jake the wrench. "I'll go fetch the spare."

In moments, Jake had the wheel off. Aaron returned with a sheepish look on his face.

"Uh Jake, we might have a bit of a problem," he said.

"Let me guess. No spare tire?"

"Bingo."

"Shit."

It was mid afternoon and it was Sunday. They were several miles east of bumfuck nowhere. In a word, they were screwed.

A dusty old Ford farm truck came into view, the first vehicle they'd seen in some time. Much to their relief, the truck slowed on approach and then came to a stop. The lanky driver and his two burley passengers climbed out. All wore tattered jeans, flannel shirts, and trucker hats, attire not much different than Aaron and Jake's. The three did not smile or speak. It brought the movie Deliverance to mind. In the movie, a group of friends found themselves abducted by a bunch of inbred, banjo plucking, pig sodomizing hillbillies.

The driver pulled a pack of unfiltered camels from his shirt pocket and tapped it on the palm of his hand before shaking one up and pulling it out with his lips. He pulled a box of wooden

Ron Fugere

matches from his pocket, struck one on the seam of his jeans, and lit his cigarette. One of the passengers who could pass for Larry the Cable Guy pulled a tin of Copenhagen out of his hip pocket, opened it, and put a pinch under his lip. The third guy just casually scratched his ass. Still nothing was said. One could almost hear the banjo playing. "Larry" spit a stream of brown tobacco juice on the ground and wiped his chin with the back of his hand. The guys began to wonder who was going have to squeal like a pig. The driver blew a smoke ring. "Got a flat?" he asked.

Duh, they thought. "Uh yeah," Aaron said.

"Where's yer spare?"

"We, uh don't have one."

"Well shoooot. I guess yer in a heap o' trouble then." He smiled.

The ass scratcher turned and headed for the truck. Visible through the windshield was an Easy Rider rifle rack, but no rifles. Could one be concealed on the floor? The guys tensed as he opened the door and reached in. He pulled out a case of Coors. "C'mon, let's have a cold one," he said and headed around the back of the truck, where he dropped the tailgate and set the beer down. Aaron, Jake, and the two passengers all reached in and cracked one open.

The driver abstained. "Nah, none fer me. Ah'm th' dezinated dryver," he said. After a while, he said, "Well drink up boys, we best ought git that tire t' town if'n ya wanna git 'er back on 'fore dark. Yer car be in a preeecarious poe-zishun. Some drunk driver liable plow right ina her." "Larry" tossed the tire in the back of the truck and he and "Ass Scratch" climbed aboard. Aaron and Jake joined the driver in the cab. He cranked up the Ford, executed a 3-point turn, and headed back toward town.

Road Tripped

They soon arrived back at Bakerville and pulled up in front of Baker and Son's Service Station. The sign on the door said closed. The business hours were listed as nine to five Monday through Saturday and ten to two Sunday. Aaron glanced at his wrist watch. It was 4: 47. Shit. A man emerged from a house across the street wearing his Sunday best. He sauntered over and asked, "What can I do for ya fellas?"

"We got a flat," Aaron said.

"Well, let's have a look at it. Bring it on in." Marv "Pa" Baker, the owner, rolled up the unlocked door to the garage. "Put it there on the changer." He turned on a breaker to start the air compressor, took off his jacket and hung it on a hook, then rolled up his sleeves while the compressor built up pressure. In a few minutes, he had the tire loose on the rim and extracted the inner tube. Remember those? He inflated the tube and dunked it in a tank of water to watch for bubbles to show where the puncture was. After marking the spot, he removed the valve stem and deflated the tube, then roughed up the area of the hole with a rasp. He wiped it off with a rag before applying glue from a tube. He struck a match and set the glue afire. He stood at the ready with the patch in hand and as soon as the fire sputtered out, he quickly applied it and rolled out any bubbles with a small roller. He re-inflated the tube and checked it again in the dunk tank. Satisfied with the repair, he reinstalled the tube in the tire, and inflated it. He dusted off his hands and asked, "Anything else I can do for you guys?"

"No, That's all we needed. Thanks."

"Well then I'll be getting' back to my supper." He washed his hands, rolled his sleeves back down, buttoned his cuffs, and slipped on his jacket.

"What do we owe you?" Jake asked.

"Well now, this bein' Sunday and all…"

Knowing they were at his mercy, Jake winced as he reached for his wallet.

"This bein' Sunday, and after hours, I ain't open for business. Putcher wallet away, son."

Fred, Larry (his real name) and Mike returned Aaron and Jake to *Gertrude* and stood by while they reinstalled the wheel. They gave them directions to their favorite camping spot down by the river and gave them the rest of the Coors. Then they hopped in the truck, honking and waving as they drove off. Down by the river, they finished the Coors for dinner.

Aaron and Jake then traveled up over the Blue Mountains onto the Idaho pan handle and its vast potato farms. A pick-up passed them. Nothing out of the ordinary about that, given that *Gertrude* often struggled to reach the speed limit. What was unusual, was the way that the shaven headed driver slowed as he pulled alongside. The scowling driver and his passenger scrutinized Aaron and Jake. Their sidelong gaze made the guys a bit uneasy. Their intentions became apparent when they pulled ahead. The tailgate, back window, and bumper were adorned with NRA stickers, confederate flags, and bumper stickers with anti-gay slogans. Perhaps they were looking for some gays to bash. Apparently, Aaron and Jake didn't look gay enough to meet their criteria. They were relieved to pass the sign welcoming them to Montana.

In Big Sky Country they noticed that theirs seemed to be the only vehicle in existence that was not a 4X4 pick-em-up truck with huge off-road tires. They stopped for groceries at a supermarket. They wandered the aisles under the baleful glare from the glass eyes of stuffed deer, elk, and antelope being attacked by cougars, black bears, and wolves. A snarling Grizzly standing erect towered over shoppers. Bobcats, lynx, and coyotes were posed with porcupines, raccoons, and possums. There was even a skunk standing on its forelegs as if ready to spray customers. Mounted heads of bighorn sheep, mountain goats, and bison adorned the walls. There was even a souvenir department where tourists could buy various bits and pieces of their favorite wild animal to adorn their man-cave. They had hoped to see wildlife in its natural element on their swing through Montana, and were appalled to see it displayed in such a manner. Back home, they were accustomed to having deer wander peacefully through the orchard unmolested. They were even tolerated when they grazed on Jake's mom's prized flowers. Once, one jumped the fence to get into the vegetable garden, and Jake's dad had thrown a rock at it. He missed, but still got a good ass chewing by his mom. When a young doe, "Lucky Lucy" was hit by a car in front of the house, Jake had nursed her back to health. To this day, her offspring and their offspring visited the orchard every year. He knew each individual deer by name. They were like family. Shooting one and having it stuffed as a trophy would be like having the family dog stuffed.

In Wyoming, they visited Yellowstone National Park, where they did get to see wild animals, but there, they would be seen trying to get into the bear proof garbage cans or approaching cars looking for a hand-out. They were going to visit Old Faithful, but found out it was closed for repair. (Actually, the road leading to it).

Next the guys headed into Utah, where they marveled at the colorfully sculpted sandstone geologic features in and around the national parks. They carefully avoided the bicycle ridin', white shirt and black tie wearin', backpack totin' pairs of zombies whose purpose in life was to "save" them by introducing them to the wonders of sacred underwear. One could only guess what horrible fate awaited our wayward travelers in the afterlife. After all, Aaron wore plaid boxers whereas Jake went commando.

The days were growing shorter and the nights cooler which drove them further south. In Nevada, they drove down the strip in Las Vegas at night, dazzled by the flashing lights, but avoiding the casinos. They had gambled enough by investing in their company and that hadn't worked out so well for them, now had it?! They sought out the Mustang Ranch, not to seek the pleasures of the ladies, but for souvenir tee shirts to add to their meager wardrobes.

Meandering back to the southwest to California, they stood in awe of the massive Redwood and Sequoia trees which dwarfed even the giant old-growth cedars in what remained of the primeval forests of their home state. They camped in Yosemite where they compared the view of Half Dome to the sepia toned photographs by Ansel Adams. In southern California, they made their way to the beach where *Gertrude* never failed to draw a crowd of admiring surfer dudes who pictured her with a roof rack filled with their surfboards. Aaron and Jake tried (and failed) at body surfing in the Pacific. Afterward, they stretched out on the sand to catch their breath. Aaron closed his eyes and enjoyed the smell of the salt air and the roar of the surf while Jake scanned the beach. A pair of deeply tanned, bikini clad girls with sun bleached hair caught his eye while they tossed a frisbee. He nudged Aaron and nodded in their direction. As if in answer to Jake's prayers, the frisbee landed at his feet. He picked it up and held it as the girls jogged over to retrieve it. The shorter of the two girls with an ample bosom said, "Sorry 'bout that!"

"No problem," Jake stammered as he handed her the frisbee.

Road Tripped

"You're not from around here, are you?"

"Nope; how could you tell?"

"You look like a Maine lobster fresh out of the pot. Don't you have any sunscreen?"

"Uh nope," he said as he looked down at his pink skin.

"Mandy has some in her car. Come on up; we better get some on you before you burn to a crisp. I'm Kailee, by the way."

"I'm Jake and this is Aaron. We're from Washington."

"I could've guessed. Don't you ever have any sun up there?"

"Not this time of year."

"Follow us," Mandy said, flashing her pearly white teeth.

"Lead away," Aaron said. The guys fell in behind the girls, giving each other a high five at their good fortune as they admired the look of the girls from behind. They were led to a white Volkswagen Golf cabriolet with the top down, where Mandy grabbed a tube of sun tan lotion from the back seat.

"Turn around," she said to Aaron and began rubbing it on his back while Kailee did likewise with Jake. Mandy took the tube back and turned Aaron around so she could rub some on his chest. She finished with a dab which she playfully put on his nose. "Feel better?"

"Yeah, much. Thanks. You girls want a beer? We've got some on ice in our car," Aaron offered.

The girls looked at each other and shrugged. "Sure; why not?" Mandy answered.

Now it was the girl's turn to follow. "Damn, today's our lucky day!" Jake whispered as they walked across the lot to *Gertrude* where a sun-bronzed Adonis said, "nice wheels Dudes!"

Aaron opened up the side doors and reached into the cooler for beers.

69

"We better get inside; it's illegal to drink in the parking lot," Mandy said as she accepted a cold one. They all hopped in and stretched out on the reclined back seat. Aaron closed the doors. It just keeps getting better, Jake thought.

When they'd finished their beers, Mandy said, "Mmm, the sunshine makes me feel kinda frisky!" Aaron and Jake broke into huge grins, but then their jaws dropped as Mandy grabbed Kailee and lay her back while they locked lips and their bodies entwined. "Mmmmm, let's go home," Kailee moaned. They swung the doors open and ran hand in hand over to Mandy's car. The guys could only watch in dismay as the girls drove away. Their hopes deflated like a popped balloon.

"Damn! What the...." Jake said

"Ya gotta admit, it was hot though, wasn't it?!"

"Damn!"

Next, in Arizona they took in the wonders of Monument Valley and the Grand Canyon which served as a reminder just how insignificant we humans really are in the grand scheme of things. Crossing the desert made them long for the forests of home.

In the Rocky Mountains of Colorado, the thin air of the high passes coupled with the anemic performance of her engine had poor ol' *Gertrude* struggling to maintain twenty miles an hour. They discovered just how useless the heater and defroster was on a vehicle equipped with an air-cooled engine. The best way to stay warm was to don more layers of clothes and wear hats and gloves. To keep the windshield clear, they tried using a towel before determining that a squeegee worked best.

The cold drove them further south into New Mexico, where the spirits of the Anasazi, the ancient ones seemed to haunt the pueblo ruins on the high plateaus.

Road Tripped

In Texas, they visited Dallas, where they sat upon the infamous grassy knoll and discussed the conspiracy theories about that fateful day in 1963. Although the Kennedy assassination had occurred before their births, it remained a controversy to this day.

In Houston, they visited the Johnson Space Center where they were amazed at what had been accomplished before the days of modern computers, that man had succeeded in putting a man on the moon with computers much less sophisticated than most wrist watches of today. Their parents had told them of being perched in front of the flickering black and white portable television set as Neil Armstrong uttered his famous phrase, "that's one small step for man, one giant leap for mankind."

Poring over their Rand McNally map, Jake asked, "Well where are we gonna head next?"

"I dunno; ya got any ideas?" Aaron replied.

"Wha'd'ya say we head for Louisiana? I've always wanted to see New Orleans."

"Sounds good! We could check out the bayou country too. Which way?" Aaron said as they drew up to an intersection.

"If ya go straight here, we could catch interstate ten."

"You know the rules. No freeways!"

Jake looked at their trusty Boy Scout compass and said, "OK; turn right here."

"You're the navigator."

After driving for a while, the guys found their way blocked by a line of cars. Aaron brought *Gertrude* to a stop. "Where are we?" He asked.

"I dunno; we must've taken a wrong turn somewhere. Maybe we oughta turn around."

Before they could do so, another car pulled up behind and another to their left, blocking them in. As they edged closer to the front of the line, no opportunities presented themselves to turn around. They came to the head of the line at a booth.

"Pasaportes por favor," the uniformed man in the booth said.

"Huh?" Aaron said.

"May I see your passports please?"

The guys rifled through their bags until they found them. Although they had not planned on needing them, they'd brought them along just so they wouldn't get lost back home. They were perplexed, but handed them over nonetheless.

"What is the purpose of your visit?" The man asked.

"We're just on a road trip."

"Road trip?"

"Vacation." "And how long will you be in Mexico?"

"Mexico?!"

His patience worn thin, the man said, "Please pull over and park there," while signaling to another man.

"How'd ya get us to Mexico?" Aaron asked Jake incredulously.

"You're the driver!"

"You're the navigator!" Aaron shrugged and said, "I guess we're already here, we might as well make the best of it."

Gertrude was set upon by one guy rifling through all of their belongings while another with a flashlight slid under her on a creeper and yet another led a German shepherd around on a leash, sniffing everything. The dog found Jake's dirty socks particularly interesting. Meanwhile, Aaron and Jake were led to separate rooms where they were asked to disrobe. When Jake started to protest, the guy snapped on a pair of latex gloves and reached for something that looked like a gynecological instrument. His look made it clear that they could do it the easy way or the hard way. Jake complied. The guard raised his eyebrows in surprise when Jake removed his jeans, revealing the anatomical feature that had been the envy of every guy in the high school locker room. His clothes were searched thoroughly, but he was at least spared the added humiliation of a body cavity search. What the agents were looking for was a mystery to them, but whatever it was, they apparently didn't find it. Next the guys were led to an office where they sat facing yet another official who demanded payment of some sort of semi-official fees, which he slipped into a drawer in his desk.

"Bienvenido a México, caballeros!" The agent said.

"Huh?"

"Welcome to Mexico Señores; now be gone!"

Chapter Seven

And so our wayward travelers came to be in Mexico. Neither of the guys spoke a word of Spanish, and most of what they knew of Mexican traditions and customs they had learned from bar stools on Cinco de Mayo. Once in Mexico, even the simplest of everyday activities presented a challenge. Where do they eat and what? Where could they exchange their dollars for pesos? Where could they buy fuel for *Gertrude*? Where does one find a bathroom? They were surprised to find that it was customary to either bring your own toilet paper or tip an attendant in exchange for the use of a roll. Fortunately, it seemed that there was always someone willing to step in and help them, sometimes for a few pesos but more often out of kindness.

As they had done in their travels through the western US, they left navigation to chance, circumstance, and whims.

Having crossed the border, they found themselves in the State of Chihuahua, Mexico. Yes, they have states there too. The state is not named for the little leg-humpin' ankle-bitin' dogs, but for the Chihuahuan Desert which they skirted and made their way up into the Sierra Madre Occidental mountain range, an extension of the Rocky Mountains. Here the cool of higher altitude was a welcome relief from the heat. They visited, Las Barrancas del Cobre, the famous Copper Canyon which is somewhat like the US Grand Canyon but is not a park. Instead, small remote villages are accessed by a train which transports locals and their livestock alongside camera toting tourists. They crossed a vast area of short grass prairies and broad river valleys sprinkled with agricultural activity.

Next they came to the State of Durango, the so-called land of scorpions, where they were sure to shake out their shoes before slipping them on. The terrain reminded them of scenes depicted in the western movies of their youth. This was no coincidence, as many such westerns were filmed here. They could easily picture Clint Eastwood facing down bands of swarthy banditos with their huge sombreros and bandoleers.

They crossed the high plateau and small mesas of Zacatecas in north central Mexico, passing through cities with colonial architecture dating back hundreds of years.

In San Luis Potosi State, they left the plateaus behind and crossed more mountains, then dropped down through pine and oak forests onto the coastal plains of the Gulf of Mexico in Veracruz. When they reached the shore of the gulf, they found a stretch of beach alongside the highway that looked inviting, and decided it was time for a swim. They waded out into the warm water but when they were hundreds of yards from shore, the water had not yet reached their knees so they gave up.

Leaving Veracruz behind, they entered Tabasco, the namesake of the famous Louisiana hot sauce. Here they turned away from the coast, heading upstream along one of the many rivers that crisscrossed the region. They crossed many other streams that emptied into the river basin. The hot moist air had the guys running with sweat day and night, so when they happened across an inviting swimming hole, they would take full advantage. A towel seemed to be of no use, as they could never get dry in the humidity, so they dressed still wet. The rivers were the only break in an otherwise endless low jungle. They were relieved when the road began to carry them higher.

In the State of Campeche, they followed the main highway east through miles of uninterrupted jungle toward Quintana Roo where they descended to the inviting coast of the Caribbean Sea. In Cancun, they encountered hordes of tourists mingling with modern day hippies. They rented snorkeling gear and explored the coral reefs in crystal clear water. It was a far cry from swimming in the waters of the Puget Sound back home, where even on the hottest summer day, the water was cold enough to bring on hypothermia and visibility was but a few feet at best. They swam among shoals of brilliantly colored fish in all shapes and sizes. When an eight foot shark swam by, they decided that they'd had enough fun. It was only a placid nurse shark and posed no threat, but sill, it was a shark!

In Yucatán, they crossed the middle of the peninsula, exploring the numerous cenotes, which are sinkholes resulting from the collapse of limestone bedrock that exposed caves and groundwater underneath. They swung from the roots of jungle trees imitating Tarzan, before dropping into crystal clear water. They visited Mérida, a city that was over 200 years old before the United States even existed as a country. Many of the colonial building were constructed from the remains of ancient Mayan ruins which were scattered across the region. They shopped in a huge public market that had been in operation for hundreds of years. It encompassed several city blocks. Dozens of vendors with similar offerings competed for customers. The guys were at a loss for how the locals determined from which vendor to make their purchases.

Beggars with hideous deformities huddled on the sidewalks with little cups, hoping for someone to toss them a few pesos, unlike the beggars in Seattle who stood at every street corner with the ubiquitous cardboard signs, many of whom would look for hand-outs before hopping in their SUV to return to their suburban homes. Although they had little to share, the guys gave them what they could.

They went to the Plaza de la Independencia on a beautiful evening to watch the street performers. Mariachi bands in full regalia wandered about while comedy troupes performed acts that would never be allowed in politically correct America. Jugglers and fire breathers too would try to attract a crowd to fill their hats. Tourists circled the plaza in horse drawn carriages along with a constant stream of cars. Along with the music of the performers, the blaring of countless horns and police whistles created a cacophony of sounds. Carried on the gentle breeze was the aroma of numerous food vendors. The evening concluded with a spectacular fireworks show that held all spellbound. As the smoke cleared, the vendors began gathering their wares, the performers concluded their performances, and all headed for home. With the evening winding down, the guys joined the rest of the crowd leaving.

They took a wrong turn and found themselves in an area where three hot girls with big hair and flashy earrings stood on the sidewalk smoking cigarettes. They wore extremely short skintight spandex dresses in shocking shades of red, blue, and yellow. The girls sized the guys up as they passed. They exchanged a few words and one wandered off, leaving a girl for each guy. A particularly comely blond shook out her flowing tresses, gave Jake a come-hither look, and purred something in Spanish. Jake stopped cold in his tracks. She crushed out her cigarette butt under the toe of her towering spike heel and with a crook of her finger, beckoned Jake to join her in the hotel in front of which they stood. Jake dutifully followed like a fish that took the worm.

From behind, Aaron called out, "Uh, Jake?" Jake ignored him, intent on the prize. "Jake!" Aaron called out more insistently.

At last Jake replied, "Get lost dude; find your own date!"

"Do ya notice anything, uh, unusual about your 'date?'"

"Yeah, she's hot as…" The girl turned and in the wash of light from the overhead streetlight, Jake could make out a five o'clock shadow and an Adam's apple. They beat a hasty retreat.

They had left *Gertrude* on a back street around the corner from a purple painted appliance store on Calle 6 They had strategically parked her there so that they could simply follow the calle and would have no difficulty finding where they'd parked her. But when they reached the spot, *Gertrude* was nowhere to be seen! Looking around, there was no mistaking that they had come to the right spot, but what could have become of her? They circled a few blocks to see if they could find her, but she could not be found.

They headed back along the calle, returning to the central plaza where they sought out a police officer. He looked perplexed when they tried to explain their dilemma and summoned another officer, who approached and asked in English, "How can I be of service, señores?"

"Someone stole our car!" Aaron explained.

"Can you describe the car, por favor?" the officer asked.

Road Tripped

"It is a green and white Volkswagen bus, like that one over there," Aaron replied while pointing at a car parked at the curb nearby with its side door standing wide open and a couple of swarthy guys leaning against it smoking. "It's not *like* that car it *is* that car!" He cried as he started toward the car with Jake and the officer following.

The guys who had been leaning on *Gertrude* nonchalantly crushed out their cigarettes under their cowboy boots and slipped away into the night.

"Aren't you gonna try to catch 'em?" Aaron asked the officer.

"Catch who?"

"The guys who stole our car."

"But is this not your car?"

"Yeah."

"So is not stolen."

"But…"

With the mystery solved, the Police officer bid them good evening and resumed his beat.

The keys were still in *Gertrude*'s ignition. Food wrappers and empty bottles littered the floor in front of the passenger seat, but that was nothing out of the ordinary. In the back were empty boxes, it appeared that the two men they'd seen had not intended to steal the car, they just needed to borrow it for a while. Aaron and Jake's few possessions had been moved aside but were unmolested. Aaron fired up *Gertrude* and drove toward the outskirts of the city to find a quiet street where they could spend the rest of the night. They would resume their journey in the morning.

As they passed from state to state, they would often encounter police or military checkpoints. Apparently, two guys traveling in a hippie van was cause for suspicion, and *Gertrude* was often subjected to search. Fortunately, the guys were spared any more strip searches.

Each day offered entirely new experiences and memories. Every dusty village they passed along the way had its own unique character.

As they continued south, they encountered much warmer weather, and spent most of their time with all of the windows down and the canvas top open. The windshield was hinged at the top so it could swing out, allowing for good flow-through ventilation. Of course this channeled the occasional insect into their laps. On one occasion, a bee blew in and under Jake's shorts, resulting in a painful sting in a most unfortunate place!

Gertrude began the long, gradual climb into the mountains of Chiapas. As they climbed ever higher, they passed through areas where the local people had hacked small plots of land in nearly vertical terrain to plant corn and other crops. American farmers would never even consider farming on this scale. They need to have land flat enough to operate huge tractors and combines. Even hobby farmers generally have invested hundreds or even thousands of dollars in a rototiller, if not tens of thousands in a tractor before they have planted the first seed.

Here, the fruit of the farmer's labor was transported from the fields on their backs or on one of the utilitarian tricycles that were prevalent throughout Mexico. These had a cargo platform in between the two front wheels with a single rear wheel driven by a chain. In the evenings, lawn chairs were placed in the cargo area and grandmother, mother, and children would pile aboard while the father pedaled away at the back. On the steeper hills, the oldest kids might get off and help push. American families have to start their SUVs just to go to the mail box.

Here and there were small clusters of homes apart from the villages, where coffee beans dried in the sun on patios and rooftops.

Often they would pass men or women who trudged along the shoulder of the road, miles from anywhere. Some carried machetes, others huge bundles of produce or firewood. Aaron's and Jake's admiration for these simple, hard working people grew with each passing mile.

Large tour busses would often overtake them on blind corners or hills oblivious of opposing traffic, which unfazed, would simply move a bit to the right and make room. Sometimes they were passed by small motorcycles bearing two, three, or even four people, crates of live chickens, or huge loads of produce.

Gertrude labored up yet another steep mountain pass and entered a small village where ramshackle shanties were scattered haphazardly along the road. A goat stood atop a shack, dining on the thatched roof, while pigs rooted and chickens scratched in the dusty yard below. An ancient native woman bathed buck naked if full view of the road with a bucket of soapy water and a rag.

The guys found their way blocked by a string tied with ribbons across the road. One end was tied to a tree, the other held by a little girl no more than five or six years of age. In her other hand she held a meager bunch of greenish yellow bananas. Her little round face was the color of weak coffee and her hair black as night. She wore a handmade cotton dress and had bare feet. Aaron was reluctant to lose their hard won momentum, but her dark brown eyes bore into his, imploring him to stop. He sighed and applied the brakes.

The little girl dropped the string and held out her hand to accept a few coins from Jake in exchange for her bananas. Aaron was not quick enough to react when their path was clear, and soon *Gertrude* was surrounded by dozens of children who appeared out of nowhere, each with something to sell. Soon *Gertrude* was weighed down with a variety of fruits and vegetables, as well as some items that the guys guessed were meant to be eaten. Most of the kids scampered happily away while the little girl set the trap for the next unwary victim.

Road Tripped

Chapter Eight

Gertrude labored up a steep incline to the top of the next pass and started down the other side. Now her speed was limited by the tight switchbacks and her overheating brakes. Rounding a tight bend, they came upon a large landslide that had blocked the road. Instead of a flagger in an orange vest, hardhat, and radio, a man in faded blue jeans, plaid cotton shirt, and a baseball cap waved them to a stop with orange ribbons tied to a stick. Aaron brought *Gertrude* to a stop behind a couple of other cars. It looked like it was going to be a long wait, so Aaron shut off the engine and set the brake. A few more cars came to a stop behind. There were no bulldozers or excavators anywhere to be seen, and the men at work used shovels not as leaning posts, but to clear the road. One particular boulder was large enough that it would ordinarily require a massive bulldozer to move. But this was Mexico, so instead a team of men were using pry bars to lever it over again and again until at last they rolled it over the edge of the precipice. The men worked slowly and steadily until without prompting, they all set down their tools and grabbed their lunches. As they ate, the work crew engaged in a lively banter.

Ron Fugere

One did not need to understand the language to know that one of them was taking the brunt of the ribbing. His response was a hand gesture that is easily recognized around the world.

The guys grabbed some of the goodies they'd bought in the village and joined the workers in the shade of a large tree. "Hola amigos, ¿cómo estás?" (Hello friends, how are you?) One of them said. The guys smiled but did not reply. "¿Gringos?" He asked. The guys looked at each other. "¿Americanos?" At last they recognized something the guy was saying. "Yes we're American," Jake replied.

The guys munched on bananas while the workers ate their lunches. They recognized some of food the workers were eating as the same as they had bought, so they watched how it was eaten and decided to try it themselves. They unwrapped the nondescript brown lump from its greasy paper package and took a bite. It was spicy, but good. They munched happily for a moment, until the habañeros kicked in. It began with a pleasant heat, like the meltdown of a nuclear reactor but milliseconds later, it went super nova. And then it got hot. The guys looked at each other in shock and watched as the red rose up their necks and faces. They puffed air and fanned their tongues to cool the fire in their mouths. One of the workers saw their distress and offered them soda bottles filled with a reddish liquid. "Agua fresco de jamaica," he said. They eagerly accepted his offer and took long pulls on their drinks. The jamaica helped a little. To show their gratitude, the guys offered some of the fruit they had bought in the village, which they accepted, saying, "Gracias."

With their lunch done, the workers laid back and pulled their hats down over their eyes for their siesta. With their way still blocked, the guys followed suit and soon all were fast asleep.

Road Tripped

Aaron and Jake were awakened by the squeal of brakes followed by the clatter of tools being thrown into the back of a truck. The workers all clambered aboard, and the truck took off heading south in a cloud of dust and smoke. The road was clear, and a neat row of stones marked the edge of the road. On the ground were two more bottles of Jamaica that the road crew had left for them. All the other cars had gone. The sun was low over the mountains as they set out the way the truck had gone.

As evening drew near, the guys looked for a likely spot to stop for the night. Sleeping in *Gertrude* allowed them to "camp" pretty much anywhere they liked; all they needed was a wide spot in the road. But with only one highway heading south, there was likely to be at least a little traffic all night, so they looked for someplace off the road. *Gertrude*'s headlights illuminated what looked like a cart path leading off into the forest. They turned off and cautiously followed the path. Soon they came to a clearing and stopped. After their long afternoon siesta, neither was particularly tired, so they sat out enjoying the cool of the night, which was a welcome relief from the heat of day. It was a new moon and with no city lights to wash the sky, the stars were brilliant. Venus shone like a jewel and they almost thought they could make out the rings of Saturn. The Milky Way galaxy looked like a broad brush stroke across the heavens.

The two old friends talked of the theories that ancient aliens had seeded the Mayan culture if not mankind in its entirety. From the Nazca Lines in Peru to the pyramids in Egypt and the Americas, from Stonehenge in England to crop circles around the world, they discussed all of the "proof" that aliens had visited Earth long ago and would someday return. With the billions of stars and galaxies visible to the naked eye from their vantage point, anything seemed possible. It was at least as plausible as the explanation promoted by the evangelists on TV. Eventually, the night grew cold and they adjourned to their sleeping bags with visions of UFOs dancing in their heads.

From a sound sleep, our two adventurers were awakened by a brilliant light and a wall of sound. Suddenly the side doors were violently flung open and they were confronted by a creature silhouetted in the dazzling light. It had a huge head with antennae. From it came a sound that could be described as electronic. Was it an alien? A robot? A cyborg? All of their work in video games came into play. They had once developed a game in which mutant cyborg alien zombies invaded a small town in Kansas. The object of the game was firstly not to be killed and secondly to fight off the invaders with the tools at hand. Without hesitation, Jake grabbed a jamaica bottle and smashed it on the head of the invader, who recoiled in surprise for a moment, allowing the heroes to make good their escape. They took off running across the clearing, Aaron in his boxers and Jake buck naked. The alien craft pursued them with its tractor beam or death ray and soon they were cornered against a stone escarpment. The aliens closed in and they were surrounded with their backs to the wall! They mentally prepared themselves for the inevitable medical experiments they were sure to endure at the hands of the interstellar visitors. Would it be the dreaded nasal probe, the rectal probe, or both?

Again they heard the electronic sound from one of the aliens. "Sí el capitán, hemos ellos," (Yes Captain, we have them.) the creature said. The aliens spoke Spanish!

"¿ Lo que en el infierno estás haciendo aquí, cabrones?" (What in the hell are you bastards doing here?) One of them shouted.

Aaron brandished a stick while Jake held a large rock over his head ready to throw it at their attackers.

"Creo que ellos son gringos!" (I think they are gringos.) One said.

Another said, "Creo que son los puñales" (I think they are gays.)

¡El aspecto gracioso uno se cuelga como un caballo! (The funny looking one is hung like a horse!)

"What are you gringos doing on a military base in the middle of the night?" another asked. The aliens spoke English too!

"We uh…" Jake stammered and lowered his rock.

Then all of the soldiers burst into laughter at the incongruous sight of the American tourists. Julio, the one who had gotten whacked on the head by Jake looked a bit sheepish; he would no doubt get a lot of ribbing. His buddies slapped him on the back and began their torment. ¡Oye Julio, tal vez debería dejar las ovejas en paz y tener una fecha con éste! (Hey Julio, maybe you should leave the sheep alone and have a date with this one!)

"¡ Hijo de putas!" (Sons of whores!) Julio grumbled.

"Son turistas americanos. Son inofensivos," (They are American tourists; they are harmless.) the one with the radio antennas said while pushing the transmit button on his radio.

The electronic voice replied, "Dígales que abandone de inmediato," (Tell them to leave immediately.) and the helicopter spun around and flew off into the night.

"I am Lieutenant Jose Fernandez of the National Defense Army. You must leave the area immediately."

The guys were allowed to slip on some clothes before departing. The soldiers all clambered into the back of their trucks and escorted the guys down the road a few miles, where the leading truck waved them onto a side road. They turned where instructed and the tailing truck followed. When they could go no further, Aaron brought *Gertrude* to a stop and the truck pulled up behind. Were they to face a firing squad for having entered a secret base? They were cornered in a remote clearing in the jungle of southern Mexico. Their only possible escape route was blocked by the truck, they were outnumbered three to one, and they were surrounded by heavily armed captors, whereas they had only a Swiss army knife in their arsenal. It would seem that their fate was sealed.

Lieutenant Fernandez approached and said, "You may sleep here. Good night." He and his fellow soldiers returned to the truck and they drove away.

Chapter Nine

Aaron glanced at the fuel gauge which had dipped below the quarter full mark. "We're gonna need to get some gas pretty soon."

"Too bad we can't use some of this," Jake said while lifting a butt cheek, squinting one eye and farting in a deep baritone.

"Damn Jake, my eyes are burnin'!" Aaron said as he rolled down the window and fanned his hand in front of his nose.

"Ah yer just jealous 'cuz I stink so pretty!"

"Holy shit, It still stinks in here! Roll down your window, will ya?"

"What, and waste it?" He sniffed the air and said, "Full bodied, robust bouquet, glowing aftertaste. Resounding report. I'd give it a nine for artistic impression, nine point nine overall!"

"You should be proud."

"Maybe I'll try out for the Olympics."

Sometimes the guys still behaved like eleven year olds.

As they climbed higher into the mountains, the air grew cooler. After the dry heat of the high desert and the stifling humidity of the lowland jungle, it was a welcome relief.

Ron Fugere

Up ahead was a rusty Pemex sign attached to the front of a cinder block shack. They turned in and shut off the engine. A short Mayan man slid out from under an aging Fiat which had had the rear of the body removed and replaced with a wooden cargo platform. He wiped his greasy hands on his pants and said, "Buenos días. ¿Cómo puedo ayudarle?" (Good morning. How can I help you?) With hand signals, Aaron indicated that they wished to buy fuel. "Sí, Señor," he said. He shuffled past the ancient fuel pumps into the shack, returning with a long funnel. He wiped the inside of the funnel with a rag and inserted it in the filler neck of the tank. He went back into the shack and returned with two six gallon jerry cans which he began pouring through the funnel. When the tank was full, he twisted on the cap. He hefted the second jerry can and tapped down its side with his knuckle to gauge how much fuel remained, then counted on his fingers in deep concentration. "Será cuatrocientos veinte pesos, por favor." (It will be four hundred twenty pesos, please.) He was met with a blank stare. He tried to indicate how much he was owed using hand signals without success. Finally he scratched the number 420 into the dirt. Jake extracted the bills from his wallet and handed them to the man. He stuffed them into his pocket, said, "Gracias; buenos días" and slid back under the Fiat.

The guys continued on their way. Another tour bus came flying past and immediately turned right onto a secondary road with a sign that said Agua Azul. The guys decided to follow and see where the tourists were headed. They came to a parking lot where several busses and many cars were parked. They shut off *Gertrude* and got out to stretch their legs. Following the crowds of people, they came to a huge waterfall cascading over a limestone cliff and another, nearly as large opposite the first. The

90

combined waters formed a huge, swirling torrent which disappeared off the edge of a precipice and disappeared into the distance. Rainbows hung where beams of sunlight pierced the mist. The roar of the water was deafening and the air was clean and fresh. They followed a boardwalk along which vendors peddled souvenirs and snacks.

"Ya getting' hungry?" Jake asked.

"Yeah I am; and I'm getting' tired of bananas. Let's see what we can find here."

One of the booths was selling whatever those spicy brown things were that had burned their mouths, so they moved on. They came upon another booth which consisted of a few boards nailed together under the cover of a blue poly tarp under which a short woman in traditional Mayan garb was preparing tacos on a fifty-five gallon drum that had been fashioned into an improvised grill. The smell set their stomachs growling. They watched while a couple of tourists took their tacos to a nearby picnic table and began eating. The guys stepped up and with hand gestures, indicated that they would like four tacos each.

The lady asked, "¿ Carne de res, cerdo, pollo o chapulínes?

The guys again gestured that they would like to have what the others had ordered. Soon they had their tacos and went to the table that the others had vacated where they began wolfing down their food.

"Damn, these are the best tacos I've ever had!" Jake exclaimed.

"Yeah, they're great! Ya wanna get some more?"

"Yeah, let's do it."

They got a few more tacos and attacked them with renewed relish. Aaron paused to pick something from his teeth with a twig. He pulled it out, and looking at it was surprised to see that it was the leg of a bug! He opened up his taco and found that it was filled with crunchy fried grasshoppers. Jake opened his as well.

"Ya mean we've been eatin' bugs?!"

"So it would seem!"

They shrugged, rolled up their tacos and finished their meal. They stopped by another booth and ordered a couple bottles of jamaica. With their drinks, they followed the boardwalk until it ended and then continued along the river trail. The roar of the waterfalls faded as they moved along, replaced by the gentle murmur of the water winding through the rocky shallows. Colorful birds of all shapes and sizes flitted through the forest, some chirping sweetly, others with ear piercing cries. Towering trees were festooned with wild orchids and draped with vines. The stumps formed broad flying buttresses. Thick jungle foliage choked the ground around the giants.

They happened across a young Mayan woman with a baby strapped to her back as she washed her clothes in the river. Wet clothes hung from branches of nearby trees. Her other children played naked in the water of the river. The trail ended at a tiny cluster of rustic hovels above the high water mark of the river. The day was growing short, so they turned and headed back down the trail. They were met by the vendors making their way home for the evening, chatting amiably in Mayan.

Although it was still early evening, the guys decided to pull off to the outskirts of the parking lot and crash for the night. Neither had gotten much sleep after the alien invasion and both were tired.

In the morning, the guys ventured back to the vendors booths and found one selling fresh ground and brewed local coffee. Starbucks has nothing on them! After their coffee, they found another booth where they had a hearty breakfast of huevos rancheros.

Back on the road again, they followed another tour bus that led them to the Mayan ruins at Palenque where for a handful of pesos, they hired a young local man, Ramón to serve as their guide. Ramón spoke fluent English, Spanish, as well as Mayan. He led them through the ruins, explaining the history of the Mayan people. From atop the highest of the ruins, they could see what appeared to be tall hills, but were in fact still more ruins that had not yet been excavated. In all directions, even more ruins stretched to the horizon. They were astonished to learn that this thriving metropolis was at its peak while Europe was in the dark ages! They wondered what the world would be like today had the conquistadors not vanquished this advanced civilization in their lust for gold. But the greatest crime of all was that all traces of their rich written language, the wisdom of the ages, was systematically sought out and burned by the church.

They followed a limestone lined aqueduct out of the temple compound and into the surrounding jungle, where nearly every stone they saw had been shaped by human hands. They came upon a waterfall where the crystal clear water cascaded over a limestone ledge. The flesh colored stone had been polished smooth into soft rounded contours by eons of water flowing over its surface giving it an organic appearance. Eventually their path led them back to the parking lot.

For his trouble, Ramón had asked only fifty pesos, less than five dollars.

Ron Fugere

Chapter Ten

Gertrude labored up another steep grade and around a corner. The outside of the corner dropped off a vertical cliff hundreds of feet tall, a rickety wooden rail all that separated vehicles from the chasm. As they rounded the corner, the guys could see a long line of vehicles stopped at the approach to another village. The sign on the side of the road said: "Bienvenido a San Gabriele." They came to a stop. Drivers and passengers passed the time smoking, chatting with acquaintances, or getting to know one another. The only people that seemed at all impatient were Americans. Just as they were in the states, they were always in a hurry to be where they weren't. The line crept ahead over a period of a few hours. Eventually, the guys struck up a conversation with Manuel, a local who spoke English.

"What's going up there?" Aaron asked.

"Oh it's just the local revolutionaries," Manuel said with a yawn.

"Revolutionaries?!" Aaron said with alarm.

"Ah they're harmless. They just block the highway to raise money. Sometimes they blow something up."

94

Road Tripped

As *Gertrude* crept slowly closer to the front of the line, the guys could see a group of men wearing ski masks milling around. As each car reached the head of the line, money was exchanged, an improvised gate was lifted, and they were sent on their way.

Meanwhile, one of the revolutionaries stood atop a crate holding court to all who would listen. A group of children played in the dirt at his feet and his gesticulation seemed to indicate that his fight was for them. He held the rapt attention of one of the generic stray dogs that the guys had seen throughout Mexico. Eventually, even the mongrel cur grew bored and wandered over to sniff at the guys. Jake reached down and scratched his head and said, "Hiya fella!" The dog licked his hand in reply.

At last *Gertrude* was the only car left of what had been a long line. The guy on the crate got down and came over to where Aaron and Jake stood. He pulled himself up to his full height of about five feet and puffed up his chest while his compatriots gathered behind him. He held out his hand and in heavily accented English, he said, "We are warriors of the Popular Front for the Restoration of Peace to the People of Mexico. I am El Supremo. You must pay tribute to the revolution to pass, señores." As treasurer, Jake stepped up and opened his wallet. He pulled out a twenty peso bill, but El Supremo shook his head to indicate that it was not enough. Jake pulled out a fifty peso bill; another shake of the head. Jake tried to stare him down. Aaron stepped up beside Jake to show his support and he too locked eyes with the revolutionary in a literal Mexican stand-off. The revolutionary gave a small affirmative nod and accepted the fifty peso note. As the bill was being passed, the eyes peering out of the ski mask were drawn away and suddenly a look of alarm came over them. The guys turned to see what had caused the alarm, in time to see *Gertrude* rolling backward down the road and gaining speed fast! They set out in hot pursuit with the revolutionaries at their heels. Moments later, *Gertrude* smashed through the rail and there was a brief moment of silence before a huge crash followed by a resounding boom was heard. The guys reached the edge of the precipice as the echo of the explosion returned and a plume of black smoke rose to meet them. They peered into the abyss to see their beloved travelling companion in her death throes. She lay on her side at the bottom of a deep ravine. One wheel was still spinning with its tire ablaze, sending a black spiral of smoke dancing into the sky.

"*Gertrude!*" Aaron exclaimed in anguish. "Oh *Gertrude.*" He stood dejectedly staring into the void with Jake at his side.

The revolutionaries caught up and joined the guys on the edge of the cliff. El Supremo took Jake's hand and returned the toll. He rolled the money into Jake's hand and patted it in sympathy. He put his arms around their shoulders and said, "Come my friends, you will drink with us." They turned and began walking back toward the village.

Up ahead, sirens could be heard approaching, while from behind, a truck approached filled with soldiers of the National Defense Army. The police, the soldiers, and the revolutionaries met at the improvised gate. The guys feared that violence was about to erupt when El Supremo stood nose to nose with Lieutenant Jose Fernandez; or more accurately, nose to chest, as the lieutenant towered over El Supremo. Both bristled for a moment and heated words were exchanged while cameras flashed. And then laughing, El Supremo slapped the Lieutenant on the arm and beckoned for him to join him in the taberna a few steps away. One of the police officers seemed incredulous and protested, but the lieutenant dismissed his objections with a wave of his hand and invited him to join them.

To the guys, El Supremo said, "Come my friends, let's have a cerveza."

The guys followed the lieutenant and El Supremo through double swinging saloon doors that would not have looked out of place in a spaghetti western, where the barkeep was already setting out many bottles of cerveza. They were joined by the Warriors of the Popular Front for the Restoration of Peace to the People of Mexico, the soldiers of the National Defense Army, the officers of the State Police of Chiapas, the National Police, a group of local citizens, some children as well as the dog, a pig and a few chickens

Inside, El Supremo stood on a chair and in a loud voice delivered a long winded dissertation punctuated by animated gesticulation that seemed to proclaim victory. Everyone grabbed a cerveza and held them high as El Supremo wrapped up his speech with a cry of, "Victoria!" Everyone pulled off their ski masks and downed their beers.

El Supremo stepped down from his pulpit and motioned for the guys to join him at the bar. He laid the collection bag with the proceeds of the days "fund raiser" on the bar and said to the bartender in English, "These are my amigos, uh....."

"What are your names?"

"I'm Aaron and this is Jake."

"These are mi amigos Aaron and Jake. They are my guests. Serve them what they want."

The barkeep asked, "What would you like, amigos?"

"Tequila!" They exclaimed in unison.

While the barkeep poured their shots, Aaron asked El Supremo, "Aren't you afraid that the army and police will recognize you without your masks?"

"Oh no; we have an understanding. We just wear the masks to scare the tourists. Today we have struck a decisive blow against the oppressors of the Ejército de defensa nacional and their lap dogs, the Policía Nacional. With this triumph over the imperialist dogs, our ultimate victory is assured!"

The guys raised their shots and said, "To your victory!" They downed their shots and asked for another round.

El supremo said to the barkeep, "Deje la botella." (Leave the bottle)

The Lieutenant ambled over to join them at the bar. El Supremo asked for more shot glasses. He raised his shot and said, "Let us drink to our vanquished enemy!"

They all downed their shots and slammed them down on the bar to be refilled.

The Lieutenant raised his glass and said, "To our glorious conquerors!"

Again the empty shot glasses were slammed down.

The lieutenant looked at his gringo drinking companions and said, "I almost didn't recognize you with your clothes on. Did you get a good night's sleep the other night?" He grinned.

"Not so good," Aaron replied.

"I didn't see your van."

"It has fallen upon misfortune," Aaron said.

"Fallen is an understatement," Jake added.

They went on to explain what had happened.

"That is most unfortunate. Let us drink to your fallen chariot!" Gulp. Slam.

El Supremo asked, "What will you do now?"

"We don't know. We don't have a car or any money now," Aaron answered.

"Ah cabrón, these things have a way of working themselves out.

The police officer that had made a fuss earlier elbowed his way through the crowd and engaged in a heated conversation with the Lieutenant, all the while gesticulating animatedly toward El Supremo. The Lieutenant listened to him for a moment before interrupting him with a dismissive wave of his hand. "Vete al carajo, Miguel poco," he said, and the officer turned and left in a huff.

"What was all that about?" Aaron asked the Lieutenant.

"Oh that is just Miguel Martinez. Que un pendejo."

"Huh?"

"In English is Michael Martin. What an asshole."

The guys looked at each other in surprise when they realized that this cop was the Mexican namesake for the cops who had given them so much grief back home. Maybe there was a secret global Michael Martin asshole cop society.

The Lieutenant said, "He seems to think I should put El Supremo in front of a firing squad. Is much the same as his father Miguel thought we should do with Markos back when he was El Supremo of the Zapatistas."

"Zapatistas?"

"They were the last band of rebels. They idolized Emilliano Zapata, a general in the revolution a hundred years ago. The Zapatistas caused quite a fuss ten years ago. Every generation has their Zapata. El Supremo here is ours."

The barkeep set out another bottle which was soon emptied and replaced by yet another as the four continued to toast one another.

Ron Fugere

The crowd of revelers gradually began to shrink, although it only grew louder, as many of those that remained broke out in song and those carrying on conversations had to shout to be heard over the din.

Aaron stood up, staggered a few steps sideways, and slurred, "Where does a guy take a leak?"

The lieutenant pointed at a door in the rear marked 'Hombres' and said, "There's the baño." Aaron took a few steps toward the door, hesitated, staggered sideways, and then stumbled through the door. Most of the remaining bar patrons flooded out into the street and the sound of their song faded into the distance. Aaron stumbled back to the bar.

The saloon doors flung open and a woman entered. She scanned the room for a moment before her fiery eyes locked on El Supremo. She strode purposely over like a torpedo locked on target. She was a bit taller than him, with black hair to the middle of her back. She wore a colorful mid-length skirt and a handmade white cotton blouse adorned with colorful embroidered patterns around the neck, garb typical of the region. She was pleasantly plump, but there was nothing pleasant about her demeanor. She lit into El Supremo in Spanish. He tried to respond, but she turned and stormed out the doors.

"Estás en la casa de perro!" the lieutenant said, slapping him on the back.

El Supremo grinned sheepishly as he poured the last round of shots. Jake got the shot with the worm. El Supremo, the lieutenant, Aaron, and Jake all lifted their glasses and the lieutenant said, "viejos amigos y nuevos amigos!" El Supremo said, "Old friends and new friends!" The four friends downed their shots. The sound of three shot glasses hitting the bar was followed by a dull thud as Jake hit the floor. The dog licked his

100

Road Tripped

face for a moment, but Jake did not respond. Then with his nose, the dog rolled Jake onto his side and lay down against his back.

The barkeep brought out a hamaca which he strung up between iron hooks embedded in the concrete walls. He gestured to Aaron to make himself comfortable. Aaron sat down into the hamaca, lifted his feet and promptly rolled out and fell to the floor where he too passed out. The barkeep laughed and shook his head as he went to the back and brought back a couple of threadbare woolen blankets which he laid over the guys.

The Secretary Treasurer of the Popular Front for the Restoration of Peace to the People of Mexico, El Supremo's second in command came over and asked his leader how much dinero had been raised. El Supremo handed him the bag with the day's booty. El segundo en commando asked the barkeep, "Cuánto le debo, mi amigo?" After he had paid the bar tab for the night, forty-three pesos remained for the cause.

The lieutenant, El Supremo, and su segundo al mando staggered out the saloon doors into the night. El Supremo said to the lieutenant, "Well my valiant enemy, we must continue our battle again soon, our treasury is depleted. How is Friday for you?"

"I have a date on Friday; how is Saturday?"

"We meet in battle on Saturday!"

Chapter Eleven

Jake stirred to a swishing sound. He opened one eye and saw a short, stout Mayan woman standing on the wall, sweeping it with a short broom, or so it appeared from his vantage point lying on his side on the dusty floor. He opened his other eye and a stabbing pain pierced his head only to be replaced by a dull throbbing ache. He closed his eyes and groaned. Someone stirred against his back. He didn't know or care who it was. The swishing of the broom kept time with the throbbing in his head and made him wish that the sharp pain would return because it was preferable to the agony that had taken its place. The bright sun beaming in above the saloon doors shined on his face, and through his eyelids, glowed blood red, then white, then red again in an endless kaleidoscope of sheer agony. Although sweat poured in rivulets from his body, he shivered. His tongue felt like a dirty sock in his mouth.

He felt a warm, wet tongue kissing his neck, but he was in no mood to get frisky. He wanted to push the woman away, but he'd been lying on his arm and it was asleep. Eventually he was able to roll over enough to allow the blood to return to his arm and he tried to brush her off, only to feel that she had a beard! He opened one eye enough to look at his bed partner only to find that it was not a comely woman, but the dog he'd befriended yesterday, and a male at that.

Then from far back in his cheeks, he began to salivate profusely. His stomach twisted and turned as nausea swept over him. He fought it for a moment before giving up hope; he crawled swiftly out under the saloon doors, across the narrow, cracked sidewalk and puked his guts out in the gutter. A tour bus roared by, belching acrid black diesel smoke. He laid his cheek on the curb and retched again. Another tour bus went by trailing a cloud of dust and litter. If he could only drag himself into the path of the next one, maybe his agony would mercifully be over.

The saloon doors flung open and Aaron fell to his knees next to where Jake lay and he too vomited in the gutter. When his stomach was purged of its contents, he continued to heave up bile until it too was exhausted. He sat with his back against the wall and his head in his hands groaning.

The dog licked Jake's face again, and Jake tried to focus on that sensation. It helped to take his mind off of his agony.

Eventually, Aaron managed to get to his feet and helped Jake up. Together, they shuffled back into the tavern, where they plopped into an empty booth in a dark corner and laid down on opposite benches. The dog came in and lay down under the table. The Mayan woman brought a tray to the table with a pitcher of water, a box of baking soda and a couple of glasses. She dumped some baking soda into the water, stirred it with a wooden spoon and filled the glasses. She put a straw in each glass and motioned for the guys to drink. They sat up and took a few tentative sips, crossed their arms on the table, and laid down their heads. Jake began snoring and drooling on the table. "Please someone just kill me and put me out of my misery!" Aaron groaned. He fought the waves of nausea and managed to take another sip.

Jake woke up with a snort and a loud groan. He took another sip of water and looked around the saloon. The lunch crowd had begun to gather. A bottle of aspirin and a plate with a couple of Mexican sweet breads sat next to the pitcher of water. He shook a few aspirin from the bottle and washed them down with a swig of water. He fought the impulse to purge. Aaron stirred but didn't lift his head. "Are we dead?" He asked. "No such luck," Jake replied. He took a small bite of one of the sweet breads and set it aside with a grimace. Ordinarily he liked them, but now they tasted like sawdust.

"Where are we?"

"In the tavern."

"What tavern?"

"Remember last night?"

Aaron paused for a moment while his befuddled mind tried to grasp the situation.

"*Gertrude?*"

"Dead."

"Shit! I hoped it was just a bad dream."

Someone ambled over to the table and said cheerfully. "Buenos días amigos!"

At last Aaron lifted his head. The face was vaguely familiar.

It was El Supremo, who laughed and said to Aaron, "You don't look so good Pendejo."

Indeed he didn't look very good. His disheveled hair stood up on one side and the course wood grain of the table top was imprinted on his face. His skin had the pallor of leftover oatmeal and what could be seen of his eyes were bright red.

Road Tripped

"You better have some agua," El Supremo said and slid a glass over. Aaron took a small sip. He picked up one of the sweet breads and then set it down again without taking a bite.

El Supremo said, "Those no good for hangover; let me get you something." He stepped over to the bar and said a few words to the barkeep and returned to sit in the booth with the guys.

"You're sure chipper this morning, El Supremo," Jake said.

"I'm sorry; we weren't properly introduced last night. I am Juan Valdez. Please, call me Juan, my friends."

Though the fog in their heads effected their short term memory, the name Juan Valdez lurked somewhere in their long term memory. "Juan Valdez? I've heard your name before." Jake said.

"Remember the Folgers adds? Handpicked by Juan Valdez? Pure Columbian?" Aaron said.

They looked at their new friend. With his bushy black mustache and Panama hat; they could see a resemblance to the guy on the can. All that was missing was the donkey.

"Si my friends. Some of the 'Columbian coffee' was grown here. My parents thought that if they named me Juan, I would always have a job picking coffee.

"Speaking of coffee, how 'bout we have some?" Jake said.

"You're the treasurer; do we have any money?"

Jake opened his wallet and pulled out a handful of bills of various denominations. He tried to count it out, but his mind simply couldn't perform even the simplest task. He laid the pile on the table. Aaron counted it out. "That's not too bad; we have over five hundred pesos. What's that in dollars?" Throughout their travels in Mexico, they had simply moved the decimal point over one digit to the left and dropped one digit for a rough conversion.

"Isn't that like around five thousand dollars?" Jake said.

"Oh no mi amigo's; that is about fifty American dollars," Juan said.

In unison, the guys exclaimed, "fuck!"

The Mayan woman brought a couple of plates with tacos and set them before the guys. Juan said to the lady, "Café, por favor."

They looked at their plates with trepidation and opened the tacos to see what they were filled with. They were relieved to see that they were filled with beef, or at least they were pretty sure it wasn't bugs. Aaron took a tentative bite while Jake watched to see if he would keep it down. When Aaron took a second bite, Jake decided to brave it. The lady brought a pot of coffee and a couple of mugs.

The fog in their heads gradually lifted as the guys finished their lunch and coffee. Aaron studied Juan's face through his bloodshot eyes and said, "I could swear that I'd seen your face before."

"Perhaps on a coffee can amigo?"

"No; somewhere else."

Now it was Jake's turn to study his face. "You were on the road crew! You gave us those drinks," he exclaimed.

"Si mi amigos. I have bills to pay and my job as El Supremo does not pay well," he said sheepishly.

"So the supreme leader of the revolution gets paid by the state he plots to overthrow?" Aaron chuckled.

"Si; is ironic; no?"

"But when we saw you there, you didn't speak English."

"If I speak English to gringos there, they never stop complaining and I can do no work."

Road Tripped

Aaron said to Jake, "So what do we do now? We can't stay in *Gertrude* anymore, and I doubt if we can afford a hotel."

Juan said, "Come mi amigos, you will be my guests." He went to the bar, paid the barkeep, and beckoned for the guys to follow. They were both unsteady on their feet, but managed to follow Juan up the hill a short distance.

The dog followed at Jake's side. Jake said, "Your dog is sure friendly, Juan."

"That is not my dog."

"Whose is it then?"

"Everyone's and no one's"

"Does he have a name?"

Juan shrugged.

"How do you say yellow dog in Spanish?"

"Perro Amarillo."

"Too long. I'll call him Rio." He reached down and patted his head. "Well, wha'd'ya say Rio?" The dog looked up at him and seemed to respond to the name.

They turned onto a side street which was lined with narrow cracked sidewalks and rows of houses, some butted tight to one another, others separated by narrow strips of bare dirt. Some of the homes were in an advanced state of decay, with adobe bricks or rough stone visible through the cracked stucco. Some had trees growing out of the remains of the roof. Others appeared to be well maintained. Nearly all had hand crafted wrought iron grates on the windows and matching gates over the tall, narrow double doors. Juan stepped up to the door of a home and inserted a long key into the lock on the gate. The gate swung open with a screech. Rio looked at Juan questioningly, and then trotted off.

Ron Fugere

Juan opened the weathered wooden doors and motioned for the guys to enter. They stepped into the dim interior of Juan's home.

"Mi casa es su casa."

Chapter Twelve

Beams of sunlight streamed in through the gaps around the wooden shutters that covered the inside of the windows, splashing light across Aaron's face, waking him. He lay in a hammock in a small room with a soaring ceiling adjacent to the foyer of Juan's house. He stretched and yawned while Jake stirred on a couch a few feet away. Both were covered with course woolen blankets. Although the days were quite warm, the nights could be chilly here in the mountains.

Through the open door, they could hear Juan talking softly to someone. The smell of coffee mingled with frying bacon drifted in. They stood and stretched before padding across the ornately glazed tile floor into the kitchen where Juan's wife, Emilia was preparing breakfast. The counter top, sink, and open shelves were all made of smooth, softly colored concrete and the floor of terracotta tiles. Occupying the rear of the kitchen was a rustic antique table set for six.

Juan greeted them, "Buenos Dias, amigo's; you are feeling better today?"

"Much better; thank you," Aaron replied.

"Did you sleep well?"

"I sure did!" Aaron replied enthusiastically. "A guy could get used to sleeping in a hammock!"

"Your couch is much more comfortable than the floor of the tavern." Jake added sheepishly while idly scratching the flea bites that he'd acquired from his bed partner in the tavern.

Emilia gestured for them to be seated and served them steaming mugs of coffee.

"Good morning Emilia; how are you?" Aaron said. She said nothing, as she spoke no English. A ready smile adorned her face. The fire in her eyes from the other night was replaced by black embers. She turned back to the small range to check on breakfast. She called out and two boys about ten and twelve years old rushed down the stairs from the loft above the kitchen and took their places. They were dressed in neat uniforms consisting of dark gray shorts, short sleeve white button-down shirts and black vests.

Emilia set out a platter with huevos ranchero, bacon, and tortillas. The boys reached eagerly for the food, and Emilia scolded them, offering Jake the serving spoon first. He took a portion and handed the spoon to Aaron. When all had been served, the boys grabbed their forks and started to attack the food. Again, Emilia scolded them.

Juan said, "These are my boys. This is Hector and this is Xavier." To the boys, he said. "Esto es Aaron y esto es Jake. Son nuestros invitados." (This is Aaron and this is Jake. They are our guests.)

"Gringos? Xavier asked.

"Si."

The family did the sign of the cross, folded their hands, and bowed their heads while Juan said grace. At last the boys were allowed to eat. They wolfed down their food, all the while exchanging barbs and jibes as siblings do. They asked to be excused, kissed both parents on the cheek, grabbed their school bags, and dashed out the door.

Aaron said, "Thank you Emilia, breakfast was delicious."

Juan translated, "Gracias Emilia, el desayuno era delicioso"

"De nada," Emilia replied.

"Well amigos, I must go to work. A tree has fallen across the highway."

The guys followed Juan out the back door into a small courtyard surrounded by high stone walls where various vegetables grew in pots and boxes and an orange tree stood. He retrieved an axe and a shovel from a corner and said, "You should go out and see our village. You will be our guests for dinner."

"But Juan, you and Emilia have already done too much!" Aaron protested. "How can we repay your kindness?" Jake asked.

"Is not necessary; I am sure you would do same."

The muffled sound of a truck clattering up the street followed by the squealing of brakes and the honking of a horn could be heard. The guys followed Juan back through the kitchen, where he grabbed a sack lunch Emilia had prepared for him. He hugged and kissed her goodbye. The guys followed Juan out the door. He threw his tools in the back of the truck and clambered aboard. The truck lurched ahead and he called, "We'll see you tonight, amigos!"

Rio greeted the guys with a wag of his tail. Jake scratched behind his ears and he whined and pawed Jake's leg in greeting. They set out together to explore the village, retracing their steps from the night before. At the highway they turned left and left

111

again onto the next adobe brick paved street, where they ambled past small shops in which one could find any number of things on display. Alongside fresh fruit and vegetables, one could find a solitary bar of soap, a chainsaw, a pig's ear, a used tire, assorted condoms (unused), and Coca Cola in a Pepsi case. They stepped into one such shop and selected a toothbrush and a tube of toothpaste.

They would have to share the toothbrush until they could find another. As treasurer, Jake opened his wallet and let the Mayan lady select the appropriate bill. She handed Jake a few coins as change. They continued along the street until they came to a central plaza. On one side stood an old church and on the other the remains of a small Mayan pyramid in an advanced state of decay. By the appearance of the stones used in the construction of the church, it was apparent that the builders had looked no farther than the pyramid for material, not knowing or caring of the historical legacy that the stones represented.

In the center of the plaza was a stone fountain surrounded by park benches in the shade of a grove of trees. The tree trunks were painted white with something to ward off insects. They found a sign with the legend baño scrawled on a weathered board, where an attendant accepted a few coins in exchange for a length of toilet paper he pulled from a roll. They took turns using the bathroom to brush their teeth. All around the plaza, people began setting up small booths and stocking their wares for the bazaar. The evening chill was gone and the temperature quite pleasant.

They continued their exploration beyond the plaza. Eventually the brick paved streets lined with concrete sidewalks and adobe homes and businesses gave way to simple dirt ruts with an occasional dilapidated wooden hut. Occasionally,

Road Tripped

another generic dog would challenge Rio. They would bark and bluster like El Supremo and the lieutenant before circling and sniffing, they would call a truce. At one hut a dog was tethered to a bush with a piece of rope. Ol' Rio took a quick sniff, then without hesitation, mounted her and began to copulate, oblivious to the Children who beat him with sticks as he was locked in the throes of passion. With Rio otherwise occupied, the guys continued their walk alone, laughing about Rio's conquest. They continued along the path until it petered out in the jungle. They reversed their path and Rio rejoined them with contentment written on his face. "Damn Rio, glad ta see one of us gets lucky sometimes," Jake laughed as he gave his head a vigorous scratch.

After a few hours, they had seen most of what the village offered, and they returned to the plaza where most of the street vendors had finished setting up their booths. The smell of food cooking at one of the booths set their stomachs growling, and they watched while a few locals bought lunch. Rolling the dice, they bought something unidentifiable and took it to a park bench where Aaron took a tentative bite. He waited a second to make sure it wasn't going to catch fire in his mouth before he pronounced it delicious and they both dug in.

After lunch they lay down on the grass in the shade of a tree and soon dozed off for a nice siesta. They were awakened by a raucous gathering of slender black birds in the tree overhead. Jake looked over at Aaron and burst out laughing.

"What's so funny?" Aaron asked.

"You look like you lost a paintball battle; but I don't think its paint!" Jake laughed.

"Ya don't look so great yourself, shithead!"

They both looked down at their guano covered bodies, then up into the canopy of the tree where hundreds of birds had gathered. They sprung to their feet and dashed out of the way just as the flock unleashed another volley.

Chapter Thirteen

The guys stood sheepishly at the door of Juan and Emilia's home where Emilia greeted them. Her face conveyed sympathy with just a touch of mirth at their appearance. She gestured for them to follow and led them to the garden in the rear where she indicated that they should have a seat on a bench. She paused for a moment obviously at a loss for what to do, when Juan walked through the door. He took one look at their condition before doubling over in laughter. Emilia scolded him for his behavior and barked an order. When Juan caught his breath, he left for a moment and returned with a couple faded pairs of jeans and tee shirts. Emilia went inside so the guys could change.

Aaron quickly stripped down to his boxers and started to dress, but Jake hesitated for a moment. He made sure that they had the garden to themselves before he too stripped. There are disadvantages to going commando! No sooner had he shed the last stitch of clothing, when through the door walked a beautiful young woman followed by Juan, Emilia, and the boys. Jake quickly grabbed the first article of clothing he could get his hands on to cover his nakedness.

Juan made introductions. "Mi amigos, this is Emilia's sister, Juanita," Juan said. To Juanita, he said, "Juanita, esto es Aaron y Jake."

Juanita offered Aaron her hand and then Jake, who clutched a tee shirt in his right hand to hide his manhood. As he awkwardly switched hands to accept hers, he was momentarily exposed for all to see. Whereas everyone else averted their eyes, Juanita brazenly peered at Jake's manhood. A look of surprise and then a devilish grin crossed her face.

Jake was dumbstruck by the vision of beauty standing before him. Aaron nudged him to remind him that he should dress. He quickly turned around and slipped on the clothes that Emilia had brought while Juanita and Emilia giggled.

They were an incongruous sight! Juan's old jeans reached only to mid-calf on the much taller Americans and due to Juan's greater girth, they had to cinch up their belts to gather excess fabric at the waist. The tee shirts hung loose but only reached to their navels.

Emilia gathered up their soiled clothes and took them to a concrete sink on the back wall of the house where she began washing them on an old fashioned washboard.

Juan asked about their day. Aaron told him where they had gone and what they had done. He asked about Juan's day and listened to his story of the arrogant gringo tourists that had grown impatient and tried to drive around the fallen tree, only to end up scraping the full length of their shiny new SUV on a rock and then acting like it was the work crew's fault. Juan had stood mute, feigning a language barrier.

Emilia finished washing their clothes and hung them to dry on the clothesline. The warm evening breeze would soon have them dry.

Road Tripped

Through the entire exchange and the dinner that followed, Jake barely spoke a word, his attention riveted on Juanita. Every man has his own personal view of what constitutes his idea of perfection in a woman's form. Although Jake had never thought about it, there could be no doubt that Juanita was his ideal. But then with Jake, his ideal woman was usually the closest at hand at any given moment, preferably one with a pulse. By any standard, she was a lovely specimen.

Juanita wore a loose mid-length skirt and a white off the shoulder blouse which accentuated her ample cleavage to best effect. The blouse was gathered with a silk sash to highlight her wasp-like waist. Her jet black hair hung in ringlets to the middle of her back and was pulled back on one side to reveal her silver hoop earrings. Her flawless skin shined like polished bronze and her eyes, like her sister's, were like shining black embers.

After dinner, Juan invited the guys to join him and his family at the plaza for the bazaar. The guys changed back into their own clothes and they all set out for the plaza. Juan's boys ran ahead to look for their friends. Juan held hands with Emilia and led the way with Aaron by his side talking. Jake sidled up alongside Juanita, but even had there not been a language barrier, he would have been speechless. Words always seemed to fail him when he was smitten.

The plaza was abuzz with activity as vendors hawked their wares and street performers entertained the throngs for a few tossed coins. Young and old couples alike walked hand in hand while others stood locked in tight embraces or passionately made out. Laughing boys of all ages chased screaming girls through the crowd. A gentle evening breeze felt deliciously cool and wafted the smells of the many different foods being prepared and sold.

With Juan occupied with Emilia and Jake following Juanita like a lost puppy, Aaron looked out over the plaza for anything of interest. All across the plaza, he saw a sea of short, dark haired men and women. Then over by the ruins of the pyramid, he caught a glimpse of a shock of blonde hair above the crowd. Since nothing or no one else stood out, he wandered over in that direction, leaving Jake alone with Juanita.

Juanita took little notice of Jake. Since they didn't share a language, there was really no way to know if they had any common interests. That did little to dissuade Jake, who continued to fawn over her. They found themselves standing by the fountain. Juanita watched the people wander by, and Jake just watched her watch.

From across the plaza, sauntered Officer Miguel Martinez of the Chiapas State Police. He twirled his nightstick like a New York cop walking his beat in a fifties movie, pausing here and there to prod a drunk with it. When he spotted Juanita, he sucked in his gut, puffed out his chest, and stood up straighter as he sauntered her way.

"Hola Juanita, ¿cómo estás?" Miguel said, ignoring Jake. Juanita batted her eyes while she and Miguel had a conversation in Spanish. They glanced at Jake and chuckled something about gringo mudo. Juanita slipped her arm under Miguel's and they wandered off leaving Jake alone in the crowd.

By the time Aaron got to the pyramid, he'd lost sight of the blonde haired woman. He climbed a few steps up for a better vantage point and scanned the crowd. What is it about blondes, he wondered? Then from above and behind him in perfect English came a voice. "What do you think you're doing standing on an archeological wonder as if it's no more than a kitchen stool?! Try to show a little respect," a woman admonished.

Road Tripped

Aaron turned to mutter an apology and found himself faced with the blonde woman, who stood with her hands on her hips glaring at him. She wore khaki shorts and a cotton blouse typical of those made by the locals. The gentle evening breeze had blown the waves of her golden hair across her face. With a wave of her hand and a flip of her head she tossed her hair over her shoulder, revealing her piercing blue eyes that bore into Aaron's. A glimmer of familiarity came over her face. She hesitated a moment, and then said, "Aaron?"

Aaron was perplexed. Where had he seen the face before, he wondered? The woman broke out in a broad smile, revealing her perfect white teeth and deep dimples in her cheeks. "Renée?"

Aaron and Renée hadn't seen each other since high school. Over the years that followed, whenever he'd driven by her home, he'd always looked over at her house in the hope he would see her and maybe work up the nerve to ask her out.

"It is you!" She said. She stepped down and embraced him. "What brings you to our little part of the world?"

"It's a long sordid story. How 'bout you; what brings you to sunny Mexico?"

"I joined the Peace Corp right after graduation. They sent me here to help build homes; kinda funny, given the fact that I can't drive a nail to save my life! I fell in love with the town and the people and haven't been home since."

"So what are ya doin' now?"

"I work at the clinic." She looked over his shoulder and exclaimed, "Oh my god! Are you two still joined at the hip?"

Aaron turned to see Jake approaching. "Look who I found," he said.

"Holy Sh-- I mean hi Renée; long time no see!" Jake said.

"What happened to Juanita?" Aaron asked. Jake looked down and grumbled something under his breath.

Looking beyond the guys, Renée said, "Look what the cat drug in!"

"Oh... My... Gawd! If it ain't double trouble!" a woman exclaimed. The guys turned to see a woman with curly red shoulder length hair. Her green eyes sparked like emeralds as she looked at Jake. It was Allison. She wore a form fitting tee shirt that accentuated her pert breasts, loose shorts, and sandals. Whereas Renée had always been the beautiful one, Allison had always been cute, in a "girl next door" kind of way. She dashed over and threw her arms around Jake in a huge bear hug. "Let me look at you!" She pulled back and tousled his hair.

"Hi Allison," Jake said. "Good ta see ya." He looked right through Allison to watch as Juanita strolled by arm in arm with Miguel.

Allison turned to see what had drawn Jake's attention. She saw a cop wander by with a pretty woman on his arm. It was Juanita and that infamous lothario Miguel. She looked back at Jake and saw by the look in his eyes that he was smitten. She was exasperated. She'd had a crush on Jake since she had first laid eyes on him on the playground in kindergarten. He had been the worldly 'older man' in the first grade. She might as well have been invisible. A few years later, he had been a regular visitor at her best friend Renée's house where he had ignored her. Just once couldn't he look at her that way? She wondered.

Renée said, "We've got a lot of catchin' up t'do. Whadya guys have goin' on tomorrow night? The guys shrugged. "Dinner at our place then. Be there," she said. She pulled a ball point pen from her bag and on Aaron's hand wrote an address: 21 Calle 2.

"You girls are roommates?" Aaron asked.

"Duh!"

"What can we bring?" he said without thinking. With nearly no money at all, his mouth was writing a check he couldn't cover. He was a bit relieved when she replied "Nothin'; just bring yerselves! Sevenish?

OK, we'll be there!

About that time Juan and Emilia arrived. Without introduction, Renée said, "Hola Juan y Emilia, ¿cómo estás?"

"Muy bien." Juan replied.

"You guys know each other?" Aaron asked.

"How could one not know of the infamous El Supremo, Juan Valdez, of the Popular Front for the Restoration of Peace to the People of Mexico?"

Chapter Fourteen

Aaron and Jake peered over the edge of the precipice above where *Gertrude* lay stricken. Over coffee they had decided that they would try to make their way down to see if any of their clothes or anything else of value could be salvaged. They held little hope that the money they had stashed under the floorboards had not burned in the fire.

"Ya think there's anything left to save?" Jake asked while surveying the burned out hulk at the bottom of the ravine.

"It doesn't look too promising, Aaron replied.

"Looks pretty steep; how we gonna get down there?" Jake asked.

"We'll head back up the road a bit and look for any trails that lead down that way." They wandered along the shoulder of the highway all the way back to the village, but no paths presented themselves. "Let's try the other way." Some distance back down the road they found what looked like a game trail leading off into the thicket.

They clambered down a steep rocky incline until they encountered an escarpment that seemed to run parallel to the road. They edged along the bottom of the escarpment in the direction they guessed would lead them to *Gertrude*. It wasn't easy going. In places the thick jungle vegetation encroached on their path and they found themselves wishing for a machete. Although they guessed that they only had to cover about a mile, a few hours had gone by and they still had not found the wreck. Finally they decided to give up and head back. It was on their way back that they stumbled on *Gertrude*. Somehow they had missed her on the first pass.

"Ah *Gertrude*, you don't look so good," Aaron said dejectedly. She lay on her left side. Much of her paint had burned away and the exposed metal was already beginning to rust. The stench of burned oil, paint and upholstery still hung in the air. From where they stood, the bottom was exposed and they could see that a fuel line had been torn loose from the engine and had probably leaked gasoline all over the place causing the explosion.

"Gimme a boost," Aaron said to Jake. Jake laced his fingers together for Aaron to step into and launched him up onto *Gertrude*'s passenger side. Aaron in turn grabbed Jake's hand and pulled him up. He swung open the rear passenger doors and they climbed in to survey the darnage. The rear seat was mostly burned away, as were the curtains that Aaron's mom had so lovingly sewn so long ago. The canvas top that Mildred had made was nowhere to be seen. Though the open roof they looked out over a shear drop of about a hundred feet.

They began to rummage through the gear that was scattered about. Jake located his old leather suitcase which was badly singed. The zipper wouldn't budge, so he opened his Swiss army knife and cut the bag open. The clothes inside were largely intact. Aaron's bag was soon located, but his hadn't fared so well. The modern nylon fabric had melted, turning his clothes into a crusty lump. They would have to share. "I guess yer finally gonna have ta learn ta go commando!" Jake chided him.

"Yeah, it sure does wonders for your love life, don't it?"

Jake climbed into to forward part of the wreck. With the engine in the rear, most of the damage from the fire had been away from the forward part of the cabin. In the glove box he found a Snickers bar still in the wrapper and it was only slightly melted. "Lunch is served!" he exclaimed. "Ya want some?"

"Nah; help yer self."

"Suit yer self," he said as he wolfed it down.

Aaron crouched down and pulled out the rubber floor mat in front of the driver's seat to expose an access panel concealed there. "Gimme yer knife." Jake handed it to him and he opened the Phillips head screwdriver. The Swiss might be pacifists, but their army had some good equipment. "Cross yer fingers!" he said and began to unscrew the panel. Three of the four screws came out easily, but the fourth wouldn't budge, so he grasped the panel and bent it back to expose the treasure within. He reached in and extracted his tin lunch box emblazoned with the images of Batman and Robin from the comic books of their youth. He held his breath and opening the lid, he pulled out a mixed handful of American and Mexican currency. "Heeyaaa!!! Jackpot!"

"Suh-weet!" Jake exclaimed.

Almost as an afterthought, Jake grabbed the old boy scout compass that hung on a leather lanyard from the rear view mirror and hung it around his neck. "Anything else we can use?" he asked.

"Nah; I think that's about it. We better get started back anyway. Remember we got dates tonight."

Oh yeah. Speakin' of which, do ya think we could go on a double date one of these nights? I could ask Juanita out now that we've got some money, and Renée could be our interpreter."

"What about Allison?" Aaron asked.

"What about her?" "I think she's got the hots for ya."

"No way; she's just bein' friendly."

Although many years had gone by, and they'd both had many girlfriends, they were still clueless when it came to the opposite sex. Too bad they hadn't ever developed a video game of love; maybe they would've learned something. Naïve? Ignorant? Call it what you will. Allison might as well have tried to convey her feelings for Jake in smoke signals.

They started their way back. It must have been about noon, because the sun was directly overhead and the temperature soared.

"Damn; I'm getting' thirsty!" Jake exclaimed.

"Yeah; I guess we should've brought some water."

"When we get back I'll let ya buy me a beer. How do ya say beer in Mexican?"

"I dunno; point at the bottle maybe?"

A cloud passed in front of the sun and it was a welcome relief from the glare. The clouds continued to gather and a short time later with a crack of thunder, the sky opened up in a tropical deluge. Plucking large leaves from a bush, they funneled the rainwater into their dry mouths. Cooled and refreshed by the rain, they continued on their way in high spirits.

"Shouldn't we have been heading up toward the highway by now?" Aaron asked.

"I guess so. Lemme see what the compass says. Well north's that-a-way, but which way did we come from?"

"OK, let's think about this. We've been heading south since we left Olalla. We were heading along the highway back the way we came, so we should have been going north. Then we turned left down the hill, so that should mean that we went west. Then we turned south toward town. So I think we should go east to find the highway," Aaron reasoned.

"That sounds logical," Jake agreed.

They looked at the compass and faced east to be confronted by a shear vertical wall.

"So much for plan 'A', what's plan 'B'? Jake asked.

"OK, remember how the highway crosses a river every so often?" Aaron said.

"Yeah."

"Well if we find the river, we can follow it downstream until we find the highway."

"That makes sense. How we gonna find the river?"

"It looks like there's a ravine down there. That must be the river."

A short while later they found it. "Damn! Lewis and Clark ain't got nothin' on us!" Aaron exclaimed. They started heading downstream. They soon found that it was much easier to wade in the shallow water of the river than to clamber along the rugged bank. The sun had burned away the clouds and the temperature again began to climb. It was very humid, so the cool water felt good. They seemed to be making good time and they were sure that they would come to the highway soon. Then they came to a fork in the river.

"Which way now, Mr. Lewis?" Jake asked sarcastically.

"I dunno, Mr. Clark. What might you suggest?"

"Ya got a coin?" Jake asked.

Road Tripped

Aaron pulled out a fifty peso coin. "Call it." He tossed the coin, caught it in his right hand and slapped it onto the back of his left. He lifted his hand to reveal the coin.

"Is that heads or tails?" Jake asked.

Together they looked at both sides of the unfamiliar coin but could not decide which side was which.

"Rock-paper-scissors?" Jake suggested.

"Fuck it! Let's go this way," Aaron said and started down the right fork. Jake shrugged and followed.

After a while, the terrain began to flatten out into a broad valley. A narrow footpath followed along the river and they no longer had to wade. Jake forged ahead, eager to put their adventure behind them. In his haste, he tripped and fell flat on his face." What the fuck?" He grasped the thin piece of twine that had tripped him and gave it a yank. They could hear what sounded like something rattling in a tin can. At least they had found signs of civilization. They followed the string and sure enough, found it tied to a tin can hanging from a tree. They looked around and saw signs of cultivation.

"You smell what I smell?" Jake asked.

"It smells like…" Aaron glanced around and saw that what had stumbled into a large field of marijuana!

Out from behind a banana plant stepped a swarthy man wearing a cowboy hat with a bandana tied across his face like a bandit in a western movie. In his left hand he held a machete, and in his right hand he held a shotgun. His finger rested on the trigger, and the barrel lay casually over his shoulder. The guys backed up a couple of steps, but found their path blocked by another man who had a rifle slung across his shoulder and in his hand a high caliber revolver. "Buenos días, Señores."

Chapter Fifteen

With their hands bound securely behind their backs and
blindfolds torn from the tails of the first man's shirt covering
their eyes, Aaron and Jake were led away, each guided by a man
grasping an arm. It was rather difficult walking blind, and they
stumbled often as they were roughly prodded along. Through the
fabric covering their eyes, they could just make out light and
dark. Eventually they were led into shadow and
unceremoniously deposited into chairs. Their legs were then
bound to those of the chairs before being bound together back to
back. There they were left. With their eyes covered, they
couldn't tell for sure if they were alone or not. They listened
carefully to see if they heard any signs of movement.
Tentatively, Aaron said, "Jake; you there?"

"I'm right here; where else do ya think I'd be?"

"Some kind mess you led us into."

"Whose idea was it to follow the river?" Jake retorted.

"I thought you were the navigator."

"So what're we gonna do?" "I dunno; ya got any brilliant
ideas?"

"Yeah, let me whip out my Swiss army knife and we'll fight our way outa here; where ever the hell here is!" Jake said sarcastically.

"Man; we are sooooo fucked!" They said in unison.

Renée and Allison wandered through the market gathering ingredients for the dinner they were going to prepare for their guests. After discussing the menu, they decided that the guys would probably like to have a dinner that reminded them of home, so they settled on the most American meal they could think of, spaghetti. They would use an old family recipe that Allison had gotten from her favorite great aunt.

In the market, they selected fresh roma tomatoes, onions, bell peppers, mushrooms, garlic, and basil for the sauce and fresh spinach for the salad. They stopped by the carniceria for sausage and from the panaderia they bought a couple loaves of crusty bread. At one of the small shops on a back street they agonized over the choice of wine to accompany the gourmet meal they planned. The vast selection of wines on offer included red or white. Lastly, they looked for the most obvious ingredient, the pasta. After checking with several of the small shops, they finally found a couple packages of dried spaghetti that was only a few years past the expiration date. They lugged their booty back to their casa to begin the preparations.

While they were preparing the meal, their cat, Frisby, rubbed against their legs. While Renée was browning the sausage, she pawed at her leg in a less than subtle hint that she's like some. Renée held a bit down for her to sample. She took a sniff and lost interest. There's gratitude for ya!

Soon the aroma of the sauce permeated the air. Meanwhile, the girls went through their wardrobes to pick their outfits.

Renée set out a slinky black dress and open toe shoes with moderate heels with her grandmother's pearl necklace and earrings as adornments.

Allison disappeared into her room for some time. When she emerged, her haute couture consisted of a soft flowing mid length skirt and a white silk blouse through which a lacy bra was visible pressing her moderate breasts together to create a little cleavage. She had pulled her hair back on one side and embellished it with a tropical flower that complimented her green eyes. For makeup, she used mascara, eyeliner, a touch of rouge, and bright red lipstick. She wore a necklace a with a simple emerald pendent and matching earrings that she'd gotten as a graduation gift from her great aunt. On her feet she wore her sexiest spike heels.

"Damn girl; you look hot!" Renée exclaimed.

Allison attempted a runway model turn. "Ya think it'll get Jake's attention?"

"I just don't know what you see in that guy. You could have your choice of any guy you want, and instead you pick him!"

"There's just something about him…"

"What, his big dick?"

"Well yeah, there's that too," she said with a small smile. "But there's a side of him I just don't think you could understand."

"Try me."

"Do you remember Lucky Lucy?"

"Who?"

"The deer that Jake saved."

"Sort of."

"Well I'd always thought he was kind of cute, but seeing him with that poor deer made me realize that he had a big heart," she said with a dreamy look in her eyes. "Sometimes he can be the most infuriating man imaginable, but then I think of him with Lucy and ..." She paused for a moment with a faraway look, then turned to Renée. "So what about Aaron, he isn't exactly an Adonis. Why do you think he's so hot?"

"I never said he was hot!"

"Oh no, not you!. C'mon Renée, this is me you're talking to. You've had the hots for him since kindergarten."

"Well he is kind of hot, I suppose."

They finished their preparations. Renée set the sauce on a low simmer, tossed the salad and set out decanters of extra virgin olive oil and balsamic vinegar as dressing. Allison put the bread in a basket and set the table with locally made stoneware and four wine glasses. She opened the bottle of red wine to allow it to breathe. On the stove, Renée set a large pan filled with water at the ready to cook the pasta after the guys arrived. With their preparations complete, Renée slipped into her outfit and put on just a hint of delicate perfume. At five to seven, she lit the candles.

In the distance, Aaron heard the approach of a helicopter. "Do you hear that?" he asked Jake. "Yeah; do you think it could be the army or the police? Maybe they've come to rescue us!"

"How would they even know we're in trouble?"

They heard the helicopter land close by and then the rotors and turbine engine spool down. After a brief pause, they heard several people approach. They felt the bindings being cut. "Stand!" a female voice barked. They stood and someone cut the last of their bindings from their wrists. Their blindfolds were yanked off and they squinted a moment until their eyes became re-accustomed to the light. They found that they were in an open, thatched roof cabana over which a camouflage net was draped. They were surrounded by surly looking men with bandanas across their faces, all heavily armed. All that was missing were sombreros, ponchos, and bandoleers across their chests to create the perfect costumes. To one side stood a slender woman in designer jeans and a silk blouse who leaned against a post smoking a cigarette. Her eyes were concealed behind very large dark sunglasses. She quietly said something to a large man in slacks and a guayabera shirt who stood respectfully at her side.

"Who has sent you here?" The man said with a note of malice in heavily eastern European accented English.

"Sent us? We were lost!"

"Do not toy with us," he said menacingly. "FBI, CIA, or DEA?

"Look man, we're just tourists," Jake protested.

"This is not a tourist area. Do you take us for fools?" To one of the thugs, he barked, "Escudriñarlas." (Search them) They were patted down. Their meager wad of cash, their wallets, and Jake's knife were set on a table.

"Where are they?" The man asked.

"Where are what?" Aaron asked.

"The microphones."

"Microphones? Why would we have microphones? I already told you; we're just tourists!" Aaron said.

The woman again spoke to the man.

"Les tira," (Strip them) he ordered.

Soon their clothes lay on the table along with the bundle of clothes they'd rescued from *Gertrude*, where one of the thugs rifled through them. Aaron stood in his boxer shorts and of course Jake again found himself naked in front of strangers. The thugs sniggered among themselves, "¡ Jesucristo, mire la tamaño de su gallo!" (Jesus Christ, look at the size of his cock!)

"Ya ready ta start wearin' underwear yet?" Aaron chided Jake.

"Silence!" the woman barked. She strode over and blew smoke into Aaron's face. Reaching down, she pulled out the waistband of his boxers to see if anything was concealed there. Of course the only thing they concealed was his pride, or what was left of it. She slowly circled around them. Pausing in front of Jake, she reached up and tore the Boy Scout compass from his neck. She tossed it to the ground and crushed it beneath her Prada heel.

"Hey; I've had that since I was eight!" Jake whined.

Now it was his turn to get the smoke in the eyes treatment. Up close, it was apparent that the woman was not Hispanic. Although she was well tanned, it was obvious that she was Caucasian, and wore a dark wig. She lifted her sunglasses enough to look under them at the source of her thugs' amusement but not high enough to reveal her eyes. "Sí es grande; Pero nuestras armas son más grandes." (Yes it is big; but our guns are bigger.)

She turned and slowly strode away, engaged in conversation with her lieutenant. Although they could not understand what was being said, they could tell by the inflection of his voice that he was asking a question while dragging his finger across his throat. She turned and cast a glance in their direction and replied with a shrug. He barked out orders, lifted the camouflage net for her to exit, and followed her out. Moments later, they heard the turbine engine and rotor of the helicopter spool up and it flew away.

One of the henchmen threw their clothes to them and they slipped them on. Another threw their meager wad of cash to the ground at their feet. It was obvious that they thought the modest sum was not worth the trouble of stealing. Jake gathered it up and stuck it in his pocket. Their hands were again bound behind their backs, but this time dark cotton bags were put over their heads. The bags reeked of pot and felt sticky with resin. They were led away, hopefully not to their execution. They were then shoved into the back of a pickup and they could feel their bag of clothes tossed in after them. They were covered with a tarp and then it sounded like a couple of thugs climbed aboard. The truck's doors opened and slammed shut, the engine started and they drove away.

The candles burned down to stubs and the girls looked at the clock again. "The assholes stood us up! Screw it; let's eat!" Renée grumbled.

"Fuck that; let's drink!" Allison exclaimed.

"Ya think Cruella DeVille told 'em to shoot us?" Jake whisperd.

"I dunno; if they were gonna, why wouldn't they have done it already?"

"Didn't wanna shit in the nest maybe?"

"Jake, whatever happens, I just want you to know that you are my best friend and always have been. I love you like the brother I never had."

"You're not gonna kiss me are ya?"

"Kiss my ass; I'm bein' serious here!"

Road Tripped

"Aw come on; I love you too Aaron. Listen; if the opportunity presents itself, I'll do what I can to draw their fire while you try to escape."

"But…"

"No buts! Just do it!"

The truck bounced over very rough terrain for some time before at last they reached a paved road. The tires squealed as they accelerated away and a whiff of tire smoke wafted under the tarp to reach their noses.

After a while, they began to feel a bit odd. Perhaps it was the effects of adrenalin wearing off or perhaps from the pot vapors they were breathing.

They drove for some time along a winding mountain road until they slowed and turned off onto another bumpy road. At last the truck came to a stop. They could hear the doors open as the tarp was pulled back. They were roughly pulled from the bed of the truck and led away down a path.

"Remember; run when the action starts," Jake said quietly.

From behind they could hear the sound of the truck idling. Their captors released their grip for a moment and they braced themselves for the volley of gunfire they expected. Instead, their bindings were cut and the bags lifted from their heads. It was dark and there was just enough starlight to see that their captors were masked to conceal their identity. They turned and headed for the sound of the truck while one remained behind to cover their exit. The remaining henchman edged back still brandishing a shotgun.

"Ready?" Jake asked.

Then the man turned and dashed to the waiting truck and it could be heard driving away.

They stood for a moment in disbelief.

"Now we're in real trouble," Aaron said.

"What kind of trouble could be worse than the bullets we just dodged?"

"We missed our date."

Chapter Sixteen

Jake asked Aaron, "So what're we gonna do now?" They stood in the dark of the clearing in which they had been unceremoniously dropped off.

"I guess we should head for the road and see if we can flag down a ride," Aaron replied and tentatively walked through the darkness in the direction of the road. Soon they reached the road and stopped.

"Which way?" Jake asked.

"Shit; I dunno; maybe we should flip a coin," Aaron replied.

"That's just what got us in the mess we're in! Maybe we should just wait here until a car comes."

They huddled shivering on a rock in the dark waiting. After a while, the horizon began to lighten with the approach of dawn, which told them which direction was east. They were pretty sure they were north of San Gabriele, so they watched for southbound traffic. At last a pair of headlights could be seen approaching from the north. They waved their arms to get the driver's attention and were glad to see the car begin to slow. They were washed in the bright lights of a gleaming new SUV with California plates as it crept by and stopped. The guys grabbed their bag of clothes and started toward the vehicle, when suddenly it accelerated away, leaving them incredulous.

"Thanks for nothin' assholes!" Jake grumbled. What is it about Americans and their aversion to getting involved? They wondered.

Soon it was daylight and the world awoke. From the surrounding jungle, a huge flock of green parrots swarmed en mass from their roost toward an unknown destination to begin their day. Where the narrow dirt road on which they had been dropped led off into the thicket, the deep tracks of off-road tires could be seen. Jake started down the path.

"Where ya goin'?" Aaron asked.

"I gotta take a leak; I'll be right back." In a few minutes, he returned saying, "Breakfast is served!" He clutched a bunch of over ripe bananas in his hand. They munched on the better looking of the bunch as they waited for the next opportunity for a ride.

Another car approached. They waved their arms to flag it down, but the car with Illinois plates didn't even slow down.

"Damn gringos! What do we look like; a couple of banditos?" Jake said.

The next southbound vehicle was a decrepit old Chevy pickup truck with tall wooden rails around the bed. The truck came to a stop. The man at the wheel shared the cab with his wife, three kids and a chicken. He signaled for the guys to hop in the back, which they shared with a goat.

It was mid morning when the truck squealed to a stop at San Gabriele. "Gracias, Amigo!" They said to the driver.

"De nada," the man said and drove away, trailing a cloud of blue smoke.

Juan greeted them at the door. "Hello Amigos; where have you been? We were worried."

Inside, they recanted the story as best they could. Juan listened attentively to their story, and then asked, "Did anyone see you come here?"

Aaron and Jake looked at each other and Aaron said, "We don't think so."

"I'm sorry my friends, but I must ask you to leave and not return here. You see it is only because you are gringos that you still live. Killing gringos causes too much attention; if you were Mexicanos, all that would be found of you is body parts. If they knew that you came here, me and my family…"

"Should we call the police?" Jake asked.

"No; you must not! The drug people have spies in the policia and friends in high places. You must speak of this to no one."

"What should we do?" Jake asked Aaron.

"Maybe we should get a room at the motel. Do we have enough money?" Aaron replied.

Jake pulled out their crumpled wad of cash and counted it out on the table. Juan looked at the pile and said, "You must not use your American dollars for a while." He pulled out his wallet and extracted all of his cash. Keeping a fifty peso note for himself, he put the rest in the pile. He explained the situation to Emilia who then pulled a clay pot from atop a shelf, extracted another wad of bills, and added those too to the pile. She then began preparing a meal.

The guys protested, but Juan insisted. At last they were able to convince Juan to take some of their American currency. He would exchange it the next time he was in another town.

Emilia set out four plates of tacos. The guys wolfed down their lunch before Juan and Emilia had even finished saying grace. It had been well over 24 hours since they had had a real meal, and both were ravenous. Emilia also prepared them a sack of food to take to the motel so that they would not have to be seen in the market.

Juan stood and waited while the guys gathered their things.

"Juan, we wish there was some way for us to repay your kindness. You and Emilia have done so much," Aaron said earnestly. "Gracias amigo," Jake added.

"De nada, mi amigos," Juan said while shaking their hands. "We will pray to the savior for your safety." Emilia gave them both hugs, and then did the sign of the cross as she returned to her chores.

Juan went to the door where he paused for a moment to listen. The sound of a car could be heard clattering down the street. When it was gone, he opened the door and looked both ways before gesturing to the guys that it was all clear.

Outside, Rio met the guys and jumped on Jake excitedly. He then followed as they made their way to the motel across the highway from the taberna, where he took up station outside the door of their room as if on guard. Soon Aaron and Jake were settled in. Their room was unfortunately facing the highway, so despite the fact that it was stifling hot, they kept the blinds closed. The dusty room was furnished with only one queen size bed. Aaron stripped to his boxers and collapsed on the bed in exhaustion. With his eyes closed, he said," don't even think of getting' on this bed naked!"

Road Tripped

"What; ya don't think ya can control yourself?" Jake said. Aaron replied by snoring. Jake rummaged through his meager selection of garments and found a pair of khaki shorts. Soon he too was sound asleep.

Aaron and Jake were awakened by Rio barking and someone pounding on the door of their motel room. They leaped to their feet and looked for a way to escape. The only possible avenue for escape was the bathroom window and it was clearly too small. They were cornered! The pounding became more insistent, and at last Aaron worked up the courage to open the door to the limit of the safety chain and hesitantly peer out. "Is it them?" Jake asked anxiously. Aaron closed the door and said, "Worse! It's Renée and Allison." He slipped on his jeans, unhooked the chain and opened the door. Renée had her arms crossed and Allison had her hands on her hips. They cast a withering glare on the guys.

Aaron reached out, grabbed the girls by the hands, and pulled them into the room. He nervously looked up and down the highway, slammed the door and put his back to it. "How did you find us?" he asked nervously.

"It's not hard; not many gringos stop here. You'd better have a damn good explanation for standing us up last night!" Renée said.

"We're really sorry girls, but, uh, we had a situation that uh…" Aaron stammered.

"What kind of situation?"

"Uh."

"We're waiting."

"For your own safety, we can't say," Jake said.

141

Ron Fugere

Now it was Allison's turn. "What a crock of shit! What, do you expect us to believe, that you're on a covert mission for the CIA or some such crap? Gimme a break!"

Aaron spoke, "I'm afraid that we're not at liberty to say more."

Renée's expression softened a bit and she said, "Ah come on Allison; they probably had a really good reason for not making it."

"Yeah, he probably had a date with that slut Juanita!" Allison retorted and cast a disdainful look at Jake.

"No, it wasn't like that," Aaron said. "Please trust me when I say that we cannot say anything more. Is there some way that we can make it up to you?"

Renée replied, "OK, you can treat us to a nice dinner out."

"We need to keep a low profile; we can't be seen around town right now," Aaron said.

"Great, not only are they unreliable, but they're cheap too!" Allison sneered.

"OK, better yet, they can take us to dinner in San Cristobal," Renée said.

"Do you have a car?" Aaron asked.

"No; we'll have to take the bus. It stops right out front," Renée said. "Be ready at eight tomorrow morning. Do not disappoint us!" With that, she strode purposely to the door. She opened it and Allison stormed out. Rio tucked his tail between his legs and scampered away. "Eight o'clock," Renée said as she slammed the door.

"Are you sure this is a good idea?" Jake asked. "We really ought to keep out of sight for a while, shouldn't we?"

"That's just why we ought to do it. We should get out of here until the smoke clears."

142

Road Tripped

The rest of the day and night seemed to stretch on for an eternity. The guys sweated in the sweltering hot stuffy room. They were bored out of their minds with not even so much as a single magazine to read, much less a TV. They sat for hours watching a small black fly flying geometric patterns in the air. Eventually the fly dropped to the floor, where it buzzed in circles until at last it was still. The high point of the day was watching a green gecko scamper across the floor, snatch up the fly, and beat a hasty retreat. With nothing whatsoever to distract them, their minds were free to dwell on their dilemma. Make that dilemmas.

Ron Fugere

Chapter Seventeen

Aaron peered out through the blinds at the sound of the bus coming to a stop. A small group of short, dark haired people milled around waiting their turn to board. Among them he could see an island of golden hair and another of red.

When the rest of the passengers had boarded, Renée signaled for the guys to come. They hastily strode from their room and followed Renée and Allison aboard. Renée handed four tickets to the driver and headed toward the rear where she found four unoccupied seats on the right side of the bus. The girls took the window seats while the guys sat on the aisle and slouched down so as to be less visible to any passing cars.

The bus lurched into motion. Rio ran behind barking until the bus gained speed at the outskirts of the village, leaving him behind. He sulked while it disappeared from sight. The bus was not one of the luxurious motor coaches that were a regular sight along the highway, but a decrepit old clunker that looked like a surplus prison bus with all the appropriate accoutrements. The seats were simple benches with fiberglass seats devoid of padding. It had obviously been some time since the dusty floor had seen the business end of a broom. Long enough that some kind of plants were sprouting in the crevasses. The windows hinged outward to allow a breeze to circulate. Many of the men among their fellow travelers pulled their hats down over their eyes and dozed while the women chatted amiably, scolded the kids, or sewed.

Once settled in, the four travelers could get reacquainted. Renée, always the inquisitive one began, "So what have you been up to since graduation? I always figured that by now you'd be a world champion motorcycle racer or something like that. The way you guys used to tear around on your bikes, I'm surprised you're still alive! I could never imagine you at a desk or behind the wheel of a truck."

"Well I certainly never did anything as exciting as that, but I did have an office."

"Did?"

He went on to explain the *Live It*, Unlimited debacle.

"Rags to riches to rags, huh?"

"That's an understatement!"

Renée looked him over and said, "I just can't picture you in a suit in an office, much less in the board room!"

"Well Jake and I weren't exactly the typical corporate droids. We were a bit like bananas on a pizza. So what about you? How'd ya go from pounding nails to being a nurse?"

"Who said I'm a nurse?"

"Well you work in a clinic, so I just kinda figured..."

"I'm a doctor."

"Really? I thought you came here right after high school. When did you find time to go to medical school?"

"Well it didn't take me long to realize that I could be of more help to the people down here if I could learn to care for their health; so I studied medicine in Mérida, Yucatán."

"So you have a Mexican license? I heard that you used to be able to buy one if you could apply a Band-Aid."

"Mérida has a great medical community," Renée said somewhat defensively. "I wouldn't hesitate to have any procedure performed there no matter how complex or risky."

Aaron told the story of their visit to Mérida and they shared a laugh.

Meanwhile, Allison was giving Jake the third degree. "So Operative Overbee, how long have you been with the CIA?"

"If I told ya I'd have ta kill ya!" Now it was Jake's turn to tell her about their venture into corporate America.

"So you could've been a millionaire?" Allison said incredulously.

"Yeah, who'd uh thunk?" He said sheepishly.

"So what about you; what do you do here?"

"I teach English at the school and sometimes I serve as interpreter when some do-gooder Americans come to town."

"So you're good at Spanish?"

"Duh!"

"Ya think you could teach me some Spanish?"

"Why, so you can go chasing after that Juanita?" Allison was still fuming over the look she'd seen in Jake's eyes when he'd looked at Juanita.

"No, no!" Jake protested, but his look gave him away; that was exactly what he had in mind. "It seems we may be here for a while, unless we can figure out how to make a buck. I guess we should learn the lingo."

Road Tripped

"You're like most gringos who just want to learn to swear in Spanish or how to order beer or a prostitute!"

"Whatever," Jake said. A stony silence ensued.

All along the roadside were countless discarded plastic water bottles and other litter. Since few locals could afford to buy bottled water, it seemed likely that it was left by tourists. As they climbed higher into the mountains, the jungle gave way to sparse pine forests. Occasionally, they would pass small clusters of homes. Where trees were plentiful, they would be constructed of wood. Where trees were scarce, they would be built of cinder blocks or poured concrete. Often, the first floor of a building had been poured and long poles of rebar projected up defining where the second floor would someday go. Some appeared as if construction had begun long ago and had been stalled indefinitely.

After a while, Renée turned and asked, "OK, we're out of town now so spill it! What's the big secret?"

"Yeah, what could a couple of video nerds from Oo-la-la be into that is such a big deal? Did you create a virtual reality cyborg that's out ta git cha?" Allison piped in sarcastically.

"Please girls, it really is better we don't talk about it," Aaron pleaded.

"I choose to remain silent on the grounds that anything I say can and will be twisted and manipulated into a torture device!" Now it was Jake's turn to be sarcastic.

"My, aren't we touchy!" Renée said.

Aaron changed the subject. "So what's this town we're goin' to; San Chrystal Ball?"

"San Crisobal. It's the closest thing we have to a city here in Chiapas," Renée explained. "You'll see soon enough; it's just a few hours south of here. It's a bit touristy, but beautiful nonetheless."

"Maybe that's a good thing; it will be easier for us to be inconspicuous where we can blend in with a crowd of tourists," Aaron said. "In San Gabriele we stand out like sore thumbs."

"You know, just because you're friends with 'El Supremo' doesn't mean you have to be afraid of the army or police; they really don't take the revolution seriously."

"I wish it were so simple."

Renée leaned close and in a low voice said,

"I won't pry any more about your secret; I'm sure you'll tell all in good time."

"Thanks, Renée; it's really for the best."

"So tell me about your love life!" She smiled.

"What if that's my secret?" Maybe I'm a world famous international lothario who is being pursued by a jilted lover and her cuckold husband!"

"So what about Jake; is he a gigolo too?"

"Nah; he's my manservant."

Jake looked at Aaron, flipped him off and, then went back to his sulking.

"No really; do you have anyone special in your life?" Renée asked.

"No, not right now," Aaron confided. "Some women thought I was a rich eccentric and would try to hook me as their meal ticket. Sometimes I'd play along, but I could usually see right through them. The worst of them usually went for the junior executives because they flaunted their wealth. Lots of silicone and trophy wives at the company picnic. So what about you?"

Road Tripped

"Kinda slim pickins in San Gabriele. Besides my career keeps me pretty busy. Renée slipped her hand under Aaron's arm and said, "Can I share a little secret with you? I always had a crush on you!"

"Me?"

"You're surprised?"

"Yeah; I always thought you were into the jocks in high school."

"There were no jocks in kindergarten."

"I didn't even know you in kindergarten! I was a year ahead."

"I didn't know you either, but I'd see you on the playground and then at home I'd play with my dolls and pretend we were married."

"Can I let you in on a secret too? I had a crush on you, although it wasn't until a few years later. Remember that summer when me and Jake got busted on our bikes?"

"Yeah."

"Reason we got busted is we only had one eye on what we were doin' and the other on you."

"So how long did you have your crush on me?" She asked coyly. He didn't answer. After a pause, she asked, "Why didn't you ever ask me out?"

"Did ya ever want something but didn't ask because you were afraid of the answer?"

"Ya mean ya thought I'd say no? You really are clueless, aren't you? Couldn't you tell I was always flirting?"

"I thought you were just teasing me."

"Let me clue you in; I wasn't."

They sat in silence for some time, each trying to process the revelation. Meanwhile, Jake and Allison sat in silence as Aaron and Renée were having their conversation. Allison occupied herself watching the scenery go by. Jake was content to just watch the other passengers or study the peeling paint on the ceiling. The motion and sound of the bus made him drowsy, but every time he nodded off, his head would fall this way or that and he would wake with a start.

At last Allison said, "I suppose I should lighten up a bit. I'm sorry if I was a bit harsh; must be the redhead in me!"

"That's alright. I guess I can see why you'd think I was just another gringo. Thing is, we may be here for a while until we can figure out a way to get home. I thought it would be easier to find some work if I spoke a bit of Spanish."

"What kind of work can you do? Not much demand for video game developers in this part of Mexico."

"I was sort of in charge of product development and marketing."

"Our idea of marketing is a cardboard sign. What else can you do?"

"We helped a little old lady with some home maintenance and repairs, we could look into that."

"There are lots of men who do that kind of work already, and they only make a few hundred pesos a day. And they probably need the work even worse than you do."

"What do you think we could do?"

"I dunno; we'll see if anything comes to mind."

The bus began yet another long decent. It passed a sign that read: "Entrar en San Cristobal."

Renée announced, "Here we are!"

Road Tripped

Chapter Eighteen

The bus proceeded downhill into San Crisobal. At the outskirts of town were small auto repair shops and tire stores interspersed with vegetable stands, carnicerias and motels. The roadside was bustling with people coming and going on foot and the traffic on the road was snarled. The bus ground to a halt. Many of the passengers took no notice of the delay, but others simply grabbed their belongings and disembarked to walk ahead. Occasionally the line of traffic would creep forward a few yards and stop.

"Reminds me of Seattle traffic!" Aaron quipped. "Only this is moving faster."

At last the bus arrived at the source of the traffic jam, a dog taking a nap in the middle of the road. Nearby, a police officer leaned on his car with its blue lights flashing, smoking a cigarette. He seemed completely oblivious to the traffic congestion. Any number of people could have shooed the dog out of the road, but it just didn't seem a high priority. Things move at a different pace in Mexico. The bus finally arrived at the terminal and the remaining passengers climbed out. At the curb, our wayward travelers stretched to limber up.

Aaron and Jake took in the new sights. San Cristobal lay in a bowl-like valley surrounded by mountains. The sun shone brightly overhead, while clouds billowed over the peaks. In the middle of the bowl, the towering steeple and bell tower of a cathedral could be seen. Throwing their gear over their shoulders, the party set out in the direction of the steeple with Allison leading.

Their path carried them down one way streets which had obviously been built many years before the automobile; they were much too narrow to accommodate two-way traffic. In places, the cobblestones had ruts worn by horse-drawn wagons. Taxis careened down the streets at breakneck speed. At stop signs, they would blow their horn and continue at unabated speed, often meeting another taxi at the intersections, avoiding a collision by a hairbreadth. The sidewalks were no more than shoulder width, so they went single file. Here and there, cars were parked with two wheels on the sidewalk, forcing pedestrians into the street in the path of the oncoming vehicles. A taxi slowed and asked in broken English, "Gringos need ride? Fifty pesos." Allison waved him off and he unleashed a torrent of what must have been colorful language to which Allison responded with a barrage of her own, accompanied by a solid kick to the driver's door panel which left a sizeable dent. He drove away, gesticulating wildly. "Dude don't know that ya don't mess with a redhead!' Jake laughed.

They continued to the central plaza which was several blocks square. On one side loomed the cathedral. A solid stream of cars, trucks, and horse drawn carriages circled the plaza. The group darted through a gap in the traffic to reach the middle of the plaza, which had lush green lawns and brick paved walkways.

Short, black haired girls and women of all ages wandered about hawking their wares. Many of the older women wore black sheepskin leggings and bare feet. They usually had a few humble items in their hands to offer. The younger girls were clad in more familiar Mayan clothing and walked in small groups, talking or texting on their modern smart-phones. Many carried huge bundles of brightly colored scarves nearly as large as they were, and would stop and spread them out for anyone who cast a glance at their offerings. If the intended customer continued to show interest, the other girls would congregate and show them their own offerings of handmade bags and jewelry. Men offered hammocks or Cuban cigars.

Aaron and Jake had not yet perfected Renée's and Allison's skills at running the gauntlet and made the mistake of making eye contact with a teenage girl. Seizing the opportunity, her and her friends besieged the guys. Renée and Allison turned to laugh at their predicament. The guys looked at them pleadingly to come to their rescue. Allison said, "No dinero, no dinero," and the girls evaporated into the crowd.

Having crossed the plaza, they were again faced with the stream of traffic. A police officer blew his whistle and signaled for the cars to stop for the pedestrians, but most drivers simply swerved around him and continued on their way. Renée stepped into the traffic, and matching her pace to that of the traffic, crossed all four lanes without slowing her stride. Allison followed suit. Aaron and Jake stopped for a moment to access their chances and stepped from the curb. A car skidded to a stop inches from Aaron and was struck from behind by another car. Meanwhile a car swerved to avoid Jake and sideswiped another car. Soon traffic was at a standstill all around the plaza. Horns blared, voices were raised, and police whistles all joined in the cacophony. "Damn; that must be what it feels like to be a prairie dog in a buffalo stampede!" Jake said as they wandered away leaving the carnage behind.

The guys joined the girls as they headed down a broad boulevard which was closed to motor vehicles. The street was paved with new bricks and the windows in the storefronts were spotless. Several stores displayed huge quantities of premium amber and sterling silver jewelry. Boutiques displayed extravagant woolen garments that would not have looked out of place on a Paris runway. Much of the art was locally made and inspired by old designs, but was adapted to suit the taste of the intended consumer, the wealthy foreigners who wandered in pairs up and down the boulevard. The attire of the tourists ranged from tailored Italian suits and shoes to khaki shorts with guayabera shirts, Panama hats, and Birkenstocks. The outdoorsy types opted for a combination of Eddie Bauer Gore-Tex with Patagonia, or LL Bean wool and REI boots.

In a single block, one might hear people conversing in French, German, or English in many different accents, accompanied by the percussion of spike heels on the pavement. Those who spoke Spanish were very much in the minority. The few native people that were there seemed ill at ease, as if expecting to be chased off at any moment.

"This kinda reminds me of Fifth Avenue in Seattle," Aaron said.

"Yeah, where's the Gucci store?" Jake piped in.

"Gawd, you are such an Olalla Billy!" Allison laughed.

"Once an Olalla-Billy, always an Olalla-Billy," Renée agreed.

Road Tripped

"Ya can take the Billy out of Olalla, but ya can't take Olalla out of the Billy!" Aaron said.

"What's an Olalla Billy?" Jake asked. Everyone burst out laughing. "What?" He looked baffled. They laughed harder still.

The foursome spent a while window shopping along the boulevard before whiling away the afternoon wandering the back streets of the city. Eventually they wound their way back to the boulevard as evening drew near.

The odor of gourmet food being prepared soon had the guys salivating; they'd only had a light breakfast and were famished. Elegant restaurants and bistros spilled out onto the boulevard, inviting couples to sample haute cuisine from the great capitols of the world.

"What say we slap on the ol' feed bag; I'm gettin' powerful hungry," Jake said starting toward a café.

Renée intercepted him and said, "Just around the corner is our favorite restaurant; follow me." She led them onto a side street and into Il Ristorante Italiano di Luigi.

Luigi's restaurant had but six tables which would accommodate no more than perhaps twelve guests. Although the sidewalk in front was wide enough for two to walk abreast, it was not wide enough for bistro seating; so the front of the restaurant was a large roll-up door which gave the impression of outdoor dining. The tablecloths were red and white checked linen with neatly folded green napkins. Each place was set with wine glasses, flatware, and a charger glazed with a grape vine motif. Candles sat at the ready in empty wine bottles covered with wax drippings. Separating the dining room from the kitchen was a large wine rack filled with dusty bottles and draped with a gnarled dry grapevine. Over hidden speakers an Italian tenor sang opera.

One of the tables appeared to be occupied by newlyweds and another by a distinguished looking man with neatly groomed silver hair and his buxom date, who could easily be mistaken for his daughter were it not for their body language which suggested a relationship of a different nature. A tall, slender young woman in a mid length black dress and apron tended to their needs. "Ciao, Sophia," Renée said in greeting.

"Ciao, Renée, e 'bella vederti!" the woman replied enthusiastically as she went about her business.

From behind the wine rack a mellifluous baritone voice called out, "Mia bella Renée, how good to see you!" Luigi stepped from behind the wine rack wearing a long white apron over his round belly and a tall chef's hat. He snatched off the hat revealing his balding pate. He strode over to embrace Renée, crushing his hat against her back.

"Luigi, this is Aaron and this is Jake. They are old friends from the states. Of course you know Allison."

"But of course. Allison you are beautiful, as always!" He kissed her hand.

"Pleased to meet you Luigi," Aaron said offering his hand. Luigi brushed it aside and gave Aaron a hug, saying, "The pleasure is all mine Aaron!" He turned to Jake and gave him a hug as well.

"Please my friends; be seated." He showed them to a table. "For you I will prepare a meal to kill for!" He gesticulated animatedly.

"You mean to die for Luigi," Renée corrected him on the proper use of the cliché.

Luigi opened a trap door in the floor by the side wall of the dining room, hooked the door open, and descended a wooden ladder while pulling the string on a bare light bulb which illuminated the earthen walls of the cellar. From below he could be heard muttering in Italian. "Ah ha!" he exclaimed and reaching up, placed first one bottle of wine and then another on the floor. He clambered up the ladder, dowsed the light, and closed the trap door. Pulling an old fashioned corkscrew from the pocket of his apron, he opened the bottle of red wine with a flourish and set it on the table to breathe while handing the cork to Jake. Jake looked at the cork, mystified as to what to do with it. Luigi took it back and took a long, leisurely whiff of its bouquet before handing it to Jake once more. Luigi kissed his fingertips and exclaimed, "Perfecto!" Jake took a few tentative sniffs of the cork, shrugged his shoulders, and handed it to Aaron who was equally perplexed as to what to do with it. He set it on the table.

"I will chill the white wine." Luigi stepped to the kitchen and returned with an antipasto platter and a baguette warm from the oven. With his bare hands, he tore chunks of the bread off and set it on the table before each guest, then wrapped the remainder of the loaf in a linen napkin and set it in a basket in the middle of the table. He then drizzled extra virgin olive oil and balsamic vinegar onto saucers. Aaron and Jake waited expectantly for butter to arrive. They watched the girls dip the bread in the saucers, and then followed their example.

Sofia came with Cesar salads and grated some fresh parmesan on each. Without asking, Luigi ground black pepper from a tall wooden grinder onto each salad. The way they moved around the table was like a well choreographed dance. Luigi draped a towel over his forearm, over which he lay the bottle of wine as he poured a small amount into Renée's glass. She held it by the stem as she examined the color and then swirled it to release the aroma, before holding it to her nose. She then took a small sip and swished it around in the mouth for a few moments before at last swallowing it. "Good color, woody nose, robust and full bodied; it is wonderful Luigi; as always."

"Hey, that's how I describe my… ouch!" Aaron jabbed Jake just in time to keep him from ruining the moment.

Luigi poured wine for the rest of the party and returned to the kitchen where he could be heard singing in harmony with the tenor on the stereo.

While they waited for the next course to arrive, the foursome watched the young couple neck at their table as if in a world of their own, while the silver haired gent ran his hand under the skirt of his date and was rewarded with a playful slap.

Through the open front of the restaurant, they could see an occasional car would go by. Many were the usual beat-up small cars seen throughout Mexico, with the occasional SUV of the tourists. A sleek black late model Mercedes stopped across the street. A swarthy looking man stepped out of the right rear door and looked around a moment before crossing to the left door which he opened to allow a passenger out. Aaron took notice due to the fact that the elegantly dressed woman who exited the car wore a mink coat; a rather rare sight in Mexico. She had short cropped blonde hair and pale gray eyes. The man followed a few steps behind as she strode assertively toward the boulevard; clearly he was not her date but rather her body guard. She reached in her handbag for a jeweled case from which she extracted a pair of sunglasses and slipped them on. When Aaron had first seen the woman, there had been a glimmer of familiarity, but he couldn't place her. When she donned her glasses, he began to suspect; but when she paused to allow her bodyguard light her cigarette, there was no doubt. It was Cruella DeVille!

Road Tripped

Aaron swiftly put his hand behind Jake's neck and physically forced his head below the table, where he leaned down to whisper, "We got trouble!"

"Yeah, I know! Can you imagine how much this meal is gonna cost us?" Jake replied.

"Not that kind trouble; the kind with guns. It's Cruella."

Jake stole a glance outside in time to see the black Mercedes drive away. He rejoined Aaron under the table. "I didn't see anything; are ya sure?"

"Did ya see a black Mercedes?"

"Yeah; it just left."

Aaron took a peek and when he saw that the coast was clear, he sat up.

"What's the matter with you guys? You look like ya saw a ghost!" Renée said.

"It was uh…" Aaron stammered.

"Probably some ex-girlfriend," Allison said.

Luigi came to the rescue by coming to clear the platter and salad plates for the main course. He returned with fresh wine glasses and pasta bowls which he set on the chargers. Soon the main course arrived. "Polo Marsala," he said while placing a large bowl of pasta in the center of the table followed by another which he proclaimed to be linguini primavera. He opened the bottle of white wine and poured a splash for Allison to sample. She nodded her approval, and he filled her glass, then the others.

It was growing dark outside, so Sophia lit the candles on the tables. Although the guys were famished and the food extraordinary, Aaron and Jake ate mechanically and said little; both were preoccupied with the appearance of the woman. When the table had been cleared again, desert was brought accompanied by the rest of the red wine.

159

The young couple left and soon the other couple followed, leaving the restaurant to the four friends.

"What time do we need to catch the bus?" Aaron asked.

"The first bus is tomorrow at eleven," Renée replied.

"Tomorrow; I thought we were going back tonight!" Jake exclaimed.

"What made ya think we were going back tonight?" Allison asked.

"I dunno; I just assumed," Jake said.

"Well it isn't like you guys have anything important to do right now," Renée said.

Luigi came to clear the desert and asked if anyone would like an after dinner drink or an espresso.

"Thank you Luigi, but I think that will be all. You really outdid yourself tonight!" Renée said.

"Siate I benvenuyi Renée," Luigi said.

As treasurer, Jake pulled out his wallet with some trepidation. He feared that he would not have enough to cover the tab. He was unaccustomed to first class dining.

"No no, my friends; you are Luigi's guests tonight. You will pay nothing!" Luigi said.

"But…" Jake was perplexed, but grateful.

"Thank you Luigi. You are a great chef and a gracious host." Aaron said sincerely.

"Un amico di Renée è un mio amico!" Luigi said. "A friend of Renée's is a friend of mine!"

After hugs all around, the party stepped to the sidewalk. Renée turned to head for the boulevard, but Aaron asked, "Renée, do you suppose we could take another way?"

"Why's that? This is the way to the hotel."

"Well, uh, we've already been that way; maybe we can see more of the town."

"But it's a lot of fun on the boulevard at night with all of the street performers."

"Please?"

Renée looked at Aaron for a moment, puzzled. She could see by the look on his face that he was anxious about something, but she had no idea what it was. She put her arm under Aaron's and led them the other way. As they walked along the sidewalk, Jake looked over his shoulder repeatedly. Allison could sense his anxiety, but did not ask what it was that caused it. Whatever it was that had frightened them in San Gabriele seemed to be haunting them here too. They turned onto another one way street. The traffic was much lighter so they walked down the middle of the street; taking to the narrow sidewalk only on occasions when cars approached. On the back streets, the guys relaxed a little.

Jake asked, "Renée, why didn't Luigi let us pay?"

"He thinks I saved Sofia's life."

"His waitress Sofia?"

"His daughter. One time when I was eating there, she fell ill. I concluded that her appendix had burst and we rushed her to the hospital. I didn't do anything at all, but he still thinks I did."

The street curved and began to climb a slope. Coming to a junction where several streets converged, they turned onto a particular street. Along the left side was a long red and yellow ochre painted stucco wall running the length of the block. Midway down the block, Renée turned into an entrance. A doorman opened a wrought iron gate, admitting them to a courtyard. Turning to the right, they stepped into the reception office. "Bienvenido a Na Bolom, ¿cómo puedo ayudarle?" (Welcome to Na Bolom, how can I help you?) The host asked.

Allison discussed the arrangements with him in Spanish, then turned to Jake and said, "OK, ya got off easy at dinner, but now ya get to make up for standing us up the other night. Cough it up!"

Jake handed her the contents of his wallet and she paid for the rooms. The host handed Jake his change and Allison two keys. She led them back through the courtyard and a dining area, then into a small intimate courtyard and a breezeway. She compared the number on the key to that on the door, opened it, and reached in to turn on a light. They all stepped in to check out the room. The room had two queen size beds covered with bedspreads fashioned by local craftsmen. A wrought iron lamp sat upon a simple handmade nightstand that stood between the beds. "The other room's right next door," Allison said.

Aaron opened the creaking doors of an armoire to reveal neatly folded woolen blankets on a shelf and empty hangers on a rod. "Check this out Jake; it's held together with wooden pegs and square nails and these hinges look like they were made by a blacksmith. I wonder how old it is."

"Well this hotel was originally a monastery and the city has been here since the fifteen hundreds, so I suppose it could be nearly as old," Renée reasoned. Aaron closed the doors and they continued to check out the room.

The walls had a smooth plaster finish painted in a warm rust color and were adorned with artifacts of the indigenous Lacandon Indians. Above their heads were exposed hand hewn beams and planks bearing the marks of the handsaw that had made them.

In the corner was a small fireplace with firewood neatly arranged awaiting only a match. Allison plucked a wooden match from a box on the mantle, struck it on the stone of the

162

hearth, and put it to a piece of kindling rich in pitch. In a matter of minutes, the fire was blazing.

"I'm kind of surprised to see a fireplace in Mexico," Aaron said.

"You'll be glad it's here; we're over seven thousand feet, and it will get cold tonight," Allison said. The guys had noticed that it was indeed already getting chilly.

Allison tossed the other key to Renée and said, "Why don't you get the fire going in the other room?"

Aaron started to follow, but Renée blocked his path with a hand on his chest. "Where do ya think you're goin?"

"But I thought…"

"You got the wrong idea!"

"Ok; I'm sorry. How 'bout a kiss g'night?"

"In your dreams! You missed your chance at the prom!"

"But we didn't go to the prom together!"

"Exactly; I rest my case."

Allison tossed their room key to Jake, followed Renée out, and closed the door behind them

"Shot down in flames!" Jake laughed.

Ron Fugere

Chapter Nineteen

Renée slowly climbed the steep steps of a pyramid, the trail of her long white gossamer gown splayed out behind, her hips swaying seductively with each step. As she climbed higher, bright red and yellow flowers sprouted in her footsteps. The iridescent feathers of her tall headdress glimmered in the sunlight and she was framed by a rainbow in a cool mist while butterflies fluttered around her. She reached the top of the pyramid and turned to face her adoring subjects, and with a single motion shed her gown, which floated away on a gentle breeze. She lay naked upon the altar where servants fanned her with palm fronds. Aaron strode purposefully up the steps to the chant of the gathered throngs. Comely servant girls removed his jaguar skin loincloth and swooned at the sight of his manhood. The sunlight gleamed upon his bronze skin, his golden armbands, and crown. Renée held out her hand, summoning him to join her on the altar and spread her legs in welcome.

The guys were awakened by a soft knock at the door. "You guys awake in there?" Renée asked. "Just a minute," Aaron

164

answered. He and Jake slipped on some pants and Aaron opened the door.

G'mornin."

"G'mornin' yerself! Coffee and breakfast in the courtyard in a half hour. See ya there!"

Jake closed the bathroom door and Aaron could hear the sound of the toilet flushing and then the shower running. In a few minutes, Jake emerged brushing his wet hair. "It's all yours."

Aaron stepped into the bathroom, then recoiled waving his hand in front of his nose while making a retching sound. "Gawd Jake! We might have to evacuate the hotel; maybe even the city!"

"Just heavenly, ain't I?"

After Aaron's shower, the guys joined the girls in the courtyard where a pot of coffee already awaited them, together with a platter of assorted sweet breads and a basket of fruit.

"Well how'd ya guys sleep?" Allison asked.

"Not too bad, except that all night long Aaron kept moaning 'Renée, oh Renée!'" Jake replied. Aaron punched him on the shoulder.

After breakfast, the four toured the casa grounds. Behind the building was an arboretum in which a few guest cabins were situated among a varied assortment of indigenous trees and shrubs. Interpretive placards and photographs served to educate visitors about the flora and fauna of the area.

Back inside the casa, they toured a museum which featured many artifacts of the Lacandon people; one of the only Mesoamerican tribes not conquered or converted by the Spanish. Another room chronicled the work of Frans and Trudy Blom, who had dedicated their lives to preserving the rainforest, protecting the Lacandon, and studying their culture. They toured Frans' library, where guests could read the very books that he had used in his studies as well as several he had penned himself.

Back in the courtyard, a few native women were demonstrating their crafts and selling their wares.

They learned that in 1950, Frans and Trudy had bought an old colonial monastery that was in ruins and restored it as their home. Casa Na Bolom, the House of the Jaguar is today used to perpetuate their vision.

"Well guys, I suppose we ought to check out and head for the bus terminal," Renée said. They returned to their rooms to gather their things and headed for the reception office. As they entered, who should they find chatting with the host in the office but Ramón, their guide of the ruins in Palenque.

"Ramón, good to see you!" Jake said enthusiastically.

Ramón looked puzzled for a moment before breaking out in a wide smile. "Hola gringos; I remember you!" He exclaimed.

"What brings you to the big city?" Aaron asked.

"I am a volunteer at Casa Na Bolom. So how did you come to be in San Cristobal"

"It is a long, sad story Ramón. But the good news is that we found our old friends from home. We'd like you to meet Renée and Allison."

"We have long known each other, my friends. Hola señoritas; it is a small world, no?"

"How do you know each other?" Aaron asked.

"It is Allison who taught me to speak English so well and Renée has long cared for my people's health." "Your people?"

"My mother is Lacandon."

"We'd never heard of the Lacandon before we came here, but we learned a lot here. Yours are a proud people." Aaron said.

Road Tripped

"We have to catch the bus soon. Be sure to stop by and say hi the next time you come to San Gabriele, Ramón," Renée said.

"I will Renée. And remember that you and Allison and your friends are always welcome in our home! Have a safe journey!"

After turning in their keys and thanking the host, they stepped to the exit where the doorman held the gate for them. They turned left and wandered through a warren of streets with Renée leading the way. Aaron and Jake had no idea what direction they were going or how far, but after walking for about a half hour they emerged from a street to find that they'd arrived at the bus terminal. Renée walked past rows of gleaming luxury motor coaches to a decrepit old clunker and climbed aboard. A hen scampered and squawked in protest as they made their way to the back of the bus. A few more passengers boarded, including a young couple from Australia and two young men from Germany, judging by their accents.

The driver closed the door, ground the transmission in gear and drove to the exit where he stopped for traffic to clear. A large box van blocked their way momentarily, and the bus driver honked his horn. A few moments later, traffic began to move, and the truck moved ahead revealing that parked across the street was a black Mercedes. Jake saw Aaron's expression and directed his gaze in the same direction as Aaron.

Leaning against the Mercedes smoking a cigarette was Cruella DeVille! The guys crouched low but continued to look, erasing any uncertainty that it was the woman from the marijuana growing operation. There could be no doubt.

The bus again found its path blocked midway across the road by a silver BMW sedan. A man got out of the passenger side and nonchalantly strode over to shake Cruella's hand while the BMW drove away, clearing their path once more. The driver of the Mercedes opened the rear door for Cruella. She tossed her cigarette to the ground, ducked in, and slid to the other side. As the bus drove past, the man from the BMW removed his sunglasses as he too ducked in, allowing the guys a brief look at his face. At the same instant, Aaron and Jake recognized the man as someone from their not so distant past; the man who had sat at the head of their boardroom table on many occasions. It was Vladimir Igor Petrovinski, former President and CEO of *Live It, Unlimited*!

Renée saw the expression on the guy's faces and knew that something was going on, but she knew by now that it was pointless to press for answers. Allison too saw their change of demeanor, but showed no such restraint. "Alright you guys; enough of this cloak and dagger stuff! What the hell is the big mystery?"

The guys did not reply or even acknowledge Allison's question; their minds were preoccupied trying to digest the significance of what they had seen.

"Fine then; you guys play your little drama. I'll be over here when you're ready to talk." She went in a huff to another seat a few rows ahead.

They rode in silence for some time as the bus passed through a few small villages. As the bus approached another village, traffic again came to a halt. From the bus, one could see over the top of the cars ahead. A number of men wearing ski masks were milling about collecting money from the drivers. The cars ahead moved off and the bus moved ahead.

The driver opened the door and a masked man stepped in. He issued a proclamation in Spanish and then repeated it in English. "We are soldiers of the Popular Front for the Restoration of Peace to the People of Mexico. I am El Supremo.

Road Tripped

We would appreciate a small donation from each of you to further our cause." He held open a bag and moved down the aisle allowing people to drop in money. An old lady had no money, instead offering the chicken. "Gracias madre, pero puede mantener su pollo," (Thank you mother, but you can keep your chicken.) He said declining her offer. El Supremo continued down the aisle. He stopped by Aaron's seat, lifted his mask, and said, "Hola Aaron; we meet again!"

Aaron leaned close and in a low voice said, "Juan, there may be a black Mercedes coming this way. If you see it, learn what you can about it."

Juan studied Aaron's face, then Jake's and said, "Si mi amigos; I will do as you ask."

"And Juan?"

"Si?"

"Be careful."

El Supremo pulled down his mask and continued his collection. When he reached the back of the bus, he peered out the back window and could see that several cars back was indeed a black Mercedes. As he made his way toward the front of the bus, he paused by Aaron and quietly said, "Just a few cars back."

"Can you delay it?"

"Si," he said without hesitation.

At the exit, he turned, and pronounced, "Gracias por su ayuda amigos! Victoty es nuestra! Thank you friends; victory is ours!"

Chapter Twenty

Allison opened the security gate and door, then waved Jake and Aaron in. Renée followed and Frisby slipped in as she closed and locked the door. Like Juan's house, an entry hall flanking the living room led back to the kitchen and dining room. Allison strode purposefully back to the kitchen, slammed her bag on the counter, pointed at the dining table, and said, "Sit!" Startled, Frisby bolted for the back door as Aaron and Jake took their seats. Renée dropped her bag to the floor and stood next to Allison. Their feet were apart and their arms crossed at their chests. The look on Allison's face was as fiery as her hair.

"Spill it; now! First you guys stand us up and give us some bullshit about a deep, dark secret. Everything is fine all the way to San Cristobal, and then you hardly say a word through dinner. You're fine through breakfast, and then you both freak out and cower like dogs and don't say a word all the way back!" Allison barked. The guys looked at Renée for sympathy but found none in her expression either.

Aaron and Jake looked at each other. It was clear that they were going to come up with some kind of an explanation. Aaron spoke, "Do you remember us telling you about how we lost our fortune? Well as we were leaving San Cristobal, we saw Petrovinski, the guy who ripped us off. What the hell he would be doing here of all places is beyond me."

"You'd think with the kind of money that asshole's got, he could buy his own damn country," Jake said bitterly.

"Are you sure it was him?" Renée asked.

"No doubt whatsoever," Aaron said. "We've known him a long time; or at least we thought we did."

"What's this guy look like?" Allison asked.

"He's probably in his mid fifties, short cut salt-n-pepper hair, a bit pudgy, a little shorter than Aaron," Jake answered.

"Hmm," Allison said. "Sounds like a guy I work for, but his name isn't Petrovinski."

"What's his name?" Aaron asked.

"I can't say; I signed a confidentiality agreement. It's not Petrovinski though."

"A confidentiality agreement? That's a bit unusual in Mexico, don't ya think?" Renée said.

Yeah, I thought so too; but then rich people can be eccentric. He pays me a lot more for one day a week than I make the rest of the week teaching school," Allison replied.

"So you're teaching him Spanish?" Aaron asked.

"That's what I do."

"What kind of car does he drive?"

"He doesn't. He has a driver. It's a BMW."

"Silver?"

"Yeah."

"Is he American?"

"He acts like an American, but he speaks with an accent; maybe Polish or Russian. I think English is his second language."

Aaron and Jake looked at each other. There seemed to be little doubt that Allison's client and V.I. Petrovinski were one and the same man. The question now was what to do with the information.

"Do you know where he lives?" Jake asked Allison.

"No; it's about an hour from here. He sends his driver to pick me up. The car has some kind of high-tech gadget so that the driver can push a button and the windows black out."

"What's his house look like?"

"I don't know that either; we enter from the garage and go straight to the library. From what I've seen of it, it's kind of... austere for someone who obviously has lots of money."

Renée, who had listened attentively to the exchange, said, "Wait a minute; you're not getting' off that easy! That explains why you were wierded out on the way back; what about before? You still haven't explained why you missed our date."

"Girls, we really shouldn't say," Aaron said. "We told Juan what happened and it scared the hell out of him. He said we shouldn't tell anyone and then he asked us to leave."

"It has something to do with drugs; doesn't it," Renée said.

The guys sat mute but their expression betrayed them. She had hit the nail on the head.

"So that's what the big mystery was. So you're not with the DEA or the FBI?"

"No."

"You saw something you weren't supposed to." They did not reply. "So you guys need to keep out of sight, huh?"

"Yeah."

"Well the motel is way too visible from the highway, so you better stay here." Renée offered.

Are ya sure that's a good idea?" Aaron asked. "We don't want to put you girls in danger."

"Well now that we kinda know what's goin' on we can take precautions," Renée said. "You should've filled us in right away."

"Where are we gonna put 'em," Allison asked.

"We'll work something out." While Renée and Allison prepared some lunch, the guys walked past the bathroom and bedrooms to the garden. Frisby emerged from hiding and began nudging Aaron for attention. He idly scratched her head without even being aware he was doing so.

"What the hell would that fuckin' asshole Petrovinski be doin' in Mexico ?!" Jake asked.

"Well you can bet that wherever that son of a bitch is, there's gotta be some kind of scam involved."

"Ya think he's in business or in bed with Cruella?"

"I'm willing to bet they're in business. We've seen some of the bimbos he could attract even before he had our millions to flaunt," Aaron said.

"She ain't all that," Jake agreed. "Ya think we oughta call agent what's his name at the FBI?" He pulled the wrinkled card from his wallet. "Special agent Mathew Cromwell."

"Not yet, we need to have a bit more info first."

"So wha'd'ya think we oughta do?"

"Well the first thing we need to do is find out where he lives. But we gotta be careful. I don't think ol' Vlad is dangerous, but if he's in cahoots with Cruella, he's in with a rough crowd."

"It'd serve the fucker right if she plugged 'im!"

"Lunch is served," Renée said, bringing a tray to the garden. They took their places at the wrought iron picnic table.

"So when do you work for Mister... your client again?" Aaron asked Allison.

"On Saturday," she answered. "Do you really think he's the guy?"

"It seems almost certain," Jake said.

"Have you ever seen him with a woman?" Aaron asked. "Probably American or European."

"Why?" Allison asked.

"When we saw him in San Cristobal, he was with… uh, a woman that … uh, we'd seen before."

"No I haven't. But I'll let ya know if I see anyone."

"OK, but be careful. Ya don't want to arouse any suspicion. She can be dangerous."

After lunch, the girls went to figure out the sleeping arrangements. They rearranged the living room furniture to make room. Like Juan's and many other houses in Mexico, the rooms had iron rings embedded in the wall from which to hang hamacas.

Renée went to fetch the hamacas that they usually used in the garden, and together, they hung them up. Allison rummaged around and found a couple of spare blankets and set them out. Renée went to the garden to invite the guys back in to check out the sleeping arrangements. "Well I see you've met Frisby. Looks like you've got a new friend!"

"Huh?" Aaron said, then looking down, he became aware that he was petting a skinny black cat with white paws. She purred loudly and licked his hand with her sandpaper-like tongue. "Friend? I don't think so! I don't even like cats," he said

Road Tripped

as he pushed her away. She responded by rubbing her cheeks against him. "What kind of a name is Frisby anyway?"

"We found her out by the highway when she was a kitten. She started to wander in front of a car and we had to rescue her. We told her that she nearly got herself flattened like a frisby and the name stuck," she explained. "C'mon, let me show you your room." She led them in.

"Well here you are," she said. "We still need to figure out where we'll put your clothes and stuff."

"No need, what you see is all we have," Aaron said.

"Gawd you guys are a pathetic pair!" Allison said. "Renée, maybe we should take them shopping at the market."

"Thank you for the offer Allison, but we really don't have very much money to spend. We'll need a lot more than we've got to make it home."

"We can lend you some money," Renée said.

"It's never a good idea to loan money to a friend," Aaron objected.

"Aw c'mon; it'll be fun! It'll be like playing with a life size Ken doll."

"Besides, it doesn't look right to have a couple of guys looking like vagrants staying here," Allison chipped in. "We have our images to uphold."

"Are you sure it's a good idea? What if we're seen?" Aaron asked.

"We'll keep our eyes out for trouble," Renée replied. "The kind of people we're talking about stick out like a sore thumb around here."

Aaron and Jake looked at each other and shrugged their agreement.

The girls grabbed their handbags and Renée said, "Let's go!"

A few hours later, they returned with their booty. Try as they might, they hadn't been able to find any jeans that were remotely close to long enough, so they had to settle for course cotton pants that the locals made only for tourists. For shirts, they each got guayaberas, shirts made of Sisal cactus fibers with very fine vertical pleats on the front and back. The guys took turns in the bathroom trying on clothes. The door refused to latch, so they just stood behind the door while they changed. Aaron made a mental note to try to fix it later. They strutted like runway models and struck poses for the girls. who responded with wolf whistles. All that was missing was a huge sombrero to complete the look of gringos on vacation.

Allison reheated the leftover spaghetti sauce from their aborted dinner while Jake kept her company.

"You clean up real nice," Renée said to Aaron and invited him to join her on the couch. "Ya want a beer?"

"Sure."

She went to the refrigerator and brought back a couple of Dos Equis. They clinked their bottles together and took a pull. Frisby plopped herself on Aaron's lap without invitation.

"It's really good to see you again Renée," Aaron said. "I've always wondered what became of you; where you were, and what you were doing with your life. I thought about you all the time," he added wistfully.

"I'm flattered! I really never thought you noticed me."

"When we were in high school, I wanted to ask you out so bad! I was just too much of a chicken shit."

"You should have."

"Really?"

"Yeah." She got up and strode to the stereo to put on some music, then turned to face him and gave him a "come hither" look. He looked at her and tapped his fingers on the couch to the beat of the music. "Aaron?"

"Yeah?"

"I saved a dance for you at the prom; are you ready to collect?"

"That was a long time ago."

"Are ya gonna keep me waiting forever?"

He shooed Frisby aside and she gave him a perturbed look. He stood and said, "May I have the pleasure?" She demurred. He took her hand in his and put his other on the small of her back. They began moving slowly to the music. "I'm sorry I'm not much of a dancer," he said.

"Just relax and feel the music."

"What music?"

"Jeez guys; git a room!" Jake said from the doorway.

The music stopped, but Aaron and Renée were slow to separate.

"Do we need to get a hose?" Allison asked. She returned to the kitchen, calling, "Dinner's ready; ya guys coming? Oops! I didn't mean it that way."

Aaron and Renée reluctantly separated, grabbed their beers, and adjourned to the dining room.

After dinner, the party returned to the living room with a few more beers. They had a lot of catching up to do.

But at last Allison stood and said, "Well guys, I've got school tomorrow, so I better call it a night." See ya in the mornin'."

"Yeah, it's been a long day," Jake said. He stood and stretched, then headed for the bathroom, leaving Aaron and Renée alone for a moment.

"I suppose I'd better say good night too; I've got patients first thing in the morning," Renée said.

They stood and moved toward her bedroom. Outside her bedroom door, they hugged. Renée pulled back and looked Aaron in the eyes. Reluctantly, Aaron released his grip and she turned to enter her bedroom. As she closed the door, she smiled and said, "Good night."

Chapter Twenty One

Aaron woke to the sound of the front door gently closing and footsteps fading away. He discovered that Frisby was asleep on his stomach. Across the room, Jake snored. He thought about the night before and smiled. Setting Frisby down, he swung down out of his hamaca. He pulled a tee shirt over his head and padded out to the kitchen in his boxers, drawn by the aroma of fresh coffee. He found a mug and poured a cup. With his coffee, he headed for the garden to enjoy the morning sun. As he neared the bathroom, running water could be heard. The door was ajar, and as he walked past, the water stopped, and Renée stepped from the shower. He stole a furtive glance that way, and saw Renée stepping from the shower, like Venus from the shell. Water glistened on her naked skin like precious jewels.

He froze, dumbstruck by her beauty. Renée was reaching for a towel when she noticed Aaron gazing at her. But rather than slamming the door in embarrassment, she returned his gaze unashamedly. She gracefully ran her hand over her head and down along her golden locks which lay across her breast. Her fingers grazed her nipple which stiffened under his gaze. A small

179

smile crossed her face as she partially covered her nakedness with the towel as she gently closed the door.

Aaron stood for a moment to allow his heart rate to return somewhat to normal, and then went to the garden with Frisby at his heels. He sat on a bench and stared into space while the image of Renée's beauty turned over in his mind's eye. Ever since he was a boy, she'd held him mesmerized. Once he'd caught Renée and Allison skinny dipping down in the creek when they were teenagers. He'd remained out of sight while they frolicked in the cold water. Then Renée had been a nubile nymph, nearing the height of desirability. Now she was a mature woman, even more lovely. She'd always been his proverbial "girl next door." Curiously, he was not physically aroused, but awestruck, as if he'd stumbled upon the Mona Lisa in the attic.

Renée joined him in the garden with her coffee, wearing a light bathrobe and her hair in a towel. She sat with him on the bench, but nothing was said. Their eyes locked in an open look of understanding. Renée seemed to intuitively know that their encounter was special, although both would be at a loss to explain in what way. She released her hair from the towel and swung her head to free her tresses. The warm sun dried her hair as she sipped her coffee.

Jake entered the garden with his cup of coffee. "Am I disturbing something?" He asked.

Aaron and Renée did not reply. They looked at each other and laughed. At last they said in unison, "Morning Jake!"

"What did I miss?" Jake asked.

Renée stood and said, "Well Guys, I better get going. Help yourself to whatever you can find in the kitchen. There are spare keys on the counter if you decide to go out; just be careful. I'll see you this afternoon." As she stepped inside, she shared a private glance with Aaron.

A few minutes later, Renée had changed into her scrubs and headed for the clinic. While the guys finished their coffee in the garden, Aaron stared off into space with Renée's image dancing in his mind.

"What planet are you on?" Jake asked.

Aaron's gaze did not deviate. Jake tried again, snapping his fingers in front of Aaron's face, "Earth to Aaron, Earth to Aaron; come in Aaron."

"Huh?"

"What's with you this morning? It's like you're not even here."

"Nothing, I'm just not awake yet."

"Don't give me that shit! There something goin' on with you and Renée?"

"Give it a rest already! First your girlfriend keeps pestering us for answers, and now it's you!"

"My girlfriend; what - who are you talking about?"

"God Jake; are you still in kindergarten? Don't you see it?"

"See what?"

"That Allison's hot for you."

"No way; I think the only reason she tolerates me is for Renée's sake 'cause she knows that she's sweet on you!"

"God you're clueless about women!"

"Yeah; and you're an expert?"

Aaron stood. "Screw it! I'm gonna go take a shower," he said and padded inside. In the bathroom, Aaron shed his boxers and tee shirt and dropped them on the floor. He turned on the water, felt for it to reach a comfortable temperature, and stepped under the shower. While he showered, the image of Renée continued to play in his mind's eye. Lost in thought, he distractedly washed himself.

From outside the bathroom door, Jake called out, "stop beatin' off and save some hot water for me, asshole!"

Snapped out of his trance by Jake's intrusion, Aaron rinsed off, shut off the water, and toweled himself dry. He wrapped the towel around his waist while he shaved. Gathering his clothes from the floor, he stepped out of the bathroom, calling, "It's all yours."

"'Bout time," Jake grumbled as he went in.

Aaron smelled his tee shirt to make sure it wasn't too funky, and slipped it over his head. He found some fresh boxers and his only pair of jeans. As he went to the kitchen for another cup of coffee, he could hear the water still running in the bathroom. A mischievous smile crossed his face, and he stepped into the bathroom where Jake was obscured behind the shower curtain. He called out, "You want hot water; you got it!" and flushed the toilet. With the cold water diverted to the toilet, only the hot water flowed to the shower.

"Ah fuck that's hot, you asshole!" Jake cried out.

"Serves ya right!" Aaron laughed.

The guys had breakfast out by the pool. Afterward, they got up to take their plates back inside. Jake said, "Here, let me take that," while taking the plate from Aaron.

"Gracias."

"De Nada!" Jake said while nudging Aaron into the pool with his hip before continuing into the kitchen.

Aaron came to the surface gasping. "You cocksucker! It's fucking cold!"

Aaron joined Jake in the kitchen, dripping all over the tile floor and Frisby, who seemed to be glued to his side.

Road Tripped

"Have a nice swim?" Jake chided him.

"I guess I had that comin'. No hard feelings?" He offered Jake his hand.

"No hard feelings," Jake replied while taking Aaron's hand. In one fluid motion, Aaron grasped Jake's hand in an iron grip, stepped under his arm, and twisted it behind his back. He then marched Jake outside, thrust him into the pool, and dove in behind. When Jake came to the surface, Aaron dunked him under again and they wrestled furiously. They came to the surface for air, to find Allison standing beside the pool, hands on her hips, shaking her head in disbelief. "Don't you guys know it's winter?" She said.

"He started it," Aaron whined like a schoolboy who had been caught misbehaving by his teacher.

Did not!" Jake whined in reply.

"Did so!" Aaron said while thrusting Jake's head under again.

Back inside, the guys retrieved their damp towels. In the living room, they stripped and rummaged around for some dry clothes while they toweled off. Aaron stepped into his boxers while Jake continued to sort through his clothes.

From the doorway, they heard a wolf-whistle, and turned to see Allison leaning against the doorjamb, her arms and legs crossed, and a snide smile on her face as she looked from Jake's face to his crotch. "Too bad I already ate, that looks like quite a meal!"

Jake quickly covered himself with his towel and blushed. Aaron went to the bathroom to brush his teeth. Jake waited a moment to see if Allison would leave so he could get dressed. She stood her ground, so he turned his back while he began to dress. He was startled by a soft warm hand on his ass. "Hmm;

that's nice!" Allison purred in his ear. Then she gave him a hard swat on the butt and strode out of the room as Aaron came back in. Aaron could see Allison's handprint emblazed on Jake's butt as Jake pulled on his pants. He laughed and said, "Somebody's been a naughty boy! Did teacher give you a spankin'?"

"Fuck you!"

In a high falsetto voice, Aaron said, "Oh Jake; you're so big! I want you! Take me! Take me now! Ohhh!"

"Fuckin' asshole." Jake grumbled while he finished dressing. Jake went to brush his teeth and shave while Aaron joined Allison in the kitchen.

"Aaron?"

"Yeah?"

"What the hell do I have to do to get Jake's attention?"

"Wha'd'ya mean?"

"Aw c'mon, you know I've always... I've always..."

"Yeah, I know."

"So what is it? He was practically tripping over his tongue for that bitch Juanita, but he won't give me the time of day."

"Ol' Jake's kinda clueless when it comes to women."

"And you're an expert?"

"Far from it. Do you think Renée uh...?"

"Duh! Now who's clueless?" Jake joined them in the kitchen.

"Well you guys are thick as thieves! Did I miss something?" They did not reply.

Aaron asked, "Do you know where I can find a toothbrush Allison? Jake and I have had to share one and it's kinda creepy."

"Eeewww! TMI!" She said. "Try the little market down on calle six."

"OK, I'll be back in a while. Two's company. You guys can catch up on things."

"See ya in a while," Allison said as Aaron closed the door.

"So Jacob …"

"Allison, I uh …" There was an awkward pause.

Choosing a safe topic, Allison asked, "So how long are you guys gonna be in Mexico?"

"We haven't even begun to figure out how we're gonna get home. I guess we're gonna need to figure out a way to earn some money. Its kinda tough since we don't even speak the lingo."

"I guess I could teach you Spanish if you'll try to act like a decent student."

"Ya think we could start with the cuss words? I got a few words for Aaron."

"I suppose we might as well get 'em out o' the way, cabrón."

"I'm not a very good student."

"I remember. Ya know, if your GPA had been just a few points lower, you might have been held back a grade and we could've graduated together."

"How do you know about my grades?"

"Call it my feminine guiles."

"So when do we start?"

"Whenever."

They stood in silence for a few moments. Jake paced the kitchen and dining room. "You and Renée sure have a nice place."

"It suits us." Another pause. "What about you; what kind of house do you have?"

"The same one I grew up in. It's gettin' kind of old."

"Seriously?"

"Yup."

They stepped to the dining room and sat next to each other at the table.

"Where are your folks living now?"

"They died in a car accident about ten years ago."

"Oh Jake; I'm so sorry! I didn't know." She clasped his hands in hers.

"It's alright; I've learned to cope. How about your folks?"

"Dad lives in Port Orchard and mom lives in upstate New York."

"You ever gonna go home?"

"I am home."

"No; I mean to Olalla."

"I miss it sometimes. It's funny; when I think of Olalla, I think of you and when I think of you, I think of Olalla."

"Ya know, when Aaron and I thought we were gonna be millionaires, we could've dreamed up any number of places that we could live; Hawaii, Europe, anywhere. But for me, I always dreamed of living right there in Olalla. Maybe build a new house back where the barn used to be." He sat with a thousand mile stare as he visualized the minute details of the piece of land that was as much a part of him as he was of it.

Allison spoke, snapping him out of his trance. "Is the tire swing still there?"

"Nah; the orchard took a beating a few years ago when we had a freezing rain. The apple tree with the swing fell from the weight of the ice. I cut it into firewood, but I just can't bring myself to burn it. I counted the growth rings; it was over a hundred years old. I can remember when it still produced fruit."

"I used to love it when your Mom's cherry tree bloomed. The blossoms looked like snow on the ground. And the aroma …" Now it was Allison's turn to adopt the thousand mile stare.

"It's funny that you called it my Mom's tree. I always thought of it that way too. The apple trees just seemed like the whole family's and the plum tree was mine, but the Cherry tree was always Mom's."

They continued to reminisce about people and places they had known. Eventually they paused to reflect on their shared memories and feelings for the place they called home. A comfortable silence ensued as they both were lost in warm thoughts of the past.

The sound of a key being inserted in the lock brought them back to the here and now. The door opened and Renée stepped in. Closing the door, she strode to the kitchen. "Aw; aren't you guys cute!" It was then that they realized that they were still holding hands. Allison reluctantly released her grip on Jake's hands.

"So what brings you home so early?" Jake asked.

"It was kind of a light day with patients, so I took the afternoon off." Renée replied.

"Jake wants me to teach him and Aaron Spanish."

"Looks like you've already got your teacher's pet. Speaking of Aaron, where is he?" Renée asked.

"He went to buy a toothbrush. He and Jake have been sharing one."

"Eeewww!" Renée said with a sour face. "How long has he been gone?"

Jake and Allison looked at each other and shrugged. "I dunno; we sort of lost track of time," Allison replied.

"Oh shit! We… I forgot all about our – uh – situation!" Jake said. "Maybe we ought to go look for him."

"You guys stay here, I'll go find him," Renée said, turning for the door. She stepped out and locked the door behind her.

"Shouldn't we help her find him?" Jake said with anxiety written on his face.

"Well whoever it is that you're afraid of is all the more likely to find you if you're both out and about." Allison reasoned.

"True," Jake agreed. "I guess we can't stay holed up in here forever. Sooner or later we'll have to venture out. She probably doesn't know that we're in San Gabriele anyway."

"She?"

"I meant 'they," he said while reaching for her hand.

She snatched her hand away. "You said she." She stood and strode into to her and slammed the door.

Outside the door, Jake asked, Allison; ya still gonna teach us Spanish?"

From behind the closed door, Allison spewed a stream of what could only be obscenities in Spanish.

Chapter Twenty Two

Renée found Aaron on a street corner looking over the meager selection of cut flowers proffered by a little girl. He selected a bouquet, and holding out his hand, allowed her to select the appropriate coins. He patted her on the head and said, "Thank you, sweetheart."

"Gracias, Señor," She replied, her little round face beaming.

Aaron stood and turned to find Renée watching.

"Are those for me?" She asked coyly, batting her long eyelashes.

Aaron handed her the bouquet. She held them to her nose and took a whiff of their fragrance "They're beautiful," she said.

"Not half as beautiful as you."

"You're so sweet," She said smiling, showing her dimples. She took Aaron's arm and they strolled back toward her house. "We were worried about you."

"Why's that?"

"Why indeed; you still haven't really given us an explanation of who or what you're hiding from."

Aaron did not say anything. They strolled in silence for a while.

"Renée, about this morning... I wasn't – I didn't... I... I'm sorry if I embarrassed you."

"It's OK; I have nothing to be embarrassed about. Besides, it's not the first time you've seen me naked."

"What do you mean?"

"In the creek. You remember."

"You knew?"

She flashed a devilish smile. "Don't ever tell Allison though; she'd be mortified!"

"It'll be our secret. You were beautiful then, but you're even more beautiful now!"

"You say the sweetest things! Can I let you in on another little secret?"

"Sure."

"Allison and I knew about yours and Jake's secret pool."

"You mean?"

"We weren't the only ones who ever went skinny dipping in the creek."

Aaron blushed.

Renée opened the door to admit them. In the kitchen, she found a vase and put the flowers in water and arranged them for best effect. "They're beautiful; thank you." She said and kissed Aaron on the cheek. He blushed again.

"Hmm; that's odd. Look at this poppy," she said pulling one from the bouquet. She held a poppy which had blossoms that were nearly the same color of green as the leaves. "I've collected a lot of the wild flowers that grow here, but I've never seen one like this." She stepped to a bookshelf in the hallway and plucked a book from the shelf. It was a book about flowers. Turning to the index, she found the section about poppies. Thumbing through the pages, she compared the poppy to those in the book. She found one that was similar, and then flipped back and forth between the pages to be sure.

"Look at this," she said, allowing Aaron to compare the flower to the picture. Apart from the odd color, the flower bore a very strong resemblance to Papaver somniferum, the opium poppy.

Jake came in from the garden to join them.

"Jake; look at this," Aaron said.

"Aw, you're so sweet Jake said in a falsetto voice. "Are ya gonna kiss me too?"

"Shut up and look at this!" Aaron showed Jake the picture.

He drew the same conclusion.

"I'm gonna take this to the clinic to analyze it," Renée said. "I have a hunch that we've stumbled on a new cash crop." She left for the clinic.

"Where's Allison?" Aaron asked Jake.

"She's sulking in her room."

"Sulking; now what did you do?"

"I didn't do anything! She's just so fuckin' sensitive. One word about Cruella and she flies off the handle," he said in an exasperated tone.

"What did you tell her?"

"Nothin', She wouldn't let me explain."

"I think we owe the girls the truth," Aaron said. "They're not dumb; I think they can read between the lines anyway." He stepped over to Allison's door, knocked gently, and "Allison?"

From behind the door, Allison said, "What is it?" irritably.

"Allison, when Renée gets back we'll give you the full story. We owe you that."

"Everything?"

"Everything." She opened the door and joined the guys in the kitchen. "It's about time you guys come clean."

"We just had to mull things over to be sure you'd be safe," Aaron explained.

"You'll understand when you hear what we have to say," Jake added.

"Sorry if I got a bit …"

"Don't worry about it," Jake said.

Allison got a pack of cards from a drawer and asked the guys to join her in a game to pass the time. "What should we play?" She asked.

"How 'bout strip poker?" Jake suggested with a taunting look, expecting her to come up with something else to play.

"You're on!" Allison said brazenly, much to his surprise. She shuffled the deck and Aaron cut. Allison won the first few hands and Jake lost. "One more hand and I'll get to see what kind of underwear you've got. I'm guessin' you're a whitey-tightey kind of guy. Hope they're clean!"

"He's gotcha there!" Aaron said with a grin. "Jake goes commando!"

"Hmm. Bonus round!" Allison said while dealing the cards. "By the way, did ya find a toothbrush?"

"Sure did! And not just any toothbrush; it's a Bugs Bunny tooth brush! Ta-da!" He produced it with a flourish.

"No fair!" Jake whined, trying to snatch it from Aaron's hand.

Road Tripped

"Gawd you guys are so mature... Not!" Allison quipped, rolling her eyes. "I better borrow the first grade edition of the text book if I'm ever gonna teach you guys Spanish."

"Huh?" Aaron said.

"Since you guys are gonna be here for a while, ya better learn the language."

"Yeah, yer probably right. Course, if Jake don't watch what he says, we'll probably out-stay our welcome soon enough," he said punching Jake on the shoulder.

Jake punched him back and wrestled him to the floor where they commenced to tussle. Renée came back in. She took in the sight of the two partially clad guys rolling around among their discarded clothes and scattered cards. Shaking her head, she said, "Do you guys need to get a room?"

The guys stood and brushed themselves off sheepishly.

"So what did you find out?" Aaron asked.

"Well the results are still preliminary, but it would appear that it's opium alright; and not just your run of the mill opium, but a very powerful variety."

"What are you guys talking about?" Allison asked.

Renée pulled another flower from the bouquet and showed it to her. "Opium."

"Where did you get the flowers?" Allison asked.

"A little girl was selling them," Aaron replied.

"Eliz, the Rodriguez girl was selling them," Renée answered. "Maybe she could show us where she got them."

"First things first," Aaron said. "We need to explain why we've been so secretive. Let's sit down."

They all sat at the table. Aaron and Jake took turns reciting the turn of events that transpired in the forest.

"OK, I can see why you guys were being cautious," Allison admitted.

"I'm gonna go see the Rodriguez's. Maybe they can tell us where they got the poppies, but they also need to be warned to stay clear of the area. They wouldn't have gotten off as easy as you guys if they'd been caught by the drug people."

After Renée left, Allison said, "OK guys, we can start your lessons today. Why don't we start by seeing what you already know."

Jake pointed at Aaron and said, "Señor Pendejo," and then putting his hand on his own chest, "Señor Cabron."

"Very good! Now tell me what they mean," Allison said.

The guys looked at each other and shrugged.

"Well Señor Pendejo, it would seem that you are known as Mister Asshole!"

Jake burst out laughing.

"You think that's funny huh, Señor Cabron?" Allison asked, rolling her Rs. "Do you know what cabron means?"

"Uh, no." Jake said.

"Well Mister Cuckold, now you do!"

"Cuckold?"

"You don't know what a cuckold is?"

"No."

"It means that your girlfriend sleeps around on you and you're too estupido to know it."

"I don't have a girlfriend."

"You really are estupido!"

Shortly, Renée returned. "Well I found out a bit of info from Esmeralda Rodriguez. Up the highway a few kilometers is a landslide. They found a trail that led to a meadow where they found lots of flowers. I told them not to go back."

Road Tripped

"So what do you think we ought to do?" Allison asked.

"Well, we could ask Juan if he's seen anything," Jake said. "He probably had to help clear the road."

"True, but he doesn't want us around his family or home. He'll be even less enthused when he hears what we found," Aaron said.

"I'll see if I can arrange something on the QT," Renée offered. She left to head for Juan's house. She soon returned to say that she'd spoken with Emilia and she would have Juan come to the Clinic about seven thirty.

A little later, the foursome went to a small restaurant on a back street for dinner. After dinner, they broke up into couples and made their way separately to the clinic to await Juan's arrival. A little after seven, through the drawn shades, Juan could be seen approaching the clinic with a pronounced limp. Renée opened the door to admit him.

Inside, Juan said, "Hola mi Amigos; is good to see you!"

"Hola Juan," Aaron said. "What happened to your foot?"

"Nada; I just need look like I hurt myself. Why else do I go to clinic?" He smiled slyly.

"We are sorry to ask this of you, but we need to know if you helped clear the landslide up the highway."

"But of course; clearing highway is my job, no?"

"Did you notice anything odd while you were working there?"

"Nothing; except…"

"Except?"

"Traffic was stopped for a while, and when we had cleared the road, everyone was anxious to be gone, except one car was slow to leave. Those behind honked their horns and cursed them.

It seemed strange. As they went by, a gringa in the back rolled down the window and stared."

"A gringa?"

"A white woman."

"Do you remember what kind of car was it?" Aaron asked.

"Si, it was the black Mercedes."

"The?"

"It was same Mercedes behind the bus… and the same Gringa. By the way, they may have had a flat tire yesterday. One never knows when a nail might end up on the road," he said with a sly grin.

Chapter Twenty Three

Saturday morning Allison stood at the bus stop by the side of the highway. At eight o'clock sharp, the familiar silver BMW came to a stop and a man got out of the passenger seat to open the door for her. "Good morning, Señorita," he said as she ducked in.

"Buenas dias," she replied.

The door closed, the driver pushed a button, and the windows turned opaque. The first time she'd encountered this feature of the car, it had been disconcerting, but she had grown used to it. She had thought it an odd feature, but had no cause for suspicion and chalked it up to the wealthy gringo's eccentricities. After the first lesson, she had begun bringing a book to pass the time on the way to and from the appointment.

She opened her book and feigned reading, while stealing an occasional glance out through the windshield for clues as to where they might be going.

From a thicket of underbrush by the side of the highway, Jake observed the silver BMW drive by. He waited a few minutes to allow it to disappear from view around the next corner, and then stepped from his place of concealment. He hurried back up the highway toward the village, and then continued on a short distance, where he put two fingers to his lips and whistled. Aaron stepped out of the forest.

"They went north," Jake said.

"Well that narrows our search, now we only have half of the state of Chiapas to cover!"

From her vantage point in the back seat, Allison could see very little, her forward view partially obscured by the two burly men in the front seat. As the car wound its way along the highway, she would occasionally catch a glimpse of a mountain peak, and see that the shadows were cast from the right. She concluded that they were driving north. As usual, the car slowed for three speed-bumps. These could often be found at the approach to a village. She stole a glance at her watch. It was eight thirty-seven. The car accelerated again and proceeded through a particularly twisty section of highway. It slowed for a very rough section of road; perhaps there had been another landslide. Eight fifty-two. At nine twenty-eight, the car slowed and turned left onto a very rough dirt road. After an abrupt right turn and an immediate left, it stopped for a moment while a tall gate opened and then proceeded onto a very smooth driveway. A few moments later, it came to a stop. Through the windshield, she could see a two car garage door open, and to the right of it, another one-car garage door. The driver pulled the car in and shut off the motor. Allison could hear the garage door close before the man from the passenger seat opened the door for her. As she followed him into the house, she "accidently" dropped her book. Turning to pick it up, she observed that the other stall in the garage was unoccupied.

Road Tripped

Inside, she was led to the study by one of the men who invited her to take a seat, and then stood as if at parade rest by the door.

As she made her way to the desk to await the arrival of her student, she nonchalantly glanced around the study. The walls were finished in a cool gray color and the furnishings were somewhat austere, not extravagant. The floor was wood rather than ceramic tiles. Although she was no expert, Allison thought the modern abstract paintings were a bit harsh for her taste. The overall impression reminded her of the waiting room of a dentist office. On one wall there stood a bookcase. Without being obvious, she noted that the titles were in English, Spanish, and some others in which some of the letters appeared to be backwards; probably Russian. She took her seat at the desk.

After a short wait, the door opened and her student entered. His highly polished shoes tapped on the hardwood as he strode to his desk. "Hola Señorita," he said; pronouncing the H.

"Hola, Señor. The H is silent, remember? It's pronounced oh-lah, not ho-lah," she corrected him shaking his hand. She noted a mole or birthmark on the back of his right hand. "Hola"

"That's better."

"I apologize for keeping you waiting. Coffee?"

"Si, por favor."

He snapped his finger and the man at the door left. A few moments later, a slender attractive Mexican woman brought a tray with two cups and a pot of coffee. She carefully set the tray on the desk and poured two cups. She set the cups with their saucers within easy reach of her boss and his guest. Napkins, sugar caddy, creamer, and spoons completed the coffee service.

"Gracias," Allison said.

"De Nada, Señorita," she replied and left the room.

"May we begin?" Allison asked.

"But of course."

The lessons proceeded as usual. Mr. Petrovinski, if that is who he was, was not what Allison would call a star student. It was clear that English was not his first language, making it more difficult to teach him yet another language. After about an hour, he stood and said, "That will be all for today, I have pressing matters to attend."

He stood and strode toward the bookcase. Although it was directly behind her, Allison could see in the reflection in the window that the right side of the bookcase silently opened like a door to reveal a safe. He waved the back of his hand in front of the safe, a green light blinked, and he opened the door to extract her fee.

From a large wad of bills he paid her the usual fee, and then pulled off an extra one thousand peso note. "This is for your patience with me."

"Gracias Señor."

He pressed a button on his desk and a man appeared to take her back to the car.

"¿ Dónde está el baño, por favor?" She asked.

"Pardon?" the man asked.

"May I use the bathroom?"

"Yes; is down hall on left," the man replied in a thick Russian accent. He waited while she used the bathroom. She "accidentally" took a wrong turn when she left the bathroom, and explored the house a bit. She noted that the windows of the sprawling rambler lacked the iron security grates common in Mexico. She suspected that the home was protected by guards and alarms.

The man found her in a living room and said somewhat curtly, "This way, please." He led her back to the garage.

As she entered the car, a black Mercedes could be seen in the other stall.

Later that evening, the four friends gathered around the dining table for a debriefing with Aaron asking most of the questions. "What can you tell us about the drive to the place?" He asked.

"They picked me up at exactly eight o'clock, as usual. After about forty minutes, we came to a village."

"About forty minutes?"

"Thirty-seven minutes; to be exact."

"How did you know it was a village?"

"There were three speed bumps."

Aaron recalled how much he'd loathed the bumps when he'd encountered them in *Gertrude*.

"It seemed as if we were going north," She added.

"How could you tell?"

"From the shadows on the mountains I could see through the windshield."

"Did the driver drive fast or slow?"

"Neither. I would say he went exactly the speed limit; hands at ten and two."

"You're pretty observant."

"At eight fifty-two, we came to a very rough section of road; maybe a landslide or construction. At nine twenty-eight we turned onto a driveway. The first short bit was rough and twisty and there was a gate, but the rest was smooth as glass. We pulled into the garage and they took me inside. Two car garage on the left and a single on the right."

"Could you see any more of the outside of the house?"

"Only that the stucco was really smooth and painted gray."

"OK so now you're inside," Aaron prompted her.

"They took me to the study. It's a cold feeling room…"

"Cold like air conditioned?"

"No cold as in stark; like a hospital waiting room. The bookcase has some Russian books in it and a secret."

"What kind of secret?"

"It hides a safe with a lot of money in it!"

"He let you see it?" Aaron asked. "You'd think he would try to keep it a secret."

"It was behind my back, but I could see him reflected on the window. He opened it by waving his hand past the safe rather than turning a dial. Some kind of electronic thingy is my guess"

"You're pretty good at all this cloak and dagger stuff!" Jake exclaimed, clearly impressed. He was seeing a side of Allison he never knew to exist.

"It's kinda fun!"

"What about your pupil?" Jake asked. "Did you see anything else than you already told us?"

"He has a birthmark on his right hand." She pointed to the back of her hand to indicate where it was. "And he has a huge gold ring," she added as an afterthought.

"It's our old friend Vlad alright; that cocksucker!"

"What about security?" Aaron asked.

"No bars on the windows; it's probably electronic."

"And guards?"

"I just saw the two men from the car plus a maid. I suspect there is probably another guard around"

"Why's that?"

Road Tripped

"I dunno, just a feeling. And I doubt if this Vlad would have all of his security people gone at the same time."

"True." Aaron said. "Jake, ya think you can pull a McGuyver?" Aaron asked.

"I'll see what I can do," he answered. He strode into the living room and returned with a dusty TV remote. He blew the dust off and said, "Can I borrow this, girls?"

The girls shrugged, and Renée said, "We don't use it anyway. It's just a cheap universal remote and the TV doesn't pick up any signal at all. It's all yours."

Jake pulled out his Swiss army knife, and with it he pried the halves of the remote apart and extracted a circuit board. "Perfect; do you have a spare flash drive for your lap-top?"

"Yeah, I'll go get one," Renée said. She soon returned and handed it to Jake.

"What are ya gonna do with 'em?" Allison asked.

"Well it sounds to me as if the gate, the garage, the security system, and the safe are all operated by remote controls. If we can record the signals, we can duplicate the remote. Do you have any other electronic gizmos around?"

"None that I can think of," Allison said.

"Is there any place in town that we could get a remote for a garage door?"

"That might be a tough one; no one has a garage, let alone with a garage door opener." Allison answered. "Maybe the guy at the hardware store could order one."

"Could you ask him?"

"Sure."

"While you're there, see if he has a soldering iron and some solder."

"OK."

"Do you think we could find an old car stereo?" he asked the girls.

"There's a junkyard east of town. If the stereos were even half decent, they're long gone though," Allison said.

"The older, the better; I'd give my left… I'd give anything for an eight-track tape deck. Aaron, ya wanna see what you can find? While yer at it, ya remember the pile of old appliances we saw on the outskirts of town?"

"Yeah."

Jake tossed him his knife and said, "I might need more diodes. See what you can find."

"I'm on it."

"I'm gonna need some batteries. AAs would be best."

"We've got some somewhere," Renée said.

With that, Aaron set out on his scavenger hunt, Renée rummaged for batteries, and Allison headed for the hardware store while Jake drew a wiring diagram of what he hoped to make.

Chapter Twenty Four

When everyone returned with their contribution to the project, Renée finally voiced the obvious question, "Just what do you plan to do with these codes and stuff anyway?"

"Petrovinski ripped us off for millions of dollars. Whatever money is in that safe is ours. We intend to get it back, put a stop to whatever scheme he's up to now, and put that fucker behind bars where he belongs," Aaron said, his resolve clear to see in his expression.

Over the next few days, Jake continued to construct and refine the recording device. The final components he extracted from a Genie garage door opener remote that had finally arrived from Mérida. Jake was confident that it would pick up the signals for the gate, the security system, and the garage. The unit, which was essentially a radio receiver, could easily be adapted to broadcast a signal as well.

Aaron concealed the device inside Allison's romance novel. She looked the book over closely, and could not tell that it had been modified in any way, that is unless you turned to page 123, where you would find a number of pages had been cut, creating a

Ron Fugere

space for the electronic gizmo that Jake had created, which looked like a high school science project. He showed her how to activate the devise by pressing a button hidden in the cover.

The safe presented a different set of challenges though. Jake suspected that it was operated magnetically, like the security gates at the Marina in Port Orchard. He remembered going there with a friend, who had just waved his wallet by the lock and it opened as if by magic. He was fairly sure he could copy the magnetic code, but not from across the room. Allison would have to get much closer. He assumed that the device that opened the safe was concealed in the huge ring Allison had observed. He could probably copy the signal from the ring, but it would take more than a few seconds, and he doubted he could develop a device small enough to be concealed in a ring with the components at his disposal. He scratched his head at a loss for how to hide the device. He voiced his concern.

"What about a bracelet?" Aaron suggested.

Over dinner, the group discussed the challenge of how to make a bracelet large enough to conceal the device and also how Allison could keep it close enough to Vlad's ring for a long enough period of time to read the code.

"One of my patients is a silversmith," Renée offered.

"Do you think he could make us a bracelet?" Aaron asked.

"And would he keep it a secret?" Jake added.

"He's a real craftsman; I've seen his work," She replied. "And as to keeping it on the QT, all I have to do is ask. I treated him for an STD and kept it a secret from his wife. He'll keep quiet."

"We can't really afford any silver though," Jake said.

Road Tripped

Allison went to the kitchen and returned with a handful of silver flatware. "These oughta do," she said, handing them to Renée.

"But how can we get it close enough to Vlad's ring for say thirty seconds?" Jake asked.

"Leave it to me," Allison said. "Ol' Vlad likes to try to peek down my blouse; I'll just unleash the girls!" She said while pushing her breasts together to accentuate her cleavage. "At least someone is susceptible to my feminine charms," she said while glancing at Jake.

"Perfect!," he replied without acknowledging Allison's barb. He set about creating a compact magnetic scanning device to fit inside a bracelet.

With Jake's work on the devices complete, the guys decided that it would be a good idea to reconnoiter their objective. The question was what to use for transportation.

"Renée, is there someplace we can rent a car?" Aaron asked.

"Sure, why don't we just run down to Hertz and rent a limo," she said sarcastically.

"I saw an old motorcycle down at the junkyard, maybe I could get it running," Jake volunteered.

If anyone can, you can," Aaron said. "Remember we just need it to run though. It doesn't have to win any races." He knew from their motorcycle days that Jake just couldn't resist the temptation to tweak the performance.

"Yeah, yeah; your still sore 'cause my Honda could always whip yer Suzuki, Jake said. "Who wants to help me push it?"

Allison volunteered and they headed for the junkyard.

With Jake and Allison gone, Aaron and Renée had the place to themselves. "How's a cold one sound?" Renée asked.

Ron Fugere

"Sounds good!"

They clinked their bottles together and took a swig. With all of their attention focused on the project, they had had little chance to be together one on one since the shower episode. Both seemed at a loss for words.

Breaking the silence, Aaron asked, "Do you have a Phillips screwdriver? I've been meaning to fix your bathroom door."

"I'll have a look," Renée said and began rifling through a kitchen drawer. She handed him the screwdriver handle first, but held the other end for a moment and said, "Was it that bad?"

"What's that?"

"Didn't you like what you saw?" Her eyes bore into his.

"It's just that…" He took the screwdriver from her hand and turned his attention to the door to escape her gaze. With his eyes on his work, he said, "Renée, ever since I first laid eyes on you I… I felt something.

"You mean when you saw me in the creek?"

"No; I mean on the playground when I was in the first grade."

"I didn't think you even knew me until what, the sixth or seventh grade?"

"I didn't know you, but there was just something about the way you looked and smiled. As I got a bit older, I tried to chalk it up to an adolescent crush."

"I know exactly what you mean. I remember you from my first day in kindergarten. Do you have any idea how cute you were?"

"Me? Cute? He finished fiddling with the door latch and opened and closed the door a few times to check his work. He turned back to Renée and met her eyes. "Renée, can I let you in on a secret? It's kind of embarrassing."

"Of course."

"When we… when I made love to my ex girlfriend, I used to fantasize about you. I would dream of you the way you were down in the creek. When I saw you the other day I… I'm sorry; I know that's kind of weird," he said and looked at the floor.

Renée stepped closer and with her index finger under his chin, lifted his face to look him in the eyes. "Can I let you in on a little secret of my own?"

He did not reply, but looked into her eyes expectantly.

"I've always fantasized about you down in the creek when I touch myself."

"You did?"

"I do."

There was a pause while Aaron processed the thought of Renée pleasuring herself.

"How did we manage to live this long carrying a torch for each other and never…" Aaron was interrupted by the sound of the front door opening.

"It wasn't my fault, you didn't have to volunteer," Jake said.

"These were my best pair of jeans; now look at them!" Allison said, pointing to a large tear on the leg.

"Just fluff up the edges a bit and make it a fashion statement."

"What is this, 1980? Where have you been?"

"Aw, quit yer whinin' and help me roll it to the back yard, will ya?"

They rolled an ancient Carabela 175cc motorcycle through the house to the garden.

Allison stormed into her room and slammed the door. Jake could be heard muttering bitterly from the garden. Aaron and

Renée, who had observed the whole exchange in silence, burst out laughing.

Allison came back out and grabbed Renée's hand, saying, "C'mon; we're going shopping," and started for the front door.

Aaron went to the garden, where Jake was hunched over the Carabela. In a matter of minutes, he'd removed and disassembled the carburetor with no more than his trusty Swiss army knife. "Don't look too bad; just a bit varnished up. Nothing a little rinse in fresh gas won't cure. Ya think the girls have a Crescent wrench?"

"I'll have a look," Aaron said. He rummaged through the kitchen drawer where Renée had found the screwdriver and returned with a wrench. "Here ya go."

Jake removed the spark plug and held his thumb over the spark plug hole. "Kick it over so I can check the compression." Aaron flipped out the kick-start lever and spun the engine over. Jakes thumb was popped off of the hole with each revolution of the engine. "Compression seems pretty good; let's check the spark." He adjusted the plug gap by eyeball, attached the plug to the high tension lead, and laid it on the cylinder head. "OK, give her a try." Another kick. "Spark's a bit weak; I guess I'll have to clean the points." He removed the ignition cover and inspected the points. "They're a bit burnt, but I think they'll do. I wish I had some emery paper."

"The girls probably have an emery board in the bathroom," Aaron suggested.

"Even better," Jake said and sent Aaron to fetch it. Jake sanded the contacts smooth. I think there's a cereal box in the kitchen; can ya tear me off a scrap of cardboard?"

"Yes doctor."

Road Tripped

Jake used the piece of cardboard to clean the filings from the contacts and adjust the gap. He rechecked the spark and satisfied with the results, reinstalled the plug and reconnected the lead. "OK, all we need is gas and oil."

Together they rolled the bike out to the Pemex station by the highway. Jake filled the tank, leaving enough room to add oil for the two-cycle engine. Surprisingly, the station had a quart of outboard motor oil on the shelf, though they were many miles from the nearest body of navigable water. Jake estimated the proper amount of oil to add to the gas and poured a bit in the tank, and then just a tad more. He twisted on the filler cap and shook the bike from side to side to mix the fuel. He turned on the petcock, waited a moment for the carburetor to fill, set the choke, and said, "Here goes nothin'!" He stabbed at the kick starter five or six times before the engine coughed. Three or four more kicks and the engine roared to life. He pulled in the clutch lever, clicked the transmission into first gear, revved the engine, and dropping the clutch, did a wheelie down the road, trailing a cloud of blue smoke. He turned around and roared past, running hard through all five gears, then locked up the brakes and slewed around to come tearing back to where Aaron stood. He skidded to a stop with a huge smile on his face.

"Ya just couldn't help yerself, could ya? Ya just had ta tweak it!" Aaron said in dismay.

"All I did was adjust the tension on the reed valves, raised the needles a bit and fiddled with the timing. I wonder where we could find an expansion chamber."

"You're hopeless."

Beside the gas station was a barrel filled with used motor oil, and the guys drizzled some on the chain. There were no paper towels to wipe their hands, so they used a discarded paper bag from the curb.

"Hop aboard; let's go find the girls," Jake said.

"Scoot back; I'm a better rider."

"You mean you *were* a better rider."

"The older I gets, the faster I was!" Aaron quipped. "Now scoot!"

They rode through town looking for the girls with Aaron at the controls. Up ahead he spotted them coming out of a shop carrying a bag. Aaron twisted the throttle wide open and went flying past the girls. He and Jake looked over their shoulders to gauge the girl's reaction, and then turned back ahead to find Officer Miguel Martinez blocking their path with his arms crossed! Aaron slammed on the brakes and lost control. The bike together with Aaron and Jake slid to a stop at the Officer's feet.

Officer Martinez looked at them through his mirrored aviator sunglasses trying to decide their fate. Then he saw Juanita across the street. "Gringos," he said, shaking his head and set out after Juanita.

The guys stood and brushed themselves off while the girls approached. "Are you guys alright?" Renée asked.

"Yeah we're fine; just a couple of scrapes and bruises." Aaron said while he picked up the bike.

"So much for keeping a low profile!" Renée said.

"Didn't you guys learn anything when ya got busted showing off when you were kids?" Allison asked.

Just then, Rio dashed up and jumped on Jake, wagging his tail. "Hey Rio; where ya been buddy?" Jake asked, scratching his head. Rio licked his face before turning his attention to Jake's wounds, which he licked clean.

"We better take you to the clinic and clean those scrapes properly so they don't get infected." Renée said.

Together the group headed for the clinic. Up ahead, a female dog yipped, and Rio dashed ahead to join her and they disappeared together.

"I guess we know what ol' Rio's been up to!" Jake said.

Chapter Twenty Five

Renée said, "be careful, you guys," while checking their gauze bandages before they pulled on their long sleeve flannel shirts.

"Yes Mom," Jake said as he wheeled the Carabela outside where Rio greeted him, tail wagging.

Aaron swept his hair back with his hand and slipped on an old John Deere cap backward.

"I wish you guys had helmets." "Our heads are harder than most helmets!"

"I mean it," she said to Aaron. "If anything were to happen to you…"

"I promise; we'll be careful," Aaron said and gave Renée a hug.

"Alright, quit playin' grab ass and let's get a move on!" Jake said looking at his watch. "It's eight already."

Aaron reluctantly released Renée from his grip. He hopped aboard and started the engine. Jake climbed on behind. They both slipped on sunglasses.

"I've gotta go too, I've got patients this morning." Renée said. She watched as they rode away with Rio running alongside barking. "I better order more gauze," she muttered to herself and headed for the clinic.

"Ya think ya can keep us upright this time?" Jake said. Maybe you should ride bitch." Aaron ignored the remark and turned north onto the highway.

Aaron tried his best to maintain the speed limit, but the low powered, heavily laden motorcycle had a hard time maintaining speed uphill, while the marginal brakes limited their speed going downhill. The shocks had long ago lost their ability to dampen the many bumps. The weather-checked old tires provided little grip, so he was cautious around the many turns, that is until another rider on an even smaller bike laden with a huge crate of live chickens overtook them. The race was on! First one rider and then the other would surge ahead, only to have the other turn the tables at the next corner. After a particularly lurid slide brought them precariously close to the edge of the road where a sheer drop of hundreds of feet beckoned, Aaron decided that discretion was the better part of valor, and slowed. The other rider zoomed past, grinning smugly.

The race had succeeded in bringing up the pace nearly to the speed limit, and it was at eight forty-three that they arrived at a village. They pogo-ed over the three speed bumps and through the village, passing the other motorcycle as its rider unloaded his chickens. He laughed and waved smugly as they passed.

At ten after nine, they came upon a stretch of road that had recently been repaired and evidence that there had been a landslide. Juan had probably been at work. They continued on their way.

At nine-thirty, they began watching for turn-offs on the left side of the road. They passed a few overgrown roads that had obviously not been used for some time, before turning onto one which showed signs of recent traffic, but it led to a corn field. They turned onto the next road and through an immediate "S" turn, and came to a steel gate. Beyond the gate, a new concrete driveway could be seen leading off into the forest. Jake checked his watch; it was nine forty six. Aaron turned around and they returned to the highway, where he turned left. A short distance up the road, he saw another overgrown path, and turned in. He continued along the path until they were hidden from view to passing cars, shut off the engine, and leaned the bike against a tree. The guys stretched to limber up after the long ride.

"OK, let's check it out." Aaron said. "If ya hear any cars coming, hide in the brush. A couple of gringos on the highway would draw too much attention and if Petrovinski came by, he'd recognize us for sure."

They swiftly made their way back toward the driveway. Only once were they forced to take to the brush as a truckload of farm laborers passed. At the entrance to the drive, they paused a moment to listen carefully. Only the sounds of the forest could be heard, so they cautiously walked along the drive to where they could see the gate. Before proceeding any further, they looked carefully for any signs of a video camera. Satisfied that none were present, they approached the gate, which was a welded steel gate like one might expect to find at a zoo or cemetery. It had an electric opener and lock instead of a chain and padlock. Rather than climbing over the gate, they followed the fence off into the woods. In hushed tones, they discussed what to do next. "Do ya think we oughta try to get a peek at the house?" Jake asked. "I don't think so; it would just improve our chances of being caught. We sure don't want to lose the element of surprise."

"So what do ya think we ought to do?"

"Nothing for now; we found what we needed to know. We should head back."

"Sounds good."

They started to head back for the drive, but stopped at the sound of a car turning onto the gravel drive. They ducked down into the brush just in time; they had not heard the sound of the car approaching until the last second. Through the brush they could see a black Mercedes stop and wait for the gate to open, before proceeding on. The gate swung closed behind the car.

The guys lay in the brush for a few moments to make sure that the coast was clear before dashing back to the bike. Before they mounted up, they discussed the latest development.

"Ya think it was Cruella?" Jake asked.

"No doubt in my mind. Aaron replied. "The question is what they're up to. First we see them together in San Cristobal, and now she shows up here."

"You don't suppose she's his girlfriend?"

"Are you kidding? Even ol' Vlad has better taste than that! Besides we both know that he likes his women young and dumb."

"What the hell's she doin' here then?"

"Gotta be business."

"You think he's in the drug business now?"

"So it would seem."

"The game just became a bit more dangerous."

"This is no game." The Carabela had gone south only a few minutes when Jake told Aaron to pull over. He dismounted and strode to the edge of the road to look out over a canyon stretching out in the direction they'd just come. Aaron joined Jake and directed his gaze where he was looking so intently. "What is it?" He asked.

Ron Fugere

Jake pointed and said, "Petrovinski's palace." Still pointing, he traced the path of the highway as it wound in switchbacks to where they stood. Although they had ridden a few miles, the highway had brought them to within no more than half a mile from Petrovinski's house as the crow flies and had given them a line of sight.

"Damn; I wish we had some binoculars!" Aaron exclaimed.

From their vantage point, a thin ribbon of water could be seen snaking its way through the jungle canyon and past the sprawling hacienda.

They had been so intent on their observations, that they'd been unaware of the approach of a car until it turned onto the gravel. They turned to see a late model Land Rover come to a stop. The passenger door immediately swung open. They looked in panic, fully expecting a thug packing an Uzi to spring from the door. They looked for a place to hide from the hail of bullets they expected to be directed their way, but no safe refuge was at hand. Resigned to their fate, they stood their ground to face their executioner.

Instead, of a thug packing an Uzi, a gringa tourist sprung from the door with a camera. She put the camera to her eye and trained its long zoom lens on a colorful toucan which was perched nearby. She twisted the lens and pressed the shutter button repeatedly.

The driver's door opened and her husband got out. "You've already got at least ten thousand bird pictures; don't ya think you've got enough?" He said with a tone of exasperation in his voice.

"You didn't seem to mind stopping for those cute Señoritas!" She replied while she kept shooting.

Road Tripped

"Fuck it; I'm gonna take a leak. He strode across the highway and stepped into the brush.

Aaron walked over near the lady and said, "Lots of exotic birds down here aren't there? Isn't that a toucan?"

"Oh! The lady exclaimed with a start. She had been so intent on her target that she had not noticed the guys standing there and had been startled. She looked at Aaron and then Jake somewhat defensively, but seeing no threat, she relaxed and asked, "Do you know anything about birds?"

"No, not really; I just like to look at them. I have a hummingbird feeder at home.

Is that a Nikon?"

"No, it's a Cannon."

"Do you mind if I have a look?"

"Sure, but be careful; this is a very expensive camera."

"I will, I promise." He slipped the strap around his neck and trained the lens on the hacienda. He twisted the zoom to bring it into focus. Through the lens he could see three garage doors opening onto a concrete driveway which encircled an oasis complete with a fountain and palm trees. A pillared grand foyer lay at about a forty-five degree angle to the garages. The roof appeared to be tile and had at least three chimneys. All in all, it had the appearance of any number of McMansions one could find in the suburbs of Seattle, where yuppies lived out their delusions of wealth and grandeur. Behind the house was a walled garden with a gate opening onto an expansive lawn. At one end of the lawn was a large greenhouse beyond which lay a cultivated field with rows of red, then orange, yellow, and finally some indistinct rows of green.

The woman's husband stepped out of the brush pulling up his zipper. He joined his wife and cleared his throat to get Aaron's attention.

"Oh, hi," Aaron said. "This is a fine camera; I'll have to get one one of these days."

"Humph. They're expensive as hell," the husband said. Looking at the guys and their mount, he could safely assume that they stood little chance of ever affording such a camera.

Aaron took the camera from his neck and handed it back to the lady. "Thank you; I hope you get lots of good photos," he said.

"C'mon Alice, we got miles t' make." The couple bickered as they returned to their SUV, slammed the doors, and sped away.

"What did ya see?" Jake asked.

"Well I think I know what Cruella and Petrovinski are up to. Let's go; I'll fill ya in later." Aaron said as he kicked the Carabela to life. They mounted up and headed back toward San Gabriele.

Now it was the girls turn to interrogate the guys. Over dinner, they discussed their reconnaissance.

"Allison, your observations were spot-on! Aaron enthused. We found his place right where we expected to."

"Were you able to scout the land?" She asked.

"No it was too risky," Aaron replied. "More risky than we thought."

"What do you mean?" Renée asked.

"Cruella DeVille showed up." Jake answered.

"You saw her?"

"No, but we saw her car arrive."

"How did you know it was her car?"

"Ya don't see very many Mercedes around here, do ya?" Jake answered.

Allison gasped. "A black Mercedes?"

"Yeah; how did you know?" Aaron asked.

"There was a black Mercedes in the garage when we left on Saturday. We had to cut our lesson short."

"Why didn't ya tell us?" Jake asked. "That bitch is dangerous!"

"I didn't know it was hers, I thought it was his!" She said defensively. "Why didn't you guys tell me to watch out for one?"

"Alright, alright you two!" Aaron said. "We already knew that they were involved in something, and now we know what it is."

"What's that?" Renée asked.

"Remember the poppies?"

"Oh yeah; by the way, the results came back from the lab," Renée said. "It was a specimen of opium poppy, alright, powerful, but nothing special other than the color."

"So that's where Vlad comes in; he must be involved in genetic engineering."

"What makes you think that?" Renée asked.

"There's a greenhouse and garden behind the house."

"So? Lots of people have gardens, and opium will grow anywhere," she said.

"How does the DEA find most drug crops?" Aaron asked.

"Helicopters." Jake answered. "They must be engineering a crop that's invisible from the air."

"Bingo!" Aaron said.

"Ya mean t' tell me that I'm working for a drug kingpin?!" Allison asked in dismay.

"I'm afraid so, Allison," Aaron answered. "This kind of changes the game. We don't want to put you at risk, so maybe we ought to call off the whole surveillance mission and just call in the police."

"No way!" She exclaimed. "The cops are probably in on it or at least looking the other way. Calling the federales could be more dangerous than spying on them."

"True." Jake said. "Besides, the money in the safe is ours. Call in the cops and I'll bet it conveniently disappears."

"I think the most important thing is Allison's safety," Renée said. "But I've also seen what heroin does to people. Allison, are you sure that you'll be safe?"

"I'll be careful," She replied. "We need to stop them."

"When the time is right, we'll call the FBI to let them know where Petrovinski is holed up and they can call in the DEA," Aaron said. "But I want to be there when they come in. I want to see Vlad and Cruella in handcuffs!"

Aaron stood and reached across the table for Jake's hand. Renée and Allison stood and clasped their hands with the guys. "We have our mission!" Aaron exclaimed.

Chapter Twenty Six

Allison and the guys boarded the bus for San Cristobal to procure supplies. When they arrived, they located a sporting goods store that catered to hikers where they spent most of their remaining cash on a pair of high powered binoculars, a Garmin hand-held GPS, and hand bearing compasses. They inquired about topographical maps, but none were available.

"I have an idea," Allison said. "Follow me." She led them to Na Bolom.

"Why would they have topographical maps at a hotel?" Jake asked.

"Remember, Na Bolom is more than a hotel; it is also a research facility, museum, and library."

At the gate, Allison asked the doorman to let them in to visit Franz's library. He was reluctant to admit them; the library was for hotel patrons, volunteers, and researchers only. They had reached an impasse, when by coincidence, Ramón walked by. He recognized his friends and broke into a broad smile. He said a few words to the doorman, who sheepishly opened the gate to admit them.

223

"Ramón, do you think that there are any topographical maps of Chiapas in the library?"

"Why would you need topographical maps?" He asked out of curiosity.

In a low voice, Aaron confided in Ramon. "We believe we've stumbled on a drug operation. We intend to destroy it."

Ramón's face grew grim. "Drugs killed my little brother. You must allow me to help. Follow me." He led them past the library and let them into a storeroom where a rack contained hundreds of rolled up charts. On the wall was a map of Chiapas on which an overlapping grid broke the state up into rectangular plots outlined in red. The red blocks were further divided into smaller rectangles outlined in green. Each block had a six digit number in the upper right corner. "Show me which charts you need."

Aaron and Jake stepped to the map and located San Gabriele. Aaron traced his finger along the highway to the next village, and then beyond. "Does this look like the stream we saw?" He asked Jake.

"It has to be; I don't see any others, and it looks like about the right area."

Aaron read off the numbers of the red and green outlined blocks and Ramón wrote them down. Instead of pulling the charts from those in the rack, he stepped to a computer on a desk. He booted up the computer, tapped in a few commands, and said, "Wait here; I'll be right back."

In a few minutes, he returned with two charts, still warm from the printer. He laid them out on the table. Aaron and Jake looked at the charts which showed topographical lines, roads, and towns, overlaid upon it. Lines of latitude and longitude broke both charts into grids and a compass rose adorned each.

Road Tripped

"Will these do?" Ramón asked.

"These are perfect!" Aaron said enthusiastically.

Ramón looked at the charts and traced his finger along the creek. "This was part of our territory before the Spanish came," he said. "We have long considered it our homeland." Not long ago, a rich gringo bought this land and made it off limits to us. He built his hacienda upon the ashes of my ancestors." He placed his finger on a spot on the chart where the topographical lines indicated a canyon through which a creek flowed.

Aaron and Jake looked closely at the spot and then at each other. "Ramón, do you know this area well?" Aaron asked.

"Like I know my own face," he replied.

"We may be able to help you reclaim your land," Aaron said. "Do you know anything about plotting a course or pinpointing a location on a chart?"

"We Lacandon needed no charts; we could find our way by reading the land, the moon, and the stars. But yes I do." He opened a drawer and extracted dividers, parallel rules, and pencils. "Are you sure this is the spot?"

"Absolutely."

While Ramón plotted the position on the chart, Aaron unwrapped the GPS and installed the batteries. "Can you give me the coordinates of the hacienda Ramón?"

Ramón read them off while Aaron entered the waypoint on the GPS. "Can you give me a spot where we could leave the highway and find our way through the forest to reach the house?"

"Of course I can; I already have. It will not be necessary though."

"Why's that?" "Because I will lead you there."

***

It was late evening when Allison, Jake, and Aaron arrived back in San Gabriele with their booty. They gave Renée an update and all retired for the night. When Aaron went to his hamaca, Frisby had left a dead mouse as an offering on the floor beneath. He disposed of the carcass and climbed in. Frisby jumped up and perched on his stomach. "What is it with you cats? Why do you pick the one person to attach yourself to that doesn't like cats?" She replied by kneading his stomach with her paws while purring loudly.

The guys were awakened the next morning by a loud knock at the door. Renée opened the door, already wearing her scrubs. "Hola Juan; ¿que pasa?"

"Buennos dias, Doctora Renée. May I speak to your guests, por favor?"

"Yes, please come in." She led Juan to the kitchen. "Uno momento; I'll let them know you're here."

"That's OK Renée, we heard him come in. Hi Juan; good to see you!" Aaron said shaking his hand.

"Hola mi amigos!"

"What brings you out to see us?"

"Some of my soldiers have reported that someone is offering them work as farm hands."

"So?" Jake said.

"The person offering the work is a gringo."

"And?"

"Gringos do not farm."

The guys stood mute for a moment, trying to grasp what Juan was getting at. "And they think that it is to grow… illicit crops?" Aaron asked.

"Si. My men want nothing to do with drug money," Juan said. "Drugs are an embarrassment to the proud people of

Mexico. We, the soldiers of the Popular Front for the Restoration of Peace to the People of Mexico will declare a truce with the government. We will join their fight to end the drug traffic in Mexico!" He pulled himself up straight and proud. His expression showed resolve.

"Juan, we have information which may help you in your fight. Please sit down." Aaron said.

"I have to head for the clinic, so you guys can talk," Renée said. "I'll see you later."

Over a pot of coffee, the guys filled Juan in on all they knew of the drug operation and their plans.

"Juan, do you have some men who would be brave enough to take the farm jobs to learn more about their operation?" Jake asked.

"Si; I know just the men!" Juan said. "Mi amigos, I must apologize for asking you to leave my home. I have brought shame to my household," Juan said looking down.

"No Juan, you had to do what was right for your family. You have nothing to be ashamed of," Aaron said. "We're proud to call you our friend."

***

Saturday morning everyone gathered at the dining room table to go over the details of the next phase of the mission. Allison looked nervously at her text book to make sure once more that it did not look suspicious. She slipped the newly crafted silver bracelet onto her wrist and absentmindedly spun it while staring into space.

"Are you gonna be OK, Allison?" Jake asked, concerned.

"Oh I'm alright; it's just that I hope everything works OK."

"Do you want me to show you again how to activate the scanner?"

"No; I've got it."

"You don't have to do this," he said. "We can always find another way."

"No, I want to do it." She stood up straight and said with determination, "I'm going to do it!" She strode to the mirror and undid one more button, cupped her breasts, and said, "C'mon girls; we got work t' do!"

Jake felt admiration for her resolve and a tiny twinge of jealousy, much to his surprise. He had never really thought of Allison as more than Renée's friend. Where was this coming from, he wondered?

"We'll be right behind you on the highway and we'll be watching from the hill while you're inside," Aaron said and began rolling the Carabela out the door.

Allison checked her watch and announced, "Game on!" She picked up her handbag, and textbook, and then headed for the bus stop. The guys took up a position just south of the bus stop where they could observe the arrival and departure of the BMW.

The car arrived at exactly eight o'clock and as usual, the man in the passenger seat got out and opened the door for Allison. The windows turned opaque, the driver did a U-turn, and they drove away. Allison had to fight the impulse to turn and look for the guys tailing them. It would have been pointless anyway, due to the magic windows. She opened up her novel to pass the time, careful not to go to page one-twenty-three. Her eyes followed the words as she turned the pages, but her mind did not comprehend the story. It was always a long, boring drive to the hacienda, but today it felt like an eternity. She checked her watch when they encountered the speed bumps; right on schedule. At about the time that they should have been encountering the rough stretch of road, they instead came upon a very smooth stretch; apparently the highway had been repaired. When the car turned from the highway onto the rough dirt road and executed the S-turn, Allison activated the scanning device. From the back seat, Allison could see the driver press a button on the sun visor, and then wait while the gate swung open. They proceeded to the hacienda, where he pushed another button to open the garage door. Inside, the men waited for the door to close before they let Allison out. She was relieved to see that the next stall in the garage was empty.

After a short wait in the study, Vlad entered and the lesson began. He was in unusually high spirits; must have stolen a little old lady's pension, Allison thought.

She turned to a page in her text book and asked Vlad to do so too. She went to his desk. Leaning over to point out a particular paragraph, she purred, "Read this paragraph for me."

While Vlad read the paragraph, Allison walked around and sat on the desk close to Vlad, allowing her skirt to hike up. She used her upper arms to press her breasts together and accentuate her cleavage to best effect and lingered a moment for her cologne to work its magic. "Now turn to page one-sixty-eight."

Vlad turned the pages. Allison pointed to a paragraph and again told him to read it. He placed his hand on hers and together they followed the words with his finger. He read a paragraph about amore. When he'd read the passage, he seemed reluctant to move his hand, which trembled as he gently ran his fingertips over the back of her hand. His ostentatious gold ring touched her silver bracelet. This is going even better than planned, Allison thought.

The door to the study swung open abruptly, and a woman with short blonde hair, wearing a sleek black dress and sunglasses strode purposefully into the room, her tall stiletto heels clicking on the floor. She crossed her arms and stood with her feet apart. "You keep me waiting," she said in a frosty voice.

"I study my Spanish."

The woman lifted her sunglasses, revealing her cold blue-gray eyes. "Yes, I can see what you study." She replaced her glasses.

Allison stood, smoothed her skirt, and buttoned her blouse.

The guys concealed the bike in the brush and climbed to a spot where they could watch the hacienda and the highway unobserved. Jake used the binoculars to look closely at the compound. "I think you're right about the greenhouse and garden," he said. "If you hadn't told me they were there, I never would have spotted the green poppies."

Aaron took a look for himself. The view with the binoculars confirmed his earlier observations. In only a week, it seemed that the crop had grown more difficult to see, which was doubtless what they were attempting to accomplish. "Fuck!" He exclaimed.

"What is it?" Jake asked.

"The black Mercedes just pulled in. Must have come from the south; we didn't see it come this way." He glanced at his watch and made a mental note of the time.

"How many people got out?"

"I don't know; they pulled into the garage."

"Ya think Allison will be OK?" Jake asked nervously.

"I hope so. I doubt if she'll even see Allison; they didn't see each other last time."

Road Tripped

"Perhaps we can continue our lessons another time," Vlad said. He pressed the button on his desk, and in an instant, the door opened and the driver entered.

"Sir?" The driver said.

"Please see our guest home."

"My fee?" Allison asked.

"Oh yes; how stupid of me!" Rather than opening the safe, Vlad pulled a large gold money clip from his pocket, peeled off a few bills, and tucked them in her hand. "There is a little extra for your trouble." His hand lingered on hers momentarily.

Allison gathered her things and strode past the woman, casting a sideways glance in her direction as if sizing up the competition. Her perfume was so heavy that it made Allison want to gag. The woman took as much notice of Allison as she would an ant.

Jake took the binoculars back from Aaron and watched as the silver BMW pulled out of the garage. He checked his watch. A short time later, it whispered past. They continued their observation for another hour to see if the Mercedes would leave. It did not. They rolled their bike out of its concealment and headed back for San Gabriele.

Chapter Twenty Seven

Aaron, Allison, and Renée watched eagerly while Jake deftly attached a USB cord to some terminals and plugged it into Renée's laptop. Aaron keyed in some commands and waited a moment for a response. He typed the commands again.

"Well?" Jake said impatiently.

"Take a look at this." The computer screen was completely filled a complex code.

"What is it?" Renée asked.

"We got a reading, but it's like they scrambled the signal."

"Can you descramble it?"

"Sure, in a couple of lifetimes."

"Did I activate it right?" Allison asked anxiously.

"You did it right, but it seems ol' Vlad is more clever than we give him credit for," Jake replied.

Let's see what we got with the bracelet," Aaron said hopefully. Jake had built a device that would take the magnetic information that the bracelet had lifted from the ring, and convert it to a bar code, which Aaron could then use to program a triggering device to open the safe. Aaron watched the computer monitor for a moment. The tension in the air was palpable. He keyed the commands again. The disappointment on his face left no doubt of the results. "I guess we're gonna have to come up with a plan 'B'."

Aaron, Jake, Renée, Allison, Juan, and Ramón all gathered around the dining table. Aaron had hung a large sheet of paper on the wall. "OK, let's start by developing the timeline," Aaron said. "Now Allison, we know that they always pick you up at exactly 08:00."

"Correct."

He denoted the action on the left column side of the page. "And you arrive at the gate at 09:28 plus or minus."

"Correct."

He marked, "09:28(+ -) arrive gate."

"Are the men ever in communication with Vlad or anyone else on the way?"

"No."

"And when do the lessons conclude?" He asked Allison.

"At about noon." Another mark on the chart.

"Now Jake, what time did you see Cruella arrive?"

"At eleven forty-nine."

"And she arrived from the north?"

"Yes."

"Allison, we know that Cruella has shown up twice now before your lessons are done. Had you ever seen her car before?"

"Yes, come to think of it; I never really thought anything of it."

"OK, so it would appear that we have a two and a half hour window of opportunity to penetrate and secure the perimeter, liberate the contents of the safe, and apprehend the target. The question now is how do we plan to do it?" They went to work filling in the timeline with each team's actions.

Rene, who had listened intently to all of the discussion in silence, at last said, "This is not the board room of a video game company, Aaron. In this game, people bleed real blood. By your own admission, this Cruella, as you call her, is dangerous. You know that she has heavily armed thugs who wouldn't blink an eye at the thought of putting a bullet through your head."

"If you don't want to be part of it Renée, no one would think any less of you," Jake said. "This is our battle."

"It's not that at all," She said. "It's just that I don't think that you take her threat seriously. With their combined resources, you are outmanned. And let me look in the armory. Now what do we have in our arsenal?" She looked around the room. "Oh, it appears we don't have an arsenal, so that would mean you're outgunned. Even if you did have guns, do you know how to use them and are you prepared to do so? And given the fact that this Petrovinski guy succeeded in absconding with your fortunes, it would appear that he has outsmarted you once. Maybe he will again." Her lip quivered as she continued, "You have just come back into my... our lives and I'm afraid of losing you. Won't you please consider bringing in the authorities? Please?"

"This is something we have to do, Renée," Aaron said. "We will bring in the authorities, you have my promise. But first we have to take back what is ours."

"Your mind is made up then." She stated it as a fact.

"Yes."

"Then if you must, I will participate, but only as medic. Just remember, 'all the king's horses and all the king's men'...," She said somberly.

"Renée has a good point about being outmanned and outgunned," Allison said. "I've only seen this Cruella bitch once, but she sent a chill down my spine. Is there a way to take her out of the equation?"

"I don't see how, and besides, we want to put her out of business too," Aaron replied. "Vlad may have stolen our money, but with her drugs, she destroys lives."

"Divide and conquer." All eyes turned to Juan.

"What do you mean?" Allison asked.

"My men and I will take her out of the equation, as you say."

"But how?" Renée asked.

"Leave it to me."

"OK, so now we have to figure out how to get in. Without the remotes for the gate and garage, we can't get in through the front door; which means that we have to come in through the back. Ramón, I believe that this is where you come in."

"Si, amigos. But when my people were at war with the conquistadors, we preferred to attack from both sides. Ours was the only tribe that the Spanish never defeated. We must attack from the front and the back."

"But we just said we can't get in through the front without the remotes," Jake said.

"And who has remotes?" Ramón asked.

"His men," Jake said.

"Then we will borrow them," Ramón said smugly.

"You haven't seen these guys!" Allison said. "Just one of them is as big as two of you!"

"And is it not said that the taller they are, the longer they fall?"

"You mean the bigger they are, the harder they fall," Allison corrected him.

"Si; as you say."

"But how?" Aaron asked.

"As Juan said; leave it to me," he said confidently.

"Does anyone else have anything to add?" Aaron asked. Everyone looked around the table at everyone else.

"I move that we adjourn this meeting until next week, same time, and same place," Aaron said.

"I second," Jake said.

"All in favor?" Everyone held up their hands.

"The motion carries; this meeting is adjourned."

With the meeting concluded, Juan and Ramón left, Juan to spend the rest of his Sunday with his family, Ramón to try to contact members of his tribe. No easy task, given that some lived in remote enclaves in the forest. Aaron and Jake's resolve grew stronger despite the complication of their failure to crack the security codes. They didn't know what Ramón had in mind, nor would they until they next met. They were encouraged by Juan's assertion that he could separate Cruella and her thugs. Perhaps his men working as farm hands would learn more of her operation. At least Juan and Ramón had tasks to perform and Renée and Allison had their jobs; whereas there was really little Aaron and Jake could do in preparation. It seemed it was going to be a long week. Aaron, Jake, Renée, and Allison went about the days somewhat mechanically, all preoccupied. Little was said as each was lost in thoughts of the mission. Allison was nervous that she might somehow arouse suspicion, jeopardizing the success of the mission. Renée worried for the safety of all involved. She felt that no one took the potential dangers seriously. Jake worried of the possible failure of the mission.

Road Tripped

They would have but one chance to reclaim their fortunes. It had been by the most remote chance that they had discovered Vlad's whereabouts; they could not hope to be so fortunate again. Should things go awry, Vlad would simply disappear, never to be seen again. He also worried for Allison's safety. He admired her fortitude and commitment to the mission. Although he would be the last to admit it, he was actually beginning to like her, even if she was a bit prickly at times. Aaron had become the de facto leader of the enterprise, and with authority comes great responsibility. He felt that he held the lives of those involved in his hands. Was he putting his friends at risk?

Chapter Twenty Eight

Sunday morning at eleven, Aaron opened the meeting. The group's numbers had been expanded by two. Juan had adopted his role as El Supremo; joining him at the table was Julio, his second in command of their revolutionary forces. Joining Ramón was a swarthy man with silver streaks in his otherwise jet black shoulder length hair. His bangs were trimmed in a severe straight line high on his brow. His deeply creased face bore tribal tattoos. His ears were adorned with wooden plugs through the lobes and a thin barb pierced the septum of his nose. He wore only a simple smock of a course fabric and his gnarled feet were bare. He did not respond as Aaron introduced the rest of the party. "I will have to serve as his interpreter," Ramón said. "This is Teo K'ha. He is an elder in our tribe. He speaks no English or Spanish, only Lacandon and a little Mayan."

"And what will his role be in the operation?" Aaron asked.

"He will lead the party along the stream to the back of the hacienda."

"Then what will you be doing?" Jake asked.

"I will accompany you in through the front."

"I see," Aaron said. "Now Allison, let's check our timeline. Were there any changes?"

"No; it was just like every other week."

"And did you see Cruella?"

"No; but I smelled her perfume. And her car was there again when we left."

"Good. It is far better that we know that she is likely to be there and when," Aaron said while looking directly at Renée. Directing his gaze at Allison, he asked, "And how was Petrovinski's demeanor? Did he behave any differently?"

"Yes."

"In what way?" "He kind of made a pass at me," She said while casting a sideways glance at Jake who tried not to respond in any way. Only a twitch of his brow gave him away.

"That's good! It means that he doesn't suspect anything."

The meeting went on for some time as the final details of the plan were developed and refined.

At last Aaron said, "I believe that we are now ready to move into the operational phase of the mission. The question is when. I propose that we execute our plan this Saturday."

"So soon?!" Renée said in alarm.

"To delay only diminishes our chance of success," Aaron reasoned.

"You promised to bring in the authorities when the time was right. What If you wait too long?"

"Perhaps the time has come to contact them. What do you think Jake?"

"I think we should, but we don't want them to arrive too soon. We need to be able to call the shots. We can't allow them to take over the operation or we'll never see the money."

"Is the money worth the risk?" Renée asked.

"That money is our future," Jake said. "With their share, Juan's army can fight the drug war. With their share, the Lacandon can reclaim some of their homeland. With Allison's share, she could improve education here. And with your share maybe you can build a new clinic."

"OK, we should make the call now," Aaron said.

"Renée, can we use the phone?"

"Of course," She said with a degree of relief.

Renée got the cordless phone from the kitchen. "Dial double-oh-one and then the number with the area code."

Aaron pulled the wrinkled card from his wallet and held it in one hand while dialing the number with the thumb of his other. He put the receiver to his ear and waited while the connection was made. "Yes; may I please speak to..." he looked at the card... "Special Agent, Mathew Cromwell? Yes; I'll hold." After a short pause, he said, "Agent Cromwell, this is Aaron Skandish. We met in Seattle during the raid on..." There was another pause while Aaron listened. "Good. I have Jacob Overbee here with me. May I put you on speaker phone?" He held out the phone and cast a questioning glance at Renée. She stepped over and pressed a button. "Can you hear me OK?"

"Yes I can. Is my voice clear?" Agent Cromwell's voice came over the speaker.

"Yes, we can hear you fine." "Mister Skandish and mister Overbee, how good it is to hear from you. How can I help you?"

"Agent Cromwell you had asked us to contact you if we learned anything of the whereabouts of Vladmir Petrovinski. We have knowledge of his whereabouts and would like to help bring him to justice."

"And where can we find mister Petrovinski?"

"He is in the State of Chiapas, Mexico."

"Can you be more exact?"

"Not at this time. We can pinpoint his location where he will be this Saturday. Is there a way that you could dispatch personnel to the San Cristobal area without raising suspicion?"

"I will see what I can do."

"And Agent Cromwell?"

"Yes?"

"Do you have any contacts in the DEA?"

"Of course."

"We have also gained knowledge of a drug operation in Chiapas producing large quantities of marijuana and opium. Can you arrange a conference call with the DEA? We would like to ask for their cooperation."

"I can. How can you be reached?"

"I will call back at this time tomorrow. Thank you."

"By the way mister Skandish, you may…"

Aaron broke the connection.

"Why did you hang up?" Renée asked.

"I didn't want to give him enough time to trace the call." He answered. "I think it would be wise for me to make another trip to San Cristobal tomorrow and call him from there. Would you like to come?"

"Yes I would; let me clear my schedule."

Ron Fugere

Chapter Twenty Nine

Aaron and Renée stood at the reception desk at Na Bolom. Renée gave the clerk her credit card and he handed her the keys. They found their room and let themselves in. The room was much like those they'd stayed in before, but this one faced the small courtyard and the arboretum from above. Sunlight streamed through the partially drawn curtains, bringing a warm glow to the soft hues of the walls and antique furnishings.

Aaron checked his watch and picked up the phone to check for a dial tone while Renée set down her things. "So here we are"

Aaron fidgeted nervously and checked his watch repeatedly as the time ground by minute by minute. At last he said, "OK, time to make the call." He pulled the card out of his wallet and reached for the receiver. He punched in the number preceded by 001 and waited impatiently for the connection to be made. "Shit! It's not going through."

"Try dialing nine for an outside line," Renée suggested.

He pushed the button on the cradle, waited for a dial tone, and entered the number again. A receptionist answered on the second ring. "FBI field office, Seattle," she said.

"May I speak to Agent Cromwell please? He's expecting my call."

"Mister Skandish?"

"Yes."

"Agent Cromwell told me to expect your call and arrange a conference call. I will connect you now."

The phone beeped three times and Agent Cromwell spoke, "Mister Skandish, Matt Cromwell speaking. I have Agent John Alexander of the DEA on the line."

"Good morning Mister Cromwell, Mister Alexander."

"Now Mister Skandish, what is this all about?" Alexander asked.

"As I'm sure Agent Cromwell has informed you, we have discovered the whereabouts of a high profile fugitive in Chiapas Mexico."

"He has."

"We have discovered that he is involved with a drug operation that may be of particular interest to your agency."

"How so?"

"They are developing a strain of opium poppies that are invisible from the air."

Agent Alexander was silent for a moment while he considered the implications of such a development. "I see. This would certainly be an advantage to those in the drug business."

"Now here's what I want you to do," Aaron said. "I will give you GPS coordinates for a position. But first I must have both of your assurances that that you will arrive there at precisely twelve hundred hours on Saturday, no sooner, no later. You'll need helicopters."

"You ask a lot, Mister Skandish," Alexander said. "The logistics of dispatching units on such short notice are considerable."

"It will be worth your trouble, I can assure you."

"I will see to it; we have units in Mérida, Yucatán."

"And you Agent Cromwell?"

"By coincidence, our agents are already checked in at your hotel, Mister Skandish. Room 203 is it?"

"You work fast." Aaron carried the phone to the window and peered out to see two men dressed in khaki slacks, guayabera shirts, and Panama hats smoking huge Cuban cigars. "The cigars are a nice touch."

"You would want us to be inconspicuous."

"Do I have your assurance; 12: 00 Saturday?"

"You do."

"OK, here are the coordinates." He read off the latitude and longitude.

After a pause while clicking could be heard over the line, Cromwell said, "The satellite image shows nothing but jungle."

"Satellite image?"

"Google Earth. The image is from a year ago," Cromwell said. "One moment while I access a different image." After another short pause, he said, "Ah that's better. I see there's a new home. Nice big lawn for us to land on."

"That's the place. Are there any other questions?"

"I believe that will be all," said Alexander. "And you, Agent Cromwell?"

"Nothing more for now. How can we reach you between now and then?"

"Just be there at noon." Aaron hung up.

Road Tripped

"So what do we do now?" Renée asked. "I dunno; I'd kind of like to get my mind off the mission for a while. We've done about all we can do for now."

"Ya wanna hit the town?"

"Sure."

"Just let me get changed."

Renée rifled through her bag and took a few garments into the bathroom. While she was changing, Aaron shed his jeans and donned the clothes Renée had bought him when he first arrived. He looked very much the tourist. When she came out of the bathroom, Renée had dressed in a lovely floral print ankle length skirt and a white silk blouse. Around her waist, she had tied a silk sash that complimented the skirt. On her feet she wore delicate sandals. She had tastefully done up her face with just a hint of makeup that enhanced her natural beauty, She had pulled her hair back on one side and fastened it with a barrette that held a wild orchid blossom. She had dabbed on a bit of fragrance that was as subtle as a field of wild flowers. The overall effect was simple yet elegant.

"Let's go!" She said while stepping out the door. Aaron drank in her beauty for a moment before he was able to collect himself and follow her out. Together they strolled down to the boulevard. If they wanted to be inconspicuous themselves, what better way to do so than to blend in with the rest of the tourist crowd?

"Would the Señor like Panama hat?" A man beckoned from a shop. "Is genuine sisal from Yucatan. Good price."

"No; no hat," Aaron said without sufficient conviction.

"Ah c'mon; try one on," Renée badgered him. "It'll be fun!"

The man whisked them into his shop. "If the Señor pleases," the man said while wrapping his hands around Aaron's head to estimate the right size. He scanned his display of hats for a moment and selected a particular style. "Ah, perhaps this! "You try." He set it on Aaron's head.

"My; aren't you handsome! Renée said. "How much?"

"For the Señor and Señorita I make good deal; only one thousand pesos!"

"Too much," Renée said and turned for the door.

"How much you willing to pay?"

"One hundred pesos."

"One hundred pesos!?" The man recoiled as if he'd been shot. "My cousin make with hand. Soak sisal in cenote. See tight weave? For you I make special deal; only five hundred pesos."

Renée again turned for the exit. The shopkeeper turned his attention to Aaron. He took the hat from Aaron's head, punched the top up, folded it flat, and rolled it up. Then he unrolled it and it quickly regained its form. "See Señor, easy to pack. You pay four hundred pesos?"

Aaron really had no interest in a Panama hat, but the persistent vendor was not about to let him escape. The man led him to a mirror and again put the hat on his head. He did look pretty good in it, he had to admit. He looked at Renée.

"Two hundred-fifty pesos; no more," she said.

"Three hundred pesos."

"Done."

Aaron and Renée continued their stroll with him wearing his new hat which perfectly complimented his garb. "You drive a hard bargain Renée. The guy's poor cousin is probably gonna starve!"

"They expect you to dicker; it's part of the game. "

"Renée, you shouldn't spend so much money on me."

"But you look so handsome in it! We'll work something out to make sure I get my money's worth," she said with an alluring smile."

"If everything goes according to plan, I'm gonna treat you to a whole new wardrobe!"

"What's wrong with my wardrobe?" She asked while executing a turn as if at the end of the runway, and then walked ahead swinging her hips like a super model. That is until she stumbled and nearly fell.

As they continued their stroll, street vendors would observe them and size up their chances. Those that sold hats looked for another customer. Those selling cigars saw a gringo in a panama hat as an easy mark, and pestered them mercilessly. Young girls and old women approached Renée shyly and showed their wares silently.

Aaron turned into a shop displaying huge quantities of amber jewelry. He took a necklace of red amber off a rack and held it up by Renée's face. He put it back and tried a gold amber necklace next.

The shopkeeper said, "The gold amber looks beautiful with your wife's hair, señor." Together they selected a beautiful necklace with matching earrings. Aaron asked her to set them aside for him.

"We'll be back in a week or so to pick it up," He assured her.

"It's very expensive, Aaron."

"Nothing is too good for my wife!"

They had a glass of wine and a bite to eat in a bistro where they made up names for all the passersby. After dinner, they had ice cream cones and exchanged licks as they wandered through the central plaza arm in arm. As darkness fell, they made one more stop for a bottle of wine, and then headed back for Na Bolom.

"Brr, it's chilly," Renée said rubbing her arms.

Aaron took off his sweater and put it around her shoulders. His hand found her waist as they strolled. At Na Bolom, the doorman held the gate open for them.

Aaron opened the door to their room and allowed Renée to enter first. She turned on a lamp, and Aaron took his sweater from her shoulders and hung it on the coat rack, along with his new hat. He struck a match and lit the fire in the fireplace while Renée opened the bottle of wine to let it to breathe.

"This is the first time we'll sleep... in the same room," Renée said. "But for some reason, it feels as if we always have."

Aaron smiled and said, "I know what you mean. Did you notice that the lady at the jewelry shop called you my wife?"

"I did. You didn't correct her, either."

"Truth is I liked the way it sounded."

"Me too."

The fire crackled and cast its flickering light though the room. Renée lit a couple of candles and turned off the lamp as Aaron poured the wine.

Aaron held up his glass and said, "To you, Missus Skandish." Renée slipped her arm with its glass through his and they drank their toast with their arms entwined, just as they did in Hollywood.

"God; would you look at us? We're like a couple of teenagers on prom night," Renée said giggling.

"Ya know Renée, I've always regretted that we didn't go to the prom together. Maybe things would have turned out different if we had."

"I don't have any regrets about it."

"No?"

"No. If we'd done things differently, we wouldn't be here right now. And I wouldn't trade this moment for a dozen prom nights."

"Don't you think it odd that we're spending the night together and we've never even kissed?"

"The night's still young," Renée said and stepped closer. Aaron took her wine glass and went to set it together with his on the mantle without taking his eyes off hers, He misjudged the distance and one of the glasses shattered on the hearth. Ignoring the mess, he placed his hand gently on Renée's cheek and searched her eyes. He brought his hand to the back of her neck and drew her face to his. Their lips came together tentatively at first. Then, like a dam bursting, all of the pent up longing and desire that they had held in check for so long came forth in a flood of passion. Their lips parted and their tongues thrashed like a pair of wrestlers in the ring. Their bodies drew together and their arms encircled each other in a frantic wrestling match of their own.

Renée pushed Aaron back and said, "We've kissed," with a smoldering look in her eyes. She released her hair and shook it out, then slipped her sandals off. She untied the sash around her waist and undid the buttons of her skirt, dropping them to the floor at her feet. Agonizing slowly, she unbuttoned her blouse while her eyes bore into the deep, dark pools of Aaron's. Her blouse joined the other garments on the floor. She now wore only her lacy silk bra and panties that she'd ordered from Victoria's Secret shortly after Aaron had come back into her life.

Aaron kicked off his shoes and slowly began unbuttoning his shirt while trying to look sexy. He undid his belt and the button of his pants. They dropped to his ankles, revealing his very favorite pair of Elmer Fudd boxer shorts. It looked like Elmer planned on doing a little camping, because he'd already pitched a tent. Renée started to take a step back toward him and stumbled over the clothing piled on the floor, falling into his arms. He lost his balance and together they fell back onto the bed with his pants still around his ankles. Her lips found his and they devoured each other's tongues, but their hunger for one another would not be sated so easily. His hands shook as he sought the clasp on her bra and fumbled with it awkwardly. Eventually, she grew impatient and sat upright on top of him and undid the clasp, releasing her breasts. The skin at her neck flushed with arousal and her pupils dilated, nearly eclipsing her sky blue irises. He reached up and gently grazed his fingertips over her nipples which stiffened to his touch. A soft moan escaped her lips as he gave her breasts a gentle squeeze as if trying to select a ripe melon. He thrashed his feet trying to kick off the pants that entangled them. Eventually, he succeeded but not without knocking the lamp from the nightstand. Renée's fingers found the waistband of his boxers. "Does he have a name?" she asked with a twinkle in her eye.

"Elmer."

"No, I mean your…"

"Elmer."

"Elmer?"

"Elmer."

"Well, Elmer, we meet at last!" She cried while frantically yanking down his boxers. His erection sprung free of its restraints. "Mmm," she hummed her approval.

He grasped her and rolled her onto her back, slid her panties off, and tossed them over his shoulder as his heart kept a staccato beat. They snagged on the ceiling fan rotating slowly over their heads, where they would remain. He now gazed upon her in all her splendor. "Does she have a name?" he asked.

"Petunia."

"Petunia like the flower?"

"Petunia like the Porky Pig's girlfriend."

At long, long last, he claimed his prize. Or maybe she claimed hers. Maybe a little of both. Maybe a lot of both.

After the first round, Aaron said, "Aren't I supposed to light us some cigarettes now like they used to do in the movies?"

"We don't smoke," Renée said while casting Aaron a look that soon had Elmer rising to the occasion. Literally. The bell rang for round two.

Renée laid their keys on the reception desk. The receptionist said, "The Señorita is particularly beautiful today. Did you sleep well?"

Renée blushed and smiled.

Chapter Thirty

With Aaron and Renée away for a couple of days, Jake and Allison were left to their own devices. When Allison got home from class, she found a scene of pandemonium in the kitchen, where Jake was attempting to prepare a gourmet meal. He stirred a large pot of red sauce, which bubbled furiously, spattering the stove and wall. A frying pan had congealed grease from the sausage he'd browned in it. Onion skins and the remains of some unfortunate bell peppers littered the cutting board.

"Hmm, it smells, uh, interesting!" Allison said. "What ya makin'."

"Ya ever heard of fusion cuisine? This is my take on it," he said while slicing a pile of tortillas into thin strips. "We're havin' Italican for dinner; or maybe that's Mexicalian."

He set the frying pan back on the burner, preparing to fry the tortilla strips. "I couldn't find any noodles, so we're using tortilla strips instead." He took the pile of strips in both hands and dropped them into the smoking grease and attempted to give them a toss as he'd seen done on TV.

Road Tripped

He popped the top off a bottle of beer, took a pull, poured, some in the sauce, and took another pull. "We didn't have any wine for the sauce, but beer oughta add some flavor!"

He turned to face Allison. "So how was your day today?"

"Oh just like any other day. Uh, Jake, ya might want to..." He turned his attention back to the stove as the contents of the frying pan burst into flames.

"Oh shit!" He exclaimed and dumped the rest of his beer on the flames.

Allison calmly put a lid over the pan to smother the flames and shut off the burners. "What say we eat out tonight? My treat."

On the way to the restaurant, Allison stopped by Maria, the housekeeper's home. They had a brief conversation in Spanish, accentuated by giggling. Maria grabbed a pail with her cleaning supplies and headed out.

"What was that all about?" Jake asked.

"Oh nothing."

They had a nice dinner of classic Mexican food accompanied by several frosty cervesas at a small restaurant in which they were the only diners.

After dinner, they headed back for the casa. Along the way they encountered Ofical Miguel Martinez and Juanita as they strolled arm in arm. Miguel tipped his hat at the other couple.

"I don't see what she sees in that pompous prick!" Jake grumbled. "It's gotta be the uniform."

"I don't see what you see in that slut!" Allison, exasperated. She stormed ahead uttering a tide of Spanish dialog punctuated by words like estupido, pendejo, and cabron. She arrived at the door just as Maria was letting herself out. She

Ron Fugere

handed Maria some money, stepped inside and slammed the door behind her. Maria walked by with a twinkle of mirth in her eyes.

Jake stood on the curb at a loss. What's with her, he wondered. If it wasn't one thing it was another.

Rio came dashing up and jumped on Jake, wagging his tail. Jake crouched low patting him vigorously while Rio licked his face. "Well Rio, it looks like it's you and me, bud." They wandered off toward the plaza where Jake sat on a park bench with Rio at his feet. "What is it with that woman, anyway," he asked Rio. "Seems like just about anything sets her off. I pity the poor son of a bitch that marries her!" Rio responded by pawing his leg. Jake reached in his pocket and pulled out a handful of coins.

"Piggy bank's almost empty, ol' buddy; hope I got enough for a beer." He stood and wandered over to small shop and started to pull a bottle from the cooler. He hesitated, and then selected the whole six-pack instead. He held out his hand for the lady to select the appropriate coins. She shook her head, took one bottle out of the six-pack, and slid the rest across the counter to Jake.

Returning to the park bench, he popped the top off a bottle, tossed the cap to the ground, and took a deep pull. He patted the bench and said, "C'mon Rio; up!" Rio hopped up and laid his nose on Jake's lap. Jake absentmindedly stroked him as he drank his beer. "Ya know old friend, you dogs got it right. Ya just bone a bitch and then ya just go about yer business. Sometimes I wish I was a dog." He tossed the empty to the ground and opened another. Another dog came by and Rio raised his head in her direction and then looked at Jake as if asking permission. "Go on buddy; have a good time." Rio hopped down and dashed off with the other dog, leaving Jake alone with his beer.

254

He belched out loud and opened another bottle. Soon dead soldiers littered the ground at his feet. He tipped the bottle back and chugged it down. He peered at the empty bottle and tossed it to the ground in disgust. "Now even the beer lets me down." He staggered over to a tree to take a leak.

"Pardon me sir, but can you not find a banyo?" Jake turned to see Ofical Miguel Martinez standing with his hands on his hips. "And you will please pick up this mess."

"Ah fuck you Mikey!"

"Pardon?"

"What; you don't understand plain English? Here, let me tell you in sign language!" Jake flipped him off.

A few minutes later, Jake was led in handcuffs to number 21 Calle 2, where Officer Martinez knocked on the door with his nightstick. The door opened and Allison peered out. "What the hell?" she said.

"I believe this man is a guest of yours, no?" Martinez asked.

"Maybe yes; maybe no; what did he do?"

Officer Martinez explained what had transpired in the plaza. "Do you wish to be responsible for him or do you wish for me to detain him until he is sober?" He asked.

"I don't know; let me think about it."

"Aw come on Allison, gimme a break, will ya?" Jake slurred.

"Maybe your precious Juanita will put you up. Oh, I forgot; she's not yours, is she?!"

"I do not understand Señorita," Martinez said.

"Oh never mind; I'll take him. Can I keep him in cuffs?"

"No Señorita, I am afraid not."

"Very well."

Officer Martinez removed the cuffs. "Perhaps next time you will think better of disrespecting our plaza Señor, no?"

Jake stepped inside and Allison closed the door. She strode purposefully down the hall, shoving Jake aside in the direction of the living room as she passed. She stormed into her bedroom and slammed the door without uttering a word to Jake.

With nothing else to do, Jake just decided to call it a night, but he found it a bit too much of a challenge getting into the hamaca. Instead he passed out on the couch.

Jake woke to the sound of the front door slamming. He groaned and shuffled to the bathroom for aspirin. Damn, I guess I just can't drink like I used to, he thought. What had he had, seven or eight beers?

He went to the kitchen to see if there was any coffee waiting. There was not. He fumbled around trying to figure out the unfamiliar coffee maker, but his head wasn't at its best. Eventually, he succeeded in brewing a pot, but more grounds had found their way into the pot than the filter.

After a while, the coffee and the aspirin had begun to have the desired effect. He looked in the fridge to see what there was to eat, but there was little to choose from. He thought about going out and buying a bite from a street vendor, but he had given most of their money to Aaron for the trip to San Crisobal and spent the rest on beer. Maybe he could stop by Juan's house and invite himself for breakfast, he thought. He walked over to Juan's and knocked on the door and Emilia answered.

"Is Juan home?" He asked.

Emilia shook her head and spoke in Spanish. Jake guessed that she was telling him that Juan was not home. Maybe he

Road Tripped

should start taking a more active interest in Allison's Spanish lessons, he thought.

Why does Allison always have to be so... prickly, he wondered? She doesn't seem to have quite such a short fuse with anyone else; he'd never seen her light into Aaron or Renée the way she did with him. Maybe he just rubbed her the wrong way.

He wandered aimlessly around town; even Rio was nowhere to be found. He found some newspapers, but of course they were in Spanish. He went back to the house for lack of anything else to do.

Out of boredom, he picked up a well worn copy of Cosmopolitan magazine. He stretched out in the hamaca and thumbed through the pages, scoffing at some of the articles. Then he happened across a dog-eared page. Several lines of text were underlined in ink and in a couple of spots, someone had drawn exclamation points. The article was titled, "When the man you desire doesn't know you're alive." He sat down to read. He began to see that some of the behavior outlined in the article could pertain to him and Aaron, particularly the text that was underlined. He knew that Aaron had always carried a torch for Renée, what if she was hot for him too? Or could it be that Allison desired Aaron too? For some reason women had always been attracted to him, so it seemed plausible.

Jake had once felt that way about Renée; when he'd first met her, he thought she was the most beautiful girl in the world, but she didn't seem to know he was alive. He had long ago gotten over his crush on Renée.

Or what if Allison had a crush on me, he wondered? That hardly seemed likely given the way she acted around him sometimes.

257

Jake awoke to the sound of the front door opening. He hadn't been aware that he was asleep. Aaron and Renée came in carrying a couple bags of groceries. "I'll get dinner started," Renée said and went to the kitchen.

"Good, I'm starving!" Jake exclaimed.

"Allison still at work?" Aaron asked.

"I guess."

"Trying to get in touch with your feminine side, I see," Aaron said grinning.

"Bite me!" Jake said as he tossed aside the Cosmopolitan. So how'd it go in San Cristobal?"

"We'll fill ya in when Allison gets home." As if on cue, she walked in the door.

"Hey, Aaron," She greeted him while ignoring Jake.

While Renée finished preparing dinner, Aaron filled Jake and Allison in about the trip. Jake and Allison both asked a few questions, but throughout the talk, Allison did not speak or even so much as look Jake's way. When Allison stepped out of the room for a moment, Aaron asked, "Something going on with you two?"

"I don't know what you mean," Jake answered.

"It feels like the next ice age has begun. Did you do something to piss her off?"

"What, like breathing, ya mean?"

A little later, Renée announced, "Well I've had a long day and I've got early appointments tomorrow, so I think I'll turn in early."

"Yeah, me too," Aaron said.

Renée took him by the hand and led him into her bedroom. Frisby slipped in as Renée closed the door.

Jakes and Allison's jaws dropped in astonishment.

Road Tripped

Chapter Thirty One

The fateful day had arrived. Allison stood at the curb in front of the bus station clutching her text book as usual. From their hiding place, Aaron and Jake observed the arrival of the BMW at 08: 00 exactly. The passenger door opened and a man stepped out, leaving the door open. As he reached for the back door handle, he suddenly slapped his hand on the side of his neck as if swatting a mosquito, then slumped to the ground in a heap. The driver looked to the right in alarm, and then he too slumped at the wheel. Aaron approached the driver's door while Jake approached the passenger door and together they drug the driver over the console into the passenger seat. Aaron slid behind the wheel and released the trunk lid. Ramón stepped out of hiding clutching a long wooden blow gun adorned with bright feathers. A quiver of darts hung from a leather thong across his chest. The tall thin basket of fine tree roots was woven with an intricate geometric pattern and had a tight fitting lid secured with a lanyard.

With Ramón's help, Jake unceremoniously thrust the first man into the trunk, and then he, Ramón, and Allison hopped in the back.

Aaron turned on the turn signal before carefully executing a U-turn and heading north out of the Village. On the outskirts of town, they drove up to an abandoned garage. On their approach, Renée rolled up the door from inside, they drove in, and she rolled it down behind them.

Soon they had the two men stretched out on the floor, where Ramón plucked darts fledged with bright yellow tufts of cotton from their necks and tossed them aside. In a matter of minutes, they had been stripped of their clothes, which concealed shoulder holsters with 9mm automatic pistols. While Renée checked their vital signs, Aaron and Jake pulled off their own clothes. Allison eyed Jake's bare ass as he undressed. The guys dressed in the other men's clothes, which were several sizes too large. Meanwhile, Ramón securely bound the arms and legs of both of the thugs. He stuffed gags in their mouths and drug them into a corner where they would be concealed from prying eyes. Jake checked for traffic while everyone else piled into the BMW. Jake rolled up the door and Aaron backed the car out. Jake closed the door, then hopped into the passenger seat. As Aaron accelerated away, Jake checked his watch.

"Better step on it; its 08:09," Jake said. It was the first words spoken since the operation began.

"How long will those guys be out Ramón?" Renée asked.

"Long enough," he said with grin. "They will have a bit of a headache when they wake up and they will remember nothing."

"What did you use on the darts?" Renée asked.

"There are many secrets in the jungle."

Road Tripped

"Do you guys know how to use the guns?" Allison asked.

"Let's just say that we hope we don't have to use them," Aaron said.

"I'll take that for a no."

"How hard can it be? Just point it and pull the trigger!" Jake said while pulling his out and looking at it with no regard for where it was pointing.

"Ya wanna point that thing somewhere else?" Aaron asked.

"What's this do?" He asked while pushing a button with his thumb. The magazine fell in his lap. "I meant to do that," he said while sliding the magazine back into place.

It was 08:42 when they arrived at the village. "OK, we still have four more minutes to make up, we're doing pretty good," Jake said.

At 08:52 they came to the stretch of highway that had recently been repaired. "Zero eight five two, we're right on schedule," Jake said. "Now let's keep to the speed limit."

Teo K'ha observed the position of the sun relative to a particular peak. In sign language, he indicated that the time was at hand. He and five other Lacandon had been following their usual and customary path along the stream of their ancestors for several days, gleaning their sustenance from the land in the old way.

As they drew near their objective, they encountered trip wires that would have easily gone unnoticed by ordinary men, but his were no ordinary men. These were Lacandon warriors. The Lacandon were a people of peace, yet long ago, they alone had defeated the might of the Spanish conquistadors. The skills of their ancestors were not forgotten. They moved like ghosts through the jungle.

Teo K'ha again checked the sun, and then he and his band peered out of the jungle to see the gleaming gray hacienda that stood where his people had once kept a winter encampment. Teo K'ha sniffed the air and detected the aroma of tobacco smoke. He remained silent in the fringe of the jungle as a sentry smoking a cigar strolled nearer. The sentry slung his machine gun over his shoulder and stepped over to the brush while unzipping his fly. He suddenly became aware that he stood face to face with a savage looking Indian who had materialized as if from thin air! Before he could react, Teo K'ha blew a cloud of white powder into the sentry's face. The man drew a startled breath and then froze in place as a urine stain grew on the front of his trousers. He slumped into Teo K'ha's arms, and though he outweighed him by nearly double, the Indian picked him up as easily as he would a baby, and carried him into the underbrush where his men silently bound him with lengths of vine. Teo K'ha pucked the cigar from the man's lips and took a few puffs before snuffing it out and tucking it behind his ear for later. His men silently fanned out around the compound and secured the rear perimeter, disarming and binding two more guards. They came to a garden area where several workers toiled, weeding rows of flowers. Teo K'ha mimicked the call of a bird, and the men abandoned their work to grab machetes. In moments, they had secured the greenhouse and detained the white lab coat clad researchers who had been at work perfecting the hybrid poppy plants that were to revolutionize the drug trade.

At 09:00 a small explosion set off a landslide several miles north of the target. Moments later, a truck with the logo of the Estado Chiapas emblazoned on the door came to a stop and a dozen men clambered out with picks and shovels to begin clearing the debris. Soon a line of cars began to back up from both directions.

Concealed in the jungle along the roadside was a small band of men wearing olive drab fatigues and ski masks. Juan Valdez, El Supremo of the Popular Front for the Restoration of Peace to the People of Mexico observed the activity with satisfaction. It would take several hours of hard work to clear the road. He noted the time, 09:27 as he removed his ski mask and fatigues to reveal the dirty jeans and tee-shirt of a road crew worker. He stepped from his place of concealment, zipping up his fly as if he had stepped away to take a leak. He picked up a shovel and began clearing the landslide. He smiled at the irony that he was getting paid by the state to clear the landslide that he had himself created.

At 09:29, the silver BMW slowed and turned onto the dirt road. Aaron steered around the S-turn and stopped at the gate. He pushed a button on the remote control built into the sun visor but nothing happened, so he pushed the other button and the gate swung smoothly open. He drove through and started down the concrete driveway.

As the gate began to close, six men in olive drab uniforms and ski masks ducked through and fanned out along the perimeter fence, their shotguns, rifles, and pistols at the ready.

Aaron brought the BMW to a stop, pushed the button on the remote, and waited while the garage door opened. He pulled inside and shut off the engine while the door rolled smoothly closed. Ramón hid in the garage, his blowgun at the ready to guard against the possibility that Cruella should arrive. Renée slid behind the wheel of the BMW ready to start the car instantly if anything should go awry. Allison led the way to the study, where she sat in her usual chair while Aaron and Jake positioned themselves out of the line of sight to await the arrival of their nemesis.

At 09:38, the door to the study opened and Vladmir Igor Petrovinski, former President and CEO of *Live It, Unlimited* strode into the room. "Hola Señorita Allison, comos das!" he said cheerfully.

"Good morning mister Petrovinski, I believe you know my friends."

He stopped abruptly and turned to see who Allison was talking about.

"Hello Vlad; long time no see!" Jake said.

"I'm sorry; you must have me mistaken for someone else. It is said that all of us Polacks look alike, no?"

"Poland, now is it? I could have sworn you were Russian," Aaron said. "I must have been mistaken. So tell me. Does everyone in Poland have a birthmark on the back of their hand?"

"So it would seem that you have got me gentlemen! Please, have a seat so we can catch up on things. I will ask Maria to bring us some coffee."

He sat at his desk and began to move his hand toward the button Allison knew was concealed under the top.

"Ah, ah, ah," Allison said. "Now be a good boy and keep your hands where we can see them."

He looked at the guys. "I see that your tastes in attire have improved; perhaps my tailor could improve the fit for you though," he said sarcastically.

"Cut the crap Petrovinski! Jake said. "Now open the safe."

"Safe? I know not of what you speak."

Road Tripped

"Ah come on Vlad; we know about the safe behind the bookcase," Aaron said. "We believe that there is something in there that belongs to us."

"Yes; of course," Vlad said as he stood and moved toward the bookcase.

"Not that one!" Allison cried in alarm.

Aaron and Jake pulled their weapons just as Vlad pressed a hidden button and the bookcase swung aside to reveal a secret passage.

"Halt or we shoot!" Jake said. "I can think of nothing I'd rather do." He held the pistol in both hands and leveled it at Vlad's chest.

Vlad raised his hands and turned to face the guys just as the magazine slid from the grip of Jake's gun and clattered to the floor. Vlad broke into a wide grin as he turned again and ducked into the passage.

"Don't make me shoot you Vlad," Aaron said menacingly.

"Perhaps I can interest you in shooting lessons, gentlemen. Your safety is on," Vlad said as the bookcase swung closed behind him.

"Fuck!" Allison cried. "Search the house, quick!"

"If he goes into the garage, Ramón will get him," Aaron said.

"He'll never make it past the Lacandon or the guerillas." Jake said.

They rushed toward the other end of the house, quickly checking rooms as they went. From behind a door in the hallway, they heard a car door slam and an engine start. "This way!" Allison cried. They rushed to the door and burst through in time to see the garage door beginning to open. Vlad sat at the wheel of a gleaming new Land Rover SUV with the engine

265

running. When he spotted them, he slammed it in reverse and floored it without waiting for the door to open completely. He smashed through the door gathering speed. He cranked the wheel hard to the right and stabbed the brakes only long enough to put the transmission into drive. Aaron, Jake, and Allison rushed out into the drive just as he stomped the accelerator to the floor. They lay directly in his path, trapped between the house and a stone retaining wall surrounding a fountain. They had no avenue of escape!

"Run!" Jake shouted and they all ran past the other garage in a vain attempt at escape.

Behind them, they could hear the powerful engine of the SUV roar and the tires spinning on the concrete of the driveway. Then ominously, the tires quit spinning and the exhaust note of the engine deepened as the vehicle got traction and began to gain speed. Suddenly there was a crash and clatter of debris as the BMW flew through the garage door directly into the path of the speeding SUV. An instant later The Land Rover smashed into the side of the BMW.

Vlad pushed aside the rapidly deflating airbag and tried to open his door, but the collision had jammed it. He threw his not inconsiderable weight against it and it sprang open. He leaped to his feet and ran in the direction of the garden, moving surprisingly fast for a man of his bulk. He'd put twenty yards on his pursuers before they had time to react. All was silent except for the sound of Vlad's expensive Italian shoes on the pavement. Suddenly Vlad fell flat on his face at a dead run. He skidded to a stop and was still.

Aaron dashed to the side of the BMW where Renée sat in the passenger seat groaning, a trickle of blood coming from a gash in her scalp. "Renée!" He cried. "Are you OK?" She'd been thrown from the wheel of the car into the passenger seat by the force of the collision. "Guys; help me get her out!" Aaron cried. There was no way to get the passenger door open, so she would need to be pulled back into the driver's seat in order to get her out.

"I'm OK Aaron; I'm OK. Just let me take it slow." She groaned as she climbed over the console and out the driver's door into Aaron's waiting arms.

"Easy big fella, don't squeeze so hard!" She said with a weak smile.

Aaron held her face and looked into her eyes. "Renée, thank God you're alright! I was afraid I'd lost you!"

"Well in my expert opinion as the medic on this mission, it's nothing that a Band-Aid, some aspirin, and a hot bath won't cure. Ya play yer card right, maybe I'll let you scrub my back," she said with a coy smile. "Let's go check on our target."

Vlad's pursuers formed a circle around him as Ramón strode calmly over and plucked a green dart from his neck.

"Shit! Now how are we gonna get him to open the safe?" Jake cried in dismay.

"Not to worry," Ramón said. "The yellow darts put a guy out completely; the green ones temporarily paralyze him, but he is still able to hear and speak. If he doesn't cooperate, we'll use a red one."

"What do the red ones do?" Aaron asked.

Ramón slid his finger across his throat to indicate that the red ones were fatal.

"Give me a red dart," Aaron said in a cold voice. "If anything happens to any of my friends, I'll stick him with it myself," He said menacingly. "Now let's get this bastard back into the study."

Aaron and Jake each grabbed one of Vlad's arms and dragged him inside. They unceremoniously dropped him to the floor in front of the bookcase.

"How do we open the bookcase?" Aaron asked.

"Fuck you!" Vlad slurred.

"I guess we'll have to do it Olalla fashion." Aaron and Jake kicked and tore the beautiful hardwood bookcase into splinters, exposing the safe.

"OK, now that we've worked that out, how do we open the safe?" Aaron asked.

"Let me see you try to open it the way you did my bookcase, you cretins!"

"It's gotta be the ring," Allison said.

"Is that how it works? The ring opens it? Aaron asked.

Vlad was silent. Jake roughly grabbed Vlad's hand and tried to prize the ring from his sausage-like finger. "Apparently someone's had too much borscht, it won't come off."

"I guess we'll have to cut it off," Aaron said. "Someone get me a knife."

"No!" Vlad screamed. "It will only work if it's on my finger! Please don't cut off my finger!" He pleaded.

"Maybe we could just cut off his hand," Allison suggested.

"Good idea, someone see if there's an axe by the fireplace," Aaron said.

"No! Please, I beg you! I will give you what you wish. Just lift me up. Please!"

"It would be easier to just lift the fat fuck's hand," Jake said.

"True, and If I stick him with a dart, we won't have to listen to him whine anymore."

Road Tripped

"Ah come on you guys, I swore an oath to preserve human life and help those who are sick or hurt at all cost," Renée said. "If you cut him up, I'll have to try to put him back together and I have a headache."

"If I stick him with the dart he'll be dead, so you won't have to try to save him anymore," Aaron said. He paused for a second contemplating the options, then said, "ah fuck it; gimme a hand you guys."

Ramón and Jake each grabbed an arm while Aaron put his arms around Vlad's chest, bearing most of his weight. Allison grabbed his hand and waved the ring in front of a sensor. A green light blinked, and there was an audible click. Renée grasped the handle and swung the door open. The guys released their grip and Vlad collapsed in a heap on the floor. Together everyone peered in the open door of the safe at the contents. Neat bundles of One hundred, five hundred, and One thousand dollar bills nearly filled the safe to capacity.

A few miles north of where the highway was blocked, Julio, second in command of the revolutionary forces, watched a black Mercedes glide past heading south. He checked his watch, it was 10:39. He waited until the car was hidden from view, and then pushed the button on a detonator, setting off a small charge which sent a landslide across the road, trapping the Mercedes. Soon a string of cars began to back up, one of which turned around and headed north, doubtlessly to alert the state that the highway was blocked.

Confronted by a string of cars at a standstill, Martina Kasparova looked impatiently at her watch, and then barked at her bodyguard in the front passenger seat, "Go see what it is that delays us." She opened her silver cigarette case and lit a smoke with her gold lighter.

After a short time, the guard returned. "There has been a landslide. It will be hours before it will be cleared," he announced.

She angrily flicked her cigarette out the window. "Turn around; we go back," She said with exasperation.

The driver executed a three point turn accompanied by much blaring of the horn to get other vehicles to clear the path. They had traveled but a short distance when the driver again brought the Mercedes to a stop. "What is it now?" Martina said impatiently.

"There is another landslide, Madam Kasparova."

"I do not like this," She said dialing her cell phone. She put it to her ear and waited while the phone continued to ring unanswered. "Do either of you have a number for any of Petrovinski's men?" She asked.

They looked at each other and the driver replied, "No madam."

She dialed another number; that of her personal helicopter pilot.

The contents of the safe were packed into a large duffle bag which Ramón heaved over his shoulder. "Be safe mi amigos, I'll see you in a couple of days and we will divide our take." He shook Aaron and Jake's hands and headed out the back of the house, where he was joined by the rest of the Lacandon. They evaporated like a mist into the jungle.

In the study, Aaron said, "I think a celebration is in order. Vlad, why don't you get us a drink?"

"I will see you all dead," He growled.

"That's OK, don't get up; I'll get it," Jake said and walked to the liquor cabinet, returning with a bottle of tequila and four shot glasses. He filled the glasses. "Care to join us Vlad?" he said while pouring a dram on top of Vlad's head. The friends clinked them together, and tipped them back. Aaron began to pour another round but stopped at the sound of an approaching helicopter. He glanced at his watch. "It's only 11: 47, the cavalry is early. Just as well, our work here is done, and someone seems to have destroyed our escape vehicle," he smiled and cast a glance at Renée with a sparkle in his eye.

The group stepped out the front door to watch the approach of the helicopter. It soon hove into view and made a quick pass around the compound at low altitude.

"I thought all US aircraft had tail numbers that begin with an 'N', Jake said.

"I think you're right," Aaron said.

"So what country does 'XB' stand for?"

"I dunno, Mexico maybe?"

The helicopter came in low again and turned sideways as a rear door slid back. Through the open door, they saw none other than Cruella DeVille, who pointed and shouted something. One needn't have a lip reader to surmise that it was a tirade laden with expletives. A man appeared with a small machine gun and without hesitation, unleashed a hail of bullets.

"Inside, now!" Aaron screamed and at a dead run, led the group back inside and into the study. He crouched low and peered over the window sill to watch the helicopter drop down to within a few feet of the ground. A man leaped down, rolled once, and came up running a zigzag course in the direction of the house with a machine gun in his grasp. The aircraft rose again and made a quick pass around the house, spraying bullets at the soldiers of the revolution who held the perimeter. Theirs was no match for the firepower held by those in the helicopter and they ducked back into the forest to regroup. They'd not been prepared for an aerial assault. Aaron stole another glimpse out the window and saw the man on the ground creeping along a wall with his weapon at the ready. With the butt of his gun, he broke out a window and leaped inside.

"Jake, try to find the release for Vlad's secret passage."

"Would you like me to tell you where it is?" Vlad asked. Everyone had all but forgotten about him.

"Tell me now or I use the dart!" Aaron said. "I mean it."

"I will, but you must take me with you."

"Why? Aren't your friends here to rescue you?"

"No, I am sure that Madam Kasparova only wishes to be assured that I do not fall into the hands of the authorities. Second shelf from top; feel along edge."

Jake found the release, and the shelf swung into the wall. "Go!' he yelled to Renée and Allison. They dashed through the opening and down a short flight of stairs into darkness. Jake grabbed the collar of Vlad's jacket and swiftly drug him thumping unceremoniously down the stairs. Aaron was last. He could hear footsteps coming down the hallway. "How do I close it? Quickly!" He whispered.

"Top right corner," Vlad said quietly. Aaron found the button and the bookcase swung shut just as the door to the study was flung open. The man leaped in just in time to see the passageway close. He leveled his gun and fired a burst.

"Move!" Aaron cried ducking as wood splinters showered him. The girls felt their way along the passage.

Jake followed, dragging Vlad behind.

"Thank you, Jacob," Vlad said.

Road Tripped

"Don't think I'm doing this for you, you bastard. You're ours. That bitch can't have you," he hissed.

Aaron crouched behind the doorway while the others made their escape. With a loud crash, the man kicked in the door. Before the man's eyes could adjust to the gloom, Aaron pricked him with the red dart and he tumbled to the bottom of the stairs.

Aaron said, "you guys keep going; I'm gonna have a look." He peered out the window, but the helicopter could not be seen. He listened a moment and peeked again. The helicopter suddenly dropped down into view and his eyes met those of Cruella. He dove down the stairs and quickly felt his way down the passage. Soon he joined the others in the garage where they all huddled in a corner, trying to be inconspicuous. The sound of the helicopter diminished for a moment, and soon the sound of someone stealthily making his way along the passage could be heard. A burst of gunfire from the passage announced the arrival of the latest threat. Aaron pulled some debris over Vlad and said, "Good luck!" as he dashed out into the open with the others, a shower of bullets on their tail. The helicopter suddenly popped up over the trees and unleashed a lethal volley in their direction. They were caught in the open in a deadly crossfire.

They sprawled along the base of the stone wall, trying to keep clear of the stream of bullets. "Where's Jake?" Allison screamed over the din.

"He must be pinned down inside," Aaron yelled in reply.

There was a brief lull while both gunmen reloaded.

In the lull, Aaron grasped Renée's hand and said, "Renée, I love you. I always have. I just had to tell you before…" Before Aaron could finish, he was interrupted by gunfire, but not that of the machine guns. He stole a glance over the wall. What he saw gave him a glimmer of hope. A man in fatigues and ski mask

273

racked another round and fired his shotgun at the tail section of the helicopter. He methodically pumped rounds into the chamber and fired again and again. A second man joined him and he too began firing his shotgun. Another man appeared and began firing a pistol. Finally a man carefully aimed his rifle and squeezed the trigger. His bullet found its mark and the helicopter suddenly spun out of control, spewing black smoke in a spiral.

The man in the garage walked out and leveled his machine gun at the group lying prone by the wall. The guerillas were their only hope, but their attention was on the helicopter. The gunman's finger began to move, and then suddenly, he collapsed to the ground where he lay with blood seeping from a gash in his head. Jake stood over him holding the 9mm by the barrel. He kicked the machine gun away and wiped the blood off of the grip of the pistol on the shirt of the gunman who groaned in pain at his feet. "Who says we don't know how to use a gun?" Jake said smugly.

The helicopter slewed left and then right as the pilot fought for control. The rotor grazed the top of the stone wall just above the group lying prone at its base, showering them with sparks and stone fragments. It then rose up, spinning so violently that a gunman was thrown out by centrifugal force, emitting his very best rendition of the famous "Wilhelm scream" as used in some 200 Hollywood movies as he plummeted down to land in the water of the fountain with a huge splash. At last, the stricken helicopter tipped on its side, and smashed to the ground with a rending crash. Fragments of the rotor became lethal shrapnel flying high into the air in all directions. Cruella rolled out of the wreckage before the last of the debris had even fallen to Earth. In her hands she held a machine gun; how she had managed to keep her grip on it during the crash was impossible to guess. She began striding purposefully across the lawn toward the group huddled by the fountain, tossing aside her sunglasses and cocking the weapon as she approached. Her pace quickened as she neared the edge of the lawn. She was but a few steps away from the driveway, when out of the sky a large piece of the helicopter's rotor plunged directly into the ground like a huge lawn dart mere inches from her and directly in her path. She was in mid step and her momentum carried her into the obstacle at unabated speed. Her forehead met the rotor fragment and she staggered backward a couple of paces, dropping the gun. Her eyes rolled back in her head and she fell to the ground in a heap.

The brave soldiers of the Popular Front for the Restoration of Peace to the People of Mexico dragged the pilot from the smoldering wreckage moments before it exploded in flames.

Jake holstered his pistol, picked up the gunman's machine gun, and strode over to Cruella. He picked up her weapon in his other hand and in a scene reminiscent of a Rambo movie; he raised them both, unleashing a victory cry, and firing a double volley into the skies of Chiapas. All eyes were on him as he lowered the guns. His finger grazed the trigger and one last round fired. He dropped the guns and hopped on one foot screaming in pain. Allison jumped to her feet and ran to him screaming, "Jake!" She hugged him and lowered him gently to the ground. "Oh my hero; my brave, brave hero; I love you Jacob Overbee!" she cried, crushing his face to her breast.

"Mrmph glrg!" He struggled for breath, so tight did she hold him.

"What my darling; what is it?"

"I can't breathe!"

Aaron stood above Jake and cried out, "Medic!"

275

Renée came and removed his still smoking shoe to reveal that he'd shot the end of his little toe off.

"Will he live?" Aaron asked trying to contain his mirth.

"He'll live," Renée said.

"Hey it fuckin' hurts! Jake said. "Do I get a purple heart, or what?"

Suddenly a black helicopter rose above the tree line! Everyone tensed in anticipation of another hail of bullets. It then turned sideways to reveal the legend "FBI" in large block letters. A voice blared over a loudspeaker, "This is the FBI. Throw down your weapons and stay where you are!" Another voice repeated the command in Spanish.

A second helicopter with the letters "DEA" emblazoned on the side flew overhead, banked and settled toward the ground. Several heavily armed men in flak jackets leaped to the ground and fanned out to secure the perimeter before the craft had even touched down.

The first helicopter then landed, and several agents swarmed out to take prisoners and search the house.

Special Agent, Matt Cromwell stepped to the ground wearing black slacks, jacket, and tie with a white shirt. He approached and shook Aaron's hand. "Mister Skandish, good to see you! He looked at his watch. "Twelve hundred hours, straight up. We're exactly on time, but it looks like the party is over."

"Must have been a mix up," Aaron said. "Maybe you're on Seattle time."

Agent Cromwell removed his mirrored Ray ban aviator sunglasses and looked Aaron in the eye. "Yeah, that must be it. Did your team take any casualties?"

"No, everyone is fine."

Road Tripped

"Hey; what about me?" Jake cried. "I took a bullet!"

"Yeah, I can see that." Cromwell said.

A man wearing a DEA uniform approached. "Perimeter is secured sir," he said to agent Cromwell. "We're gathering the last of the prisoners. Several guerrillas in camouflage escaped into the jungle though."

"Gather all of the prisoners here."

"Yes sir."

"I think you'll find the body of one man in a passageway under the house," Aaron said.

"Gunshot?"

"Bee sting."

All of the prisoners that could stand were in a line, their hands in handcuffs behind their backs. Those that couldn't stand lay at their feet. Aaron, agent Cromwell, and the DEA Lieutenant strolled along the line like generals reviewing prisoners of war. Aaron pointed out three of the men. "These are our inside men; you can release them. They can probably provide you with some useful information about what these guys were up to," He said pointing at the men in the lab coats." Oh; before I forget, there are a couple more prisoners back in San Gabriele. They're probably gettin' kinda hungry and thirsty by now."

Aaron stopped in front of Cruella DeVille where she sat holding a damp cloth to her forehead. "This is…"

The DEA Lieutenant interrupted. "No introduction necessary; we know Martina Kasparova all too well."

Agent Cromwell paused by a man lying on the ground. "This is the man you thought was dead. We found him in the passageway. He doesn't feel too good though. Must be allergic to bees," He said. "You wouldn't by chance know anything about the empty safe in the library, would you?"

"Safe? What safe?"

At last they stood above Vladmir Igor Petrovinski. "Mister Petrovinski; we meet at last!" Agent Cromwell said. "Well mister Skandish, how does it feel to be a rich man?"

"What do you mean?" Aaron asked. Did he know about the money from the safe? He wondered.

"Oh, I didn't get a chance to tell you before," He said. "The company that wanted to buy yours posted a reward for information leading to the arrest of this man. You and mister Overbee are going to be wealthy. Very wealthy. They have also expressed an interest in seeing your resumes."

Road Tripped

Chapter Thirty Two

Several days had passed before the group consisting of Aaron, Jake, Renée, Allison, Juan, and finally Ramón met to celebrate the success of their mission and divide their booty. They gathered around Renée's and Allison's dining table and exchanged warm greetings. They were unable to meet sooner due to the fact that it had taken Ramón and his band of Lacandon as many days to hike out of the jungle while evading detection.

Cynics might have thought that the temptation of several million dollars in a backpack would prove too much for a man to resist, but anyone who knew him would never entertain such thoughts. Ramón was nothing if not a man of integrity.

"So tell me Ramón, how is it that the man I pricked with the red dart survived?" Aaron asked.

"Ah mi amigo, the red darts are no different than the yellow ones; I only said they were fatal to scare our target," he said with a gleam in his eye. Even men of integrity are known to regress.

"And how was your journey?" Jake asked.

"I think that it was the greatest reward of all! I was able to walk in the footsteps on my ancestors with Teo K'ha, a man who lives as they did!'

"Speakin' of rewards, wha'd'ya guys say we have a look at our take?" Allison said eyeing the coarse woven bag Ramón had dropped on the floor.

Ramón obliged, by dumping the contents on top of the table. All stood in silence, dumbstruck by the sight of a pile of money so vast that one would only expect to see it in a movie.

"Before we begin, I think a toast is in order," Aaron said. He filled six shot glasses with tequila. "Who would like to make the toast?"

Juan raised his glass. "Please mi amigos, I wish to speak." He cleared his throat. "I have lived my whole life here in San Gabriele. The village is much as it always has been. But not long ago, two men came to us by fate; two men who will forever be remembered as changing our lives for the better. Two men who I am proud to call my friends. To you Aaron and you Jake!" All downed their shots.

"Thank you Juan; we are proud to be your friend."

"How should we do this?" Jake asked.

"I used to be a waitress," Allison said. "Let me do it." She began by separating the bundles of one hundred, five hundred, and thousand dollar bills. She then made six even piles of bundles of thousands. The left over bundles she set aside. Next she did the same with the bundles of five hundreds, and finally the bundles of One hundreds. In no more than five minutes, she had divided the money into six piles of $ 480,000 and a seventh pile of $ 270,000. "See, that wasn't so bad, now was it?"

Road Tripped

"So what do you guys think we should do with the leftover bundles?" Renée asked. We could break the bundles and count all the bills, but that sounds like a lot of work."

"I think it would be nice to do something for the people of Chiapas with it," Aaron said. "Juan, and Ramón, do you guys think you could find a way to put it to good use?"

Juan and Ramón looked at each other and Juan answered, "Si; we would be glad to do this."

A few days later, Aaron and Renée returned from San Cristobal. They rushed into the house and called out, "Allison? Jake? Are you guys home?" They came in from the garden smiling.

"Hey Guys, we're glad you're back. We've got some exciting news!" Allison said.

"We do too!" Renée said. Renée was wearing the amber necklace and earrings that Aaron had picked out on their last rip, along with a beautiful skirt and blouse tailored to fit her form perfectly.

Damn Renée, you sure look nice!" Jake said. Allison jabbed him in the ribs.

"Don't you ever quit gawkin' at other women?"

"So what's the big surprise?" Renée asked.

"You first!"

"No, you first!"

"OK, here goes!" Allison held out her left hand to reveal a diamond ring, humble, yet beautiful. "Jake and I are going home to Olalla!"

"Oh my god!" Renée screamed and embraced Allison in a crushing hug. "But… Oh my god!"

"OK, so now it's your turn; what's your big surprise?"

"You didn't really think you were gonna beat us to the draw now did you?" Renée held out her left hand, revealing a simple band of gold. "Aaron and I have decided to make our home here in San Gabriele. We want to have a family, and this is where we want to raise our kids."

"Oh Renée, I'm so happy for you! I always knew this day would come for you. I just never thought this bone head would ever come through for me though."

"Sometimes even a blind pig finds a truffle," Jake said.

Aaron and Jake drew together and hugged, congratulating each other.

Jake said, "Well old buddy, it looks like our road trip is officially over."

"Don't be so sure; there's someone we want you to meet," Aaron said and beckoned them to the front door. They stepped outside, where a beat up old Volkswagen beetle idled at the curb. The paint was several different shades of yellow and the fenders had obviously gotten the worst of contact with other cars. A puddle of oil had already formed under the engine in the few moments that they'd been inside. The canvas sun roof was rolled back. Lying behind the car tied to the rear bumper with pieces of twine was a bunch of tin cans. "Jake and Allison, meet *Trudi!*"

"*Trudi?*"

Yeah Trudi; think of her as *Gertrude's* daughter!" He opened the driver's door. "C'mon, let's go for a ride!"

Renée and Allison climbed into the back seat and Jake hopped in the passenger seat. Aaron climbed behind the wheel and slammed the door. It didn't latch, so he slammed it again harder. He pushed in the clutch and ground the transmission into first gear. He let out the clutch and stalled the engine. He hit the starter button and was rewarded only with a whirring noise as the starter spun but did not engage. "Ya mind givin' me a push?"

Jake groaned.

They drove a few blocks and as they turned onto a side street, where Eliz, the little Rodriguez girl was selling flowers. Aaron brought Trudy to a stop. "Wait here guys, I'll be right back." He knelt down by Eliz and picked out a flower. He reached in his pocket and pulled out a thousand dollar bill, which he put in her hand and rolled her pudgy little fingers around it. He tousled her hair and returned to Trudi, where he put the flower in the bud vase on the dash.

Ron Fugere

Epilogue

Vladimir Petrovinski returned to the United States to face a number of charges. Aaron and Jake were spared having to testify at a trial, as Vlad had pleaded guilty to charges that would assure that he have a lengthy stay in federal prison. His legal team had made it clear that he stood little chance of fighting the charges and that an American prison was like a country club compared to a Mexican prison. Even that would have been preferable to facing charges in Russia, where he had many unfriendly acquaintances who would assure that he meet an untimely and gruesome fate.

Martina Kasparova was not as fortunate. She was convicted of drug trafficking charges and sentenced to life in a Mexican federal prison. Through go-betweens, she planned to hold the reins of her empire while she was incarcerated and plotting her escape. What she didn't know was that one of her lieutenants who had eluded arrest had in fact turned evidence in exchange for clemency on the condition that he operated as a mole within her organization. Her involvement in the day to day operations of her empire would ultimately lead to its demise as the details

284

were passed onto the federales, resulting in many more convictions within and without her organization.

Aaron and Jake were offered their old positions with *Live It, Unlimited*, which would be operated as a wholly owned subsidiary of the company that purchased it. They would be free to develop and market their games as they saw fit and would receive huge signing bonuses, ridiculous salaries, and lucrative fringe benefits. Best of all, they could live and work where they wished.

In June, Aaron and Renée flew home for Jake and Allison's wedding. Joining them in the first class cabin were Ramón, Juan, and Emilia.

Upon arrival, Aaron and Renée went to the mobile home dealer from which he had purchased his new house. In the rear of the lot, he could see the home which had been repossessed. He strode purposefully into the office, where he found the manager at his desk. The man recognized Aaron and tensed, expecting trouble. Aaron dumped a pile of cash on his desk and said, "Count it." The man counted it twice. "Give me a receipt," Aaron said curtly. The manager scrawled a receipt on a pad and handed it to Aaron. "Deliver my house next week." He said as he and Renée turned for the door.

Outside, Renée asked, "What do we need with a mobile home since we're gonna live in Mexico?"

"We're gonna need a place to stay when we come to visit. Besides, I just had to see his face when I gave him the cash," he replied.

Jake's bachelor party was a typical Olalla affair, with a huge bon fire and several kegs of beer and a few barnyard animals. There were no strippers though. They just knew that if Allison got wind of it, there would be hell to pay.

For the big occasion, Jake had been persuaded to wear a tux for the first time in his life. The tailor that fitted him had had to explain that a cummerbund was not a breakfast pastry. Aaron hired him to come from Seattle on the morning of the wedding just to tie Jake's bow tie.

Allison wore a simple yet elegant gown together with her cherished emerald necklace and earrings that had been given to her so long ago by her favorite Great Aunt Mildred. Yes, the very same Mildred that the guys had grown to love.

Jake and Allison were wed in a small, private ceremony held in the shade of a weeping willow tree down by the creek where it meandered through Jake's land. Dear ol' Mildred sat in the front row in a place of honor with Abner by her side. Rounding out the guests were such families as they had well as a few close friends, some of which they had known since they were toddlers.

Mildred had suffered a stroke while they were away and was restricted to a wheelchair. It had severely affected her physically, but her mind was as sharp as ever. Although her speech was slurred, she was able to express her wish to live out her days in the home she had shared with her Henry. Unfortunately, she was no longer physically able to care for herself. The couples resolved that they would see to it that Mildred would never live in a nursing home.

Renée sent for Maria, the daughter of her receptionist, Alejandra back in San Gabriele. She dreamed of becoming a doctor like Renée, whom she idolized. She would stay with Mildred and care for her while she attended medical school at the University of Washington. Her tuition would never be a problem, Renée assured her. Some day she would return to San Gabriele and take over the new clinic when Renée retired. Aaron and Jake hired a friend who was a contractor to update, repair, and modify Mildred's home for wheelchair accessibility.

When he was done with Mildred's home he would begin construction of a new house for Jake and Allison. Allison specified a spot with a view of the creek. Jake had a different spot in mind, but Allison's wishes would prevail. There was just no reasoning with that woman!

As a wedding present, Aaron gave the couple his most prized possession: *Ingrid*. He had contacted the city of Seattle only to find that his trusty Volvo had been sold at auction. He coerced Deputy Michael Martin Jr. to use his connections to track down the buyer. Aaron bought the college coed a brand new Volvo in exchange for good ol' *Ingrid*. She thought he was nuts. She may be right.

The End

Ron Fugere

Made in the USA
Middletown, DE
26 May 2019